THE PERFECT
FAMILY

ALSO BY SHALINI BOLAND

The Secret Mother
The Child Next Door
The Silent Sister
The Millionaire's Wife
The Perfect Family
The Best Friend
The Girl from the Sea

THE PERFECT FAMILY

SHALINI BOLAND

bookouture

Published by Bookouture in 2018

An imprint of StoryFire Ltd.

Carmelite House
50 Victoria Embankment
London EC4Y 0DZ

www.bookouture.com

ISBN: 978-1-78681-525-5
eBook ISBN: 978-1-78681-524-8

This book is a work of fiction. Names, characters, businesses,
organizations, places and events other than those clearly in the
public domain, are either the product of the author's imagination
or are used fictitiously. Any resemblance to actual persons, living or
dead, events or locales is entirely coincidental.

For my perfect family xxxx

PROLOGUE

I gaze through the kitchen window. A gust of wind shakes the sepia leaves on the grapevine twisting across the pergola. A sparrow hops lightly along the rattan sun lounger. It's so pretty. So domestic. So perfect.

Sometimes I forget myself. I let myself relax and believe that everything is okay.

But it's never okay.

And I can never relax.

CHAPTER 1

Strange – I don't remember seeing the front door open when I came down earlier. I peer outside, frown and push it closed with a click.

'Girls! Come on, get your shoes on, we're going to be late!'

Moments later, my ten-year-old daughter Eva bounds down the stairs, her caramel hair tied back off her face in a ponytail.

'Is your sister ready too?' I ask.

Eva shrugs.

'Katie!' I yell up the stairs, but there's no reply. I sigh. My six-year-old is such a little dreamer. I kiss Eva's forehead. 'Can you run back up and tell Katie to get a wriggle on?'

Eva does as I ask while I slide my feet into two-inch heels and check my reflection in the hall mirror. I have an important meeting this morning with a potential new client. I need to look professional and I absolutely cannot be late. The school run must go like clockwork.

'She's not in her room,' Eva says, reappearing in the hallway.

'Try the bathroom.' I smooth my eyebrows and turn away from the mirror.

'I looked. She's not there either. Or in my room.'

'What about—'

'She's not up there,' Eva interrupts, a look of panic darting across her face. 'I even looked under the beds and in the wardrobes in case she was hiding.'

'Katie!' I begin marching through the downstairs rooms of our shabby Victorian fixer-upper that we've never quite managed to fix up, with its draughty hallway and rattling windows. My husband Robert and I had such grand designs for this place when we bought it. Maybe it'll happen one day. My heels tip-tap across the stripped floorboards as I search the lounge, the kitchen, utility room, dining room, the downstairs loo… but there's no sign of my youngest daughter. Back in the hallway, I freeze, remembering the previously open front door. Katie is a curious child. With a stab of pure terror, I think of the busy main road beyond the driveway and my skin goes cold. 'Eva, check upstairs again – look in every single room.'

'I already did that.'

'I know, but can you do it again?' As I bark out instructions to Eva, I'm almost falling over myself to reach the front door.

'Mum, are you okay? What are you doing?'

'I'm fine,' I cry, but my heart has suddenly started beating like a machine gun. As Eva disappears back upstairs, I wrench open the front door and step out onto our driveway, scanning the small front garden as rush-hour traffic thunders past beyond the hedge. The sky is clear and blue, but there's a nip of autumn in the air, a damp chill that makes me shiver. I weave between our two cars, checking my youngest daughter is not hiding behind either of them. Then I call Katie's name and stare blindly around, trying to keep calm, but it's plain to see she's not out here. Shaking away images of cars screeching to a halt and my daughter's little body tossed up over a car bonnet, I stride down onto the pavement and peer up and down the road, praying that I'll catch sight of her. But there's no sign, and despite her absent-mindedness, she surely wouldn't leave the safety of our driveway. I've told her enough times that the road is dangerous. But she's not out here, so she *must* be back in the house. *She has to be.*

Back inside, I check the downstairs rooms once again with Eva at my side. Katie's not in any of them. Perhaps she went into the back garden for some reason. I ask Eva to keep searching the house while I go into the utility room and try the back door. It's locked and the key is still on the hook, so it's highly unlikely Katie is out there. But maybe she went out of the front door and then came around the side of the house, distracted by something or other. I slip the keys off the hook and open the back door, stand on the threshold scanning the garden – the mossy patio, the overgrown rectangle of grass, the fruit trees at the back, and the ramshackle, sage-green summer house.

'Katie!' I cry, my voice disappearing into the still morning air. 'Katie! Are you out here? Time to go!' I cross the stone patio and step onto the grass, my heels sinking into the soft earth. 'We're going to be late for school!' My voice is definitely wobbly now, but I'm determined not to let my mind jump ahead again and imagine the worst. I make my way across the dew-soaked lawn to the summer house, try the door – it's locked   and peer through one of the windows. Empty. Just the kids' bikes and some gardening equipment.

'Hello, Gemma, everything okay?'

I snap my head round to see my retired neighbour's round face peering at me over the garden fence. 'Sherry, hi. I don't suppose you've seen Katie? I can't seem to find her…' I give a short laugh to show that I'm not really worried. But I don't know why I did that because I *am* really worried. I make my way back down the lawn towards her.

Sherry frowns. 'No, sorry. I'll go in and ask Paul. I take it she's not in the house then?'

I shake my head and bite my lip.

'I'm sure she won't have gone far.'

'Mum?'

I gasp and look up, hopeful that it's Katie. But it's Eva standing by the back door, white-faced. 'Did you find her?' she asks.

'Not yet, darling, but she's got to be around here somewhere.' My voice sounds hollow and bright.

'Maybe she went to school on her own,' Eva suggests.

I turn as Sherry clears her throat discreetly behind me. 'Let me know if you need any help looking. And try not to worry. I'm sure she'll turn up any minute.'

'Thanks, Sherry. I appreciate it.' I step off the grass, take Eva's hand and we go back inside. 'This is ridiculous,' I mutter. 'She can't have just disappeared.' I turn to Eva with another thought. 'She's probably hiding. You know how much she loves to play hide and seek. Let's check the house again. Have a proper scout around.' I stomp up the stairs, calling Katie's name. Eva follows, and I try to keep my panic in check. I don't want her to see how freaked out I'm becoming. It's already been five minutes since I first realised Katie was missing.

'Where is she, Mum? Is she going to be okay?'

'Of course,' I reply, trying to keep my voice from trembling. 'Katie!' I yell. 'It's not funny any more. We're going to be late for school. Come on!' I march into her bedroom, the floor a tangled mess of cuddly toys and discarded clothes. What I would give to see her lounging around on her bed right now. Her PJs are strewn across her pillow, her favourite book left open – everything looks so normal.

I crouch down and look under the bed, even though Eva said she'd already checked. But Katie's not there. It's just an empty black space. If only I had been paying more attention to her this morning instead of spending ages getting myself ready. I shouldn't have taken my eyes off her for a second. But we're at home. Surely we should be safe here. How can she have vanished into thin air? Robert and I are always in a rush, always doing a million things at once. Right now, he's out with his regular Tuesday-morning client. He's a personal trainer and works odd hours so, between the two of us, looking after the girls always manages to end up a messy and unpredictable affair with one or the other of us getting stressed and running late.

I get to my feet again and run my fingers through my short hair, not caring that I'm messing up the careful style that took me ages to perfect earlier.

'Mum?' Eva stares up at me. 'Mum, where is she? I'm scared.' Her eyes start to pool with tears.

I'm scared too. I take my precious daughter's hand in both of mine. 'Don't worry. Don't cry, she's fine. I'm sure she'll show up any second, and we'll give her a big fat hug and tell her off for scaring us senseless.'

I've looked everywhere. It can't be more than ten minutes since I first found she was missing, but it already feels like hours. If she's not in the house she must have gone out the front door. But I already looked on the driveway and on the road beyond. There was no sign of her. She wouldn't have run off, would she? Did she go out of her own accord?

Or did somebody take her?

I shiver at the sickening thought. Suddenly the seriousness of the situation slams into me like a truck. My normal life has turned into every mother's nightmare in a matter of moments. I rush into my bedroom, kick off my muddy high heels, slip on some trainers, hitch up my skirt and run down the stairs.

'Mum! What are you doing?' Eva cries as I yank open the front door. 'Where are you going?'

'Stay in the house!' I yell back. 'I won't be long. I'm going to look for your sister!' Every second matters now. It could be the difference between finding Katie... and not.

CHAPTER 2

I head out onto the driveway, trying to quell the rising dread. To suppress the terror that's threatening to bubble over. It will be fine. Katie's just wandered off and I'll spot her any minute and wonder why I was getting in such a state. On the pavement, I glance up and down the road again. I see a gaggle of teenage school kids on the opposite side of the street and I call out to them over the sound of rumbling traffic.

'Excuse me!'

They don't hear me.

'Hey! Excuse me!'

One of them looks over. He nudges his friends, who all glance up at once, like meerkats.

'Have you seen a little girl?' I put my hand out to show her height. 'Blonde hair?'

They shake their heads.

'I live here.' I point to the house. 'If you see her can you come and let me know?'

They give me blank-eyed nods.

I realise I'm panting, shaking. Which way would she have gone? I turn left and start running. I should have brought my phone with me to call Robert. To call the police. I try not to think about the speeding cars. About a fact, stuck in my mind, that the main cause of child deaths in this country is traffic accidents. And then there are the other reasons. Darker possibilities. *Don't think about those.*

Any minute now, I'll see my baby girl, I'm sure of it. I glance up a side street but there's no sign of her, so I keep running.

When we first viewed our house, Robert had misgivings about the road. He said it was too busy. Could be dangerous for the girls. But I said it would be okay. What if I was wrong? What if she's been knocked over by a car? It would be all my fault. I glance up the next side street. That's empty too. What if I'm running in the wrong direction and she went the other way? I could be moving further from her all the time. And I've left Eva home alone. I should have asked Sherry and Paul to watch her. What if she decides to come out looking for me and gets lost too? This is hopeless.

I turn back, my breathing ragged, sweat gathering in my armpits and across my back. *Katie, where are you?* I turn around. I'll go back home, get Eva and we'll start searching, in the car this time. We can cover more ground that way. I'll call Robert too. This can't be happening… can it?

As I turn back into the drive, I try to compose myself. I don't want Eva to see how upset I am. I have to play down my fear. I spot her little face at the window, and then she disappears. Seconds later, she throws open the front door.

'Did you find her, Mum?'

'Not yet, sweetie. Let me get my phone and we'll get in the car and go looking.'

'But she'll be okay, won't she?'

I turn my face away, my voice sticking in my throat. 'Yes, of course, we'll go and find her.'

Eva follows me as I snatch up my phone and keys. I take a steadying breath and we leave the house. What if I never see my little girl again? How will I tell Robert?

As I'm unlocking the car, I see a familiar figure striding up the pavement towards me, immaculate in her white trousers, striped shirt and pearl earrings, dark brown hair curling at her shoulders.

Diane? That's all I need. What's my mother-in-law doing here? She's never a smiley person at the best of times, but today she has a face like thunder. And then I see who's with her…

'Katie! Katie!' I run down to meet them, noting my daughter's tear-streaked face before crouching down and giving her the biggest hug. As I feel her thin quivering body in my arms, I send up a silent prayer of thanks, inhaling the scent of her and feeling her wet tears against my cheek. 'Where have you been? I was worried to death! We were just about to come searching for you.'

'Katie!' Eva cries, following me. 'Where were you?' She puts her hands on her hips. 'Me and Mum were *really* worried!'

Katie buries her face in my skirt.

'I couldn't believe it!' Diane cries, looking over my head. 'I was driving along, on my way to the doctor's surgery to pick up a prescription, and I saw Katie two streets away from here, walking unaccompanied and crying her eyes out. I nearly crashed the car! But I can't get any sense out of the girl. Did you have a row?' She finally honours me with an icy glare.

I glance away from my mother-in-law's accusing stare and look instead into Katie's eyes, pushing her hair off her face and tucking it behind her ears. 'Katie, darling, what were you doing out of the house?'

'I'm sorry, Mummy. Are you really cross with me? Grandma said I shouldn't be on my own, but I got lost.' Katie's lower lip wobbles.

'But why did you go outside?' I press.

'I wanted to see Daddy before we went to school.'

'Daddy's working. You know that.'

'But sometimes he comes back in time, so I went out to see. You know, if he was going to come running up the road. But he wasn't there, so I walked for a bit to see if he was round the corner. But then I got lost…' Her lip begins to tremble again.

'You must never ever go out without telling me or Daddy,' I say, before crushing her small body to my chest once more, and kissing the silky hair on top of her head. The smell of her berry shampoo makes me want to cry. 'You could have been run over, or…' I dread to think what else could have happened. 'That goes for you, too, Eva.' I hold my arms out to her. 'No one is to leave the house without Mummy or Daddy.'

'I wouldn't do that,' Eva replies with an eye roll, stepping into my embrace for a too-short moment. 'Well done, Grandma, for finding her.'

Diane makes a harrumphing sound and purses her lips. But I don't care how snooty my mother-in-law is being. Thank goodness she showed up when she did.

I straighten up. 'Thank you, Diane. I… I don't know what would have happened if you hadn't spotted her.'

'Yes, well, let's not dwell on that, shall we?' she replies with a dismissive sniff. 'Shouldn't these two be at school by now?'

I check my watch. It's already eight thirty. 'We're late. I'll have to cancel my meeting.' But that's not important now. What's important is having my girls back home, safe and sound. I hold out my arms and both girls come close, letting me hug them. Eva likes to think she's too grown up for cuddles, so I'm making the most of this opportunity.

'Do we still have to go to school?' Eva asks with a pout, finally having enough of my over-squashy hug.

'Of course you do,' Diane replies for me.

Eva wrinkles her nose. 'But we've just had a *drama*. I thought people had to rest after a drama.'

I give a little snort of laughter.

'I'll take them to school, if you like, Gemma. So you can get to your meeting.'

'What about your prescription?'

'My grandchildren are more important than a silly prescription. I can pick it up afterwards.'

'Are you sure?' I ask, wishing I could decline her offer. I don't want to let the girls out of my sight. But I have to be practical. Accepting Diane's help is the only way I'm going to get to work on time.

'Of course. I do wish you'd let me help out more, Gemma. Come along Katie, Eva, get your school bags.' As Diane walks past, I get a waft of her perfume, Arpège.

We chaperone the children back inside the house and again I try not to think about what would have happened if Diane hadn't driven past Katie when she did. Hopefully I would have found her anyway, but there are all kinds of dangerous people in the world. What if one of them had been passing while Katie was out there alone? I should have been more careful. More vigilant. The fact is, someone opened the front door. And even if it was Katie who let herself out, the door was still left open. Anyone could have come into our house… I shudder and take Katie's hand. 'Let's go and wash that teary face,' I say, taking her into the downstairs loo and running the tap. 'No more crying, okay? You're home, safe and sound, and you'll see Daddy when you get home from school.'

'Okay,' she says in a small voice as I help to splash her face with water.

I pat her skin dry and hang up the towel. 'Now, let's see a happy face.'

She gives me a lopsided smile and I seriously consider the possibility of blowing off work, keeping the girls home from school and putting on a Disney movie. But then my responsible head kicks in and I realise that this would be sending out a terrible parenting message, as well as missing out on quite possibly the most important meeting of my career.

A few minutes later, I watch from the front door as my mother-in-law strides down the driveway with my daughters in tow. Once again, I feel like a crappy parent. I bet Diane never had these crises when Robert and his brother James were little. She was probably the perfect mother. I check my watch again, but I'm not really concentrating. I think I'm still in shock. I'm really not sure the girls should have gone off to school.

Okay, I can either stand here beating myself up, or I can get myself together and go win this new client. I square my shoulders and take a deep breath.

CHAPTER 3

It's the middle of the night when an insistent banging jerks me upright. I take a deep breath and exhale slowly to get my suddenly thundering heartbeats under control. But they won't obey.

'I know you're in there!' he cries, his voice twisted and rough. Nothing like the adoration and gentleness he used to show me. 'Come on, you little bitch! Open up!' His voice is still muffled. Good, he hasn't broken through the door yet. I still have time.

This is why I always rent a ground-floor flat with a back door. I've never needed it up until tonight, but now that he's found out where I live, I'll have to abandon the place before he gets to me, or who knows what he'll do.

As the hammering on the door gets louder and the insults worsen, I slip out from beneath the covers and pull a warm sweater over the top of my pyjamas. I grab my phone and my laptop from the dressing table and shove them into my bag. A ready-packed holdall sits at the foot of the bed. No point bothering with the rest of my stuff. It's not important. Just a few clothes in the wardrobe and some food in the fridge. I've never stayed anywhere long enough to accumulate anything of any worth.

Turning the key in the French doors, I briefly wonder how he managed to find me. It's been over a month since I last saw him. Over a month since I left his beautiful home. Since I got the hell out of there. So how did he manage to track me down? I've used an alias to rent this place, like I always do. Not that it matters how he found out. What matters is that he's here, and if I don't get my arse moving, he's probably going to kill me.

'Open the fucking door!' More banging, and then an almighty crash.

Shit. I draw the curtains and slip out through the door, closing it and locking it firmly, checking it really is locked. I'm annoyed to find that my fingers are trembling. I can't afford to be scared. To be weak. It will slow me down. Make me vulnerable.

I'll need to find a new place to stay. Somewhere far from here. I don't have anyone I can go to. No family of my own. It was always just me and Mum – a team. But since Mum died it's just been me. Sometimes I really wish I could have a perfect little family of my own.

As the light flashes on inside, I bite back a squeal, trying not to let the fear consume me. Instead, I shoulder my holdall and slip around the side of the building, breaking into a practiced run. My car is parked two streets away but I can cut through an alley to get there.

I realise I've misjudged this entire situation. I won't ever make the same mistake again.

Next time, I will be more careful.

CHAPTER 4

When I finally reach my office building in town – a plain 1980s red-brick building with blue windows (hideous, but practical and convenient) – my heart sinks at the sight of a workman's van parked lengthways across the front of my reserved space. I beep my horn a couple of times, but no one comes and I'm too late to deal with this now, so I reverse out of the car park and luckily manage to find a metered space in a side street around the corner.

My meeting was scheduled for nine thirty, but I'm already ten minutes late. Maybe he'll be running behind schedule too? All I need is a few extra minutes to reach my office and get myself together. I'm still shaky from Katie's disappearing act and I can hardly walk in my heels – I messed up my others in the garden looking for her, so I've had to wear a different pair which are higher and far less stable. I wasn't expecting to have to walk this far. Finally, I make it in through the entrance of the building that houses my company, GB Facilities, on the third floor.

I greet the receptionist as I make my way over to the lift. 'Morning, Cassie.'

'Morning, Mrs Ballantine. Your nine thirty is already up there. I said he could wait outside your office.'

'Okay, thanks. What time did he arrive?'

'Only about ten minutes ago. Hope you don't mind me saying, but he didn't seem too happy that you weren't here yet.'

Damn. Mick Cosgrove is a big deal. He contacted me out of the blue. He owns a couple of huge commercial buildings at the Lansdowne. It would be great for business if I could land him as a client and the last thing I wanted to do was keep him waiting. This pitch is really important to me, but I'm still shaken from this morning's incident with Katie. I hope she's okay. I'm half expecting the school secretary to call me to collect her because she's too upset to stay in class. But I can't allow my worries to take control. I need to focus on winning Cosgrove over.

The lift dings and the door opens. I step in and examine my reflection in the mirror, smoothing my hair and checking my teeth for lipstick. Luckily, I look quite calm on the outside, so hopefully he won't notice any traces of anxiety. My career has always been important. When I left school, I got a job as a PA at a facilities management company and worked my way up to a management position that involved looking after local office buildings, making sure they had adequate security, cleaners, catering, maintenance – all the boring behind-the-scenes stuff that keeps businesses ticking along. I discovered that I was really good at my job. I enjoyed making sure everything was running smoothly. I was respected, appreciated, had a decent salary. Anyway, I was in line for a big promotion when my boss was suddenly arrested for tax fraud and the company went under. I thought that was the end of everything.

One of my ex-boss's clients persuaded me to go solo and take over his contract. I got a bank loan and set up a new business – GB Facilities – with just that one contract. Now, nine years later, I have contracts with various local firms who rely on me to look after their office buildings. But Cosgrove is one of the biggest fish in the area and could propel my business out of the small-time and into the big league. I want to land him and I'm determined to win him over this morning.

The lift opens onto the third-floor lobby and I see a man in a well-tailored suit standing in the doorway to the kitchen, having a cup of coffee with Damien, my PA, and Dave, my head of security. I've never actually met Cosgrove in person, but I'm guessing this must be him. He and Dave seem to be having a laugh about something. Thank goodness he doesn't seem to be in a bad mood. I mouth a thank you to Dave before Cosgrove turns towards me.

My potential new client is tall, dark and charismatic, his brown eyes full of humour. But when he sees me, Cosgrove's smile disappears and he gives me a frosty nod. Straightening my shoulders, I hold out my right hand.

'Mr Cosgrove? Hello, I'm Gemma Ballantine. I'm so sorry to keep you wait—'

'You're late,' he replies, leaving my hand floating in mid-air.

'You're right,' I say, hoping he doesn't decide to leave. 'It's absolutely inexcusable. Please accept my apologies. Honestly, I don't make a habit of keeping people waiting. There was a van blocking my parking space and… but you don't want to hear the details of my commute.' I'm aware I'm babbling like a demented person, but I can't seem to help myself. Looks like I should have stayed home with the girls after all.

'Luckily, your head of security kept me entertained,' Cosgrove says, his manner softening a little. 'Seems we've got a few acquaintances in common.'

'That's good to hear. Dave's great. And again, so sorry I'm late, Mr Cosgrove.'

'As long as it doesn't happen again. I'm a busy man. And I was under the impression that you're supposed to be organised and on top of things.'

'Of course. I am. Today was… out of the ordinary.'

'Okay, well let's start over. Call me Mick,' he adds with a slight upwards quirk of his mouth.

I allow myself to relax a little. 'Thanks. Okay… Mick.' I gesture down the corridor. 'Shall we go to my office? Damien can get you another drink, if you'd like?'

'I'm fine.'

Once in my office, I tidy a space on my desk and pull my laptop out of my bag.

'Nice view,' Mick remarks, gesturing to the distant sea glimpsed beyond the other three rows of buildings – mainly low-rise apartments and hotels.

'It's not bad, is it? I've got my eye on the next floor up. You can see the Purbeck Hills from up there.' Although I've meticulously prepared everything in advance for our meeting – PowerPoint presentation, facts, figures etc. – I had banked on having at least half an hour to set up and get myself into the zone. Right now, I'm on the back foot. It's not a great start. Luckily, it looks like Mick hasn't been put off. After a couple of minutes of small talk about our professional lives, I launch right into my pitch about the business and what GB Facilities can do for him. Once I start talking, my nerves disappear and I actually begin to relish the challenge of winning Mick over.

We're in the middle of a complex discussion about figures when, annoyingly, my phone starts buzzing on the table. I ignore it, but then it pings several times and resumes its buzzing.

'Feel free to get that if you need to,' Mick says, leaning back in his chair and staring at me.

'Oh,' I shake my head, 'no, that's okay. I'll just…' I reach over and turn off my phone. After my terrible first impression this morning, I need to keep him sweet.

Mick smiles. 'Annoying things, aren't they?'

'Tell me about it.'

'You're not allowed to talk to just one person any more,' he muses. 'You have to have multiple conversations. I'll be talking to you in person while you're replying to someone on messenger…'

'… and tweeting about who you're talking to,' I add.

'… while taking a selfie.'

'… to put on Insta.' I grin.

'Well, thank you for turning off your phone,' he says. 'I'm happy to have your undivided attention.'

'You're welcome.'

'Look, I have to shoot off soon,' Mick says, 'but do you want to finish this meeting over dinner tonight? I'd like to go over that information I asked for regarding those security systems. Will that give you enough time to get prepared?'

Dinner tonight with a client will not go down well with Robert. And I really wanted to spend time with the girls this evening. I'm so worried about Katie. A knock at my office door saves me from answering. It's Damien.

'Phone call for you, Gemma.'

'Can you take a message? I'm in a meeting.' Damien should know not to disturb me. He's aware of how important this pitch is.

'It's the school,' he says in an apologetic whisper.

'Can you take a message?'

'They won't let me. She's insisting she speaks to you.'

'Can you call Robert for me?'

'He's not answering.'

'Please,' Mick chips in, 'take the call.'

'Is that okay? I'm sorry.'

'No problem.' Mick tactfully gets to his feet. 'I'll wait outside.'

'Thank you. I'll be quick. Damien will look after you.' I turn to my PA. 'Okay, put the call through.'

'They're already holding,' he replies.

As Damien ushers Mick out of my office, I pick up the phone, half annoyed at the school, half worried what it could be about.

'*Mrs Ballantine?*'

'Speaking.'

'*This is Hayley from the school office. We've been trying to reach you for the past half hour.*'

My pulse begins to race. 'Is it Katie? Is she okay?'

'*Katie? Yes, as far as I'm aware, Katie's fine.*'

'So, what's the problem?' This better not be a call about missing uniform or a school project.

'*Miss Chalmers has asked me to contact you. It's Eva. You need to come and pick her up.*'

'Pick her up? Is she okay? She's not hurt, is she?'

'*No. Don't worry, she's not hurt or ill, but Miss Chalmers is insisting you come in.*'

Miss Chalmers is the headmistress and I've never met a scarier woman in my life. She's good with the children, but is formidable with the parents. 'It's a bit tricky at the moment. I'm in a meeting at work,' I explain. 'Is something wrong?'

'*Can you please come in? Miss Chalmers will explain once you get here.*'

'But—'

'*As soon as you can please.*' The line goes dead. Hayley has ended the call.

Bloody hell. What's all that about? I've never had a call like that before. I put the receiver back in its cradle, get to my feet and start chewing my lip. I've now got to tell Mick Cosgrove that we can't carry on with our meeting. But that's the least of my worries. What can have happened to Eva for the school to want me to come in and collect her? Is it something serious? Did someone upset her? I hope it's not something to do with Katie going missing this morning. It just seems too much of a coincidence to have two separate incidents with my children in one morning. I should have insisted that Hayley tell me what's going on. She's power mad, that one. I gather up my phone, laptop and paperwork, and stuff everything into my bag. Taking a deep breath, I leave my office.

Mick is talking to Damien about AFC Bournemouth and their chances of avoiding relegation, but when I appear he breaks off and raises his eyebrows. 'Everything okay? Shall we carry on?'

'I'm so sorry. I'm going to have to go. Got to collect my eldest from school – some kind of emergency.'

'Oh, I'm sorry to hear that. So, shall I make dinner reservations for seven tonight?'

'Can we make it another day?' I ask, praying he won't be too put out. 'It's just... I'm not sure whether I'll be free this evening, what with my daughter...'

Mick frowns. 'I'm busy tomorrow. How about lunch on Friday?'

'Sounds good.' I nod. 'Damien, can you...'

'Of course, you go. I'll work out timings with Mr Cosgrove.'

'Thank you. Apologies again, Mick. I'll see you on Friday.'

'Looking forward to it.' He leans in to kiss my cheek, which is slightly inappropriate, and we bump heads. Luckily, Damien starts talking about suitable appointment times just as the lift door opens and I'm able to get away.

As I hasten back to the car in my crippling heels, I can't stop my mind going into overdrive, wondering what's happened with Eva. They said she's not hurt or ill, so what on earth can it be about? Why couldn't they have told me on the phone? I turn the corner and shiver as a gust of autumn wind hits me. Buttoning up my jacket, I try to remember where I parked my Honda CR-V. I've got so much going on in my head that I can't even remember which side of the road I parked on. Eventually, I spy it hiding behind a minibus. But as I draw closer, my skin goes hot and my jaw drops open. I can't quite believe what I'm seeing.

Someone has sprayed graffiti along the side of my car, its silver paintwork scarred with the damning words:

Bad Mother

CHAPTER 5

'Bad mother?' I murmur, my breath stolen from my body. I take a step closer to check the car's number plate and confirm that this actually is my Honda, that I haven't got it confused with someone else's. Unfortunately, it really is. My car has been graffitied. Is this a deliberate, personal attack on me, or simply some random act of vandalism?

I glance around to see if I can spot some youth in a hoodie running away, spray can in hand. But of course there's no one. Whoever it was is long gone. With shaking fingers, I unzip my bag and scrabble around for a tissue. I locate one and start rubbing at the edge of the awful words, trying to erase them, but they won't come off. They've fused to the paintwork. I spit on the tissue to see if that might help, but the words are indelible. Permanent. Who could have done such a thing? *Bad mother.* Am I really a bad mother? I'm not the best. I know that. I work too hard. I'm always busy. But I love my children. I feed them, clothe them, provide for them, hug them, kiss them. I would do anything for my girls.

I blow out a steady stream of air in an attempt to stop the threatening onslaught of tears. But I don't have time for tears or for any kind of self-pity. I have to get to school to collect Eva. She's a good girl. She never gets into trouble. So what could it be about? And how am I supposed to get to school now? There's no way on earth I'm driving anywhere with the words 'Bad Mother' emblazoned across the side of my car. I'm certainly not turning up at school advertising my inadequacies as a parent. At least no one is here to witness my humiliation. Luckily this is a quiet side street, not a main road. Although, maybe if I'd parked somewhere busier, this would never have happened. It's that stupid van's fault for blocking me out of my parking space at work. I feed the meter, grab my phone, leave my defaced car and walk a little way up the street to call a cab.

The woman says they'll be here in five minutes. My feet are killing me, but I can't bring myself to go anywhere near my car, let alone sit in it. I lean on a wall, slip off one of my shoes and begin rubbing at my stockinged toes. Who invented high heels, anyway? They might look good, but I'm not enjoying the pain. I'm sure pinched toes must contribute to stress.

The taxi finally shows up. I get in, mumble a pleasantry to the driver and settle back while he drives me to my daughters' school, fifteen minutes away. The journey feels slower than it is. I should probably call Robert while I have some time, but it'll be better if we speak later, once I'm home. There's too much to discuss in one phone call.

The cab drops me off outside school and I make my way across the car park to reception. It feels strange being here in the middle of the day, without the manic traffic jams and cliques of parents. Instead, it's still and silent. No movement or sound save for the leaves rustling and the sound of distant cars from the main road. I press the buzzer to the main entrance and the door is released, letting me into the building. Hayley looks up from behind the glass screen which separates school from the parents. I idly wonder why they need to have the glass there. Is it to prevent germs? Noise? Violence? All three? Hayley looks pointedly at her watch. I know it's over half an hour since she called, but there's nothing I can do about that.

'Hello, Mrs Ballantine,' she says without a smile. 'Miss Chalmers has been expecting you. I'll let you in.'

'Thanks.' I wait for the buzzer and push open the inner door which leads to the headmistress's office. Now that I'm here, I'm beginning to feel a little apprehensive. Could my usually well-behaved daughter be in trouble? Or has she told them what happened to her sister this morning?

Miss Chalmers has popped her head out of her office and when she spots me, she takes a deep breath. This looks ominous.

'Mrs Ballantine.' She holds out a hand and we shake. I follow her into her office and we both take a seat. I'd guess that Miss Chalmers is a decade or so older than me, in her forties. She has a no-nonsense attitude that makes me feel like a small child myself.

'What's this about?' I ask, folding my hands into my lap.

'Unfortunately, we've had a bit of an incident today.'

'Is Eva okay?'

'Eva is fine.' She pauses for a moment. 'Unfortunately, Lauren Taylor is not.'

'Lauren? What's happened with Lauren?'

Lauren Taylor is Eva's best friend. I hope they haven't had a disagreement. The past two years have been a tricky time with Eva's friendship groups. Lots of teasing and ostracising, tears and drama. But Eva and Lauren always manage to make up in the end. Lauren's mum, Rebecca, is a friend of mine. I say 'friend', but our relationship is probably too complicated for that label. Ever since Eva got the part of Mary in the Year 1 nativity play, things have been somewhat competitive. Not from *my* point of view. I will always congratulate Rebecca, rather than embark on a game of one-upmanship where, for example, she would say Lauren came first in a maths test and I would counter with the fact that Eva won an award for a short story. Life's too short for all that crap.

Rebecca used to have a high-flying job in the city but gave it all up to be a stay-at-home mum, and is extremely 'alpha', throwing all her mental energy into being the most dedicated parent on the planet. She's traded her power suits for boho chic and she's ditched her car for a bicycle. As chair of the PTA, she's fully immersed herself in school life, and her two kids, Lauren and Ethan, are the recipients of constant holistic, organic micro-management, cherished to within an inch of their young lives.

'Unfortunately, Eva hit Lauren,' Miss Chalmers says calmly.

'I'm sorry, what?!'

'It happened earlier today when they were getting changed for PE.'

'She *hit* her?' I ask, my muscles tensing.

'I'm afraid so. Yes. We tried calling you immediately after the incident, but, as you know, we've had some trouble contacting you and Mr Ballantine this morning. We also left a message on…' she looks at a piece of paper on her desk '… on Mrs Diane Ballantine's voicemail. She's listed as one of your alternative contacts.'

That's all I need – Robert's mother's judgement on top of everything else. 'Are you absolutely sure Eva did this? It's just, it's so out of character. She's never been violent in her life.'

'It's true, I'm afraid. She hit Lauren in the face and gave the poor girl a nosebleed.'

'No! A nosebleed?' My mind starts racing with possible explanations. 'Where's Eva now? Did you speak to her? There must be some mistake… she must be covering up for another child.'

'I'm sorry, but there's no mistake. Eva admitted to it, and all the girls in her class saw what happened.'

'Where is she?' I say, getting to my feet, my fists clenching at my sides. 'Where's Eva? If she really did do this, then it must have been in self-defence. She would never hit someone for no reason.'

'Eva wouldn't tell us. She's refusing to talk about it. But, whatever the reason, there's no excuse for violence. Please, won't you sit back down, Mrs Ballantine. I know this must have come as a bit of a shock. Eva has never been in this kind of trouble before.'

'It's just so out of the blue!' I'm desperate to find out what really happened. I need to speak to Eva. To get her side of the story. 'Where's my daughter now?' I ask, walking towards the door, desperate to speak to her.

'She's in isolation with one of our teaching assistants.'

'Isolation?' Sounds like something from a prison drama. 'What's that? Sorry, I don't mean to snap, but this whole situation sounds crazy.'

'I understand it's a bit upsetting. Think of it as a time out. She's in a quiet classroom reflecting on what she's done. Please, come back and sit down for a moment more. Would you like some water? A cup of sweet tea?'

'No, I don't want anything, thank you.' I force myself back to the blue felt chair. If Miss Chalmers doesn't get Eva here in the next five minutes, I'm going to go searching for her myself. 'And what about Lauren?' I ask, swallowing. 'Is she okay?'

'The school nurse said she'll be fine. Nothing's broken. But you should know… her mum's taken her to A & E to get her checked out, just in case.'

'A & E!' A flare of adrenalin sets my heart racing. 'Is it that bad?' I'm horrified by this whole situation. Rebecca must be furious. I'll have to apologise. Eva will have to apologise. It will be all round the school by this afternoon.

'There's another thing…' Miss Chalmers says, shifting in her chair.

'What other thing?' My palms are sweating and I wipe them down the sides of my skirt.

'Mrs Taylor is contemplating reporting the incident to the police.'

'What?' How can my quiet-as-a-mouse, good-as-gold daughter be reported to the police for violence? It's like I've stepped into some alternate universe. This can't be happening.

CHAPTER 6

'Rebecca Taylor wants to report Eva to the police?' I ask, hoping I've misheard.

'Yes,' Miss Chalmers replies, crushing my hopes. 'I did ask her not to. And, to be perfectly honest, I think it was simply an initial, angry reaction. I don't really think she'll go through with it.'

'But she might! She might report my ten-year-old child to the police.'

'She won't have a criminal record. Please try not to worry. Like I said, I'm sure it was just said in the heat of the moment. But I wanted to make you aware that it's a possibility.'

A wave of nausea hits me. I pull my phone out of my bag. 'I'll give her a call. Apologise.'

Miss Chalmers shakes her head. 'I'd leave it for a few hours. She's at the hospital right now. Once Lauren's been given the all clear, Mrs Taylor will probably feel less... emotional about the situation.'

'And you really think Lauren's okay?'

'I'm sure she's fine. It was a nosebleed, nothing more. That doesn't excuse Eva's behaviour, though.'

I try to relax my shoulders, and drop my phone back into my bag. 'Okay. Thank you. You're right. I'll speak to Rebecca later.'

Miss Chalmers gives a satisfied nod, her shiny bobbed brown hair swinging forward and back. 'For now, you'll need to take Eva home.'

'Okay, yes, sure. She must be so upset.'

'Yes, but you must understand that what Eva did has consequences. Striking another pupil is unacceptable behaviour. We have a zero-tolerance policy on violence. And with that in mind, she'll be excluded from school until Monday.'

'You're suspending Eva from school?' My heart thuds uncomfortably against my ribcage. Never in a million years did I think either of my children would be in such trouble.

'I'm afraid I have to,' Miss Chalmers replies. 'But it's also in Eva's interest. By this time next week the incident won't be as fresh in everyone's mind. And Lauren's mother will know that the school is taking this seriously.'

'I suppose that's true,' I concede. 'It might appease her. Will this exclusion... will it go on Eva's school record?'

'Yes.'

I nod and chew my lip, thinking that this could affect Eva's application to senior schools.

'Let's bring Eva in for a chat. See if she'll open up about why she did it, now that you're here.' Miss Chalmers picks up her phone and asks someone to bring my daughter to her office.

The wait is a little awkward, and we talk about how we can't believe this is Eva's final year at primary school, and how quickly the time has gone. All I can think about is that it's such a shame this has happened. I hope it doesn't ruin her whole memory of her time at school.

When the door finally opens, a white-faced Eva walks in, trailing her schoolbag along the floor. I get to my feet and hold out my arms. Eva's lower lip wobbles and she presses herself against me with a couple of muffled sobs.

'Shall we all sit down?' Miss Chalmers says. 'Eva, you can sit next to your mum.'

I peel my daughter off me and she slouches into the chair by my side like a deflated balloon.

'Hey, Eva, what happened today?' I ask. 'Miss Chalmers says you hurt Lauren.'

Eva tenses up and scowls.

'Eva?' I prompt.

'I didn't mean to!' she cries.

'So it was an accident?'

She pauses. 'Sort of.'

'Why don't you just tell me what happened, and then we can put this all behind us and go home.'

'Go home? But it's only lunchtime.' She sighs. 'I'm sorry I made her nose bleed, but she was being really mean to me. I just wanted her to stop. I didn't mean to hurt her so badly.'

'I know you didn't. How was she being mean?' I ask gently.

'I didn't bring my PE kit in today,' Eva replies.

'Well, that's not your fault. That's because of what happened with Katie this morning. We were all a bit rushed and you probably forgot to—'

'I didn't forget it,' Eva says. 'I didn't bring it in cos it was in the basket, still damp, because—'

'Because I forgot to put it in the drier,' I finish. 'I'm sorry. My fault. But what's that got to do with Lauren?'

'Well,' my daughter continues, 'I had to borrow some kit from the spares box. And Lauren started calling me Stinky Eva. Everyone was laughing and Lauren said that everyone had to call me Stinky Eva for the rest of term.' Eva's face is bright red and she's biting her lip really hard to stop herself from crying.

'Did you tell Lauren to stop calling you those names?' I reply.

'Yes. But she ignored me and then everyone said I smelled.'

I feel my temper rise on Eva's behalf. I can totally understand why she wanted to punch Lauren. But at the same time, I know she should never have reacted like that. 'Well,' I say to Miss Chalmers, 'I suppose that explains why Eva lashed out.'

'Did you tell Mrs Slade about the teasing?' Miss Chalmers asks.

Mrs Slade is Eva's class teacher. I'm a little miffed at the head referring to Lauren's behaviour as 'teasing'.

'No,' Eva replies.

'Don't you think it would have been better to tell your teacher, rather than hit someone?' Miss Chalmers asks.

Eva shrugs. But it's not a defiant shrug, it's more like an I'm-exhausted-can-this-stop-now shrug.

'At least we know that it wasn't unprovoked,' I say. 'Eva was being picked on.'

'I agree, it can't have been very nice,' Miss Chalmers says with a sympathetic expression. 'But it's still no excuse for such a violent outburst.'

'But surely—' I begin.

'I suggest you take Eva home, and take some time to reflect on what's happened. With any luck, Lauren's nose will be fine and everything can go back to normal on Monday.'

'Will you be having a word with Lauren about her behaviour?' I ask.

'I think Lauren's had enough of a lesson today, don't you?' Miss Chalmers says, glancing from me to Eva.

With a tense jaw and a hardening in my stomach, I get to my feet and give Miss Chalmers a curt nod. I don't want to have an argument with her in front of Eva, but I'm not happy that Lauren isn't going to be reprimanded about the way she treated Eva and got the other girls to gang up on her. 'So, she'll be back on Monday then?' I ask, double-checking that my daughter's punishment still stands.

'I think that's best. The school will send you a letter laying out the reasons and the terms of the temporary exclusion.'

I wish I could storm out, but I know that won't help my daughter's cause. So instead, I grit my teeth and shake Miss Chalmers hand before leaving the office with Eva. My mind whirling with everything that's happened, my daughter's small hand in mine.

Outside, I see that the sky has darkened and fat, cold drops of rain have begun to fall, plopping onto the tarmac with lazy deliberation. And it's now I remember that I don't have my car with me. It's still parked in town with a bloody awful insult sprayed across its side. Those two words, which right at this moment feel like they're absolutely true. An uncomfortable thought starts to take shape... could it have been Rebecca who vandalised my car? No. Surely not. That's not her style. *Is it?*

CHAPTER 7

I sit up and press the heels of my hands into tired, scratchy eyes, the events of last night driving into my brain like an express train pulling into a station. I'm not stupid, I knew it was only a matter of time before something like this happened, but it was still a shock to hear the absolute fury and violence in his voice. To realise that I was the cause of it.

Glancing around the room as grey morning light filters in through cheap polyester curtains, I arrive at the conclusion that this place is an absolute dump. If the room were nicer, I'd like nothing more than to close my eyes and sink back into oblivion for a few more hours. But it's not, so I throw off the musty blankets and get to my feet. I need to get a new job as soon as possible so I can get out of this shithole. If I hadn't screwed up so badly, I'd be getting paid right about now. Instead, I can kiss that pay cheque goodbye.

I remember climbing into the lumpy hotel bed in the early hours of the morning, my heartbeats crashing around my ribcage like metal balls in a pinball machine. I still feel antsy even now, despite the fact I dumped my phone and drove over 100 miles to get away. Surely there's no way he can find me again. Not now.

Hugging my knees to my chest, I try to summon up a smidgeon of enthusiasm for the day ahead... Nope. Nothing. But I'd better find some reserves from somewhere because I need a new plan and I need it fast.

Once again, I shudder to think what might have happened if he had got hold of me – he definitely sounded mad enough to kill.

I locate a socket under a table, next to a wastepaper basket. I plug in my laptop and wait for it to fire up. While I'm waiting, I make myself a cup of coffee using the kettle and sachets provided on the white melamine tray. I hate instant coffee, but I suppose it's better than nothing. Eventually, my home screen populates with all its colourful little icons. I hold my breath while I open my emails, hoping to see the message that will save me.

CHAPTER 8

Eva and I finally stagger into the driveway, soaked through to the skin, Our breaths coming in gasps and our teeth chattering. It was too short a walk from school to call a cab, but maybe I should have done it anyway, because it feels like we've both just battled our way through a hurricane.

I insert the key into the lock, dreaming about warm clothes and a hot cup of tea. But strangely the key doesn't seem to want to go in. I jiggle it about, but it only goes part way. I check it's the right one. It is. It's the only brass key on my fob, the rest are silver. Perhaps the rain has made the lock swell up? But that doesn't sound right. The wood might swell, but not the metal lock, surely?

'Mum, can we go in?' Eva asks, her voice partially whipped away by the wind.

'I'd love to, but I can't get the key to work.' I try again, but it's no good.

'Mum, I'm cold.'

'I know, I'm trying!'

'Sorry.' She looks down at her shoes.

'No, *I'm* sorry.' I kiss the top of her soaking-wet head. 'I didn't mean to snap, sweetie.' I take a deep breath and try the key once more.

'Maybe Dad's home?' she asks hopefully.

'He's out working.' I ring the doorbell a few times, just in case, but, as expected, no one answers. I feel like screaming. This morning has been a series of disasters from start to finish. It really seems like someone has it in for me.

'Mum? Mum!'

I give myself a shake. Eva is looking up at me like I've lost the plot.

'What are we going to do?' she asks. 'I want to go in.' Her face is pale and drawn, little tributaries of rainwater slipping down her forehead, cheeks and chin.

'I'll give Dad a call.' Although he hasn't returned any of my calls this morning, so I hope he's between clients and his phone is switched on. I pull out my mobile and thankfully Robert answers on the third ring. I briefly explain about being locked out. He's at the gym, but says he'll be here in ten minutes.

It's more like twenty minutes before we see the welcome sight of his VW Golf turning into the driveway. I suppose I could have asked next door if we could wait at theirs, but I couldn't face making small talk with anyone. Not after the morning I've had. And we would then have had to explain why Eva isn't at school. In the end, we found shelter under an overhanging laurel bush in the drive, huddling together to keep warm, like a couple of stray cats.

Robert emerges from the car dressed in his work gear. 'What are you two doing home?' he asks, light brown hair flopping down over one eye, his smile faltering when he sees our expressions. 'Are you all right? You're soaked.'

'Haven't you checked your phone messages?' I ask.

'My messages? No. Why? I've had back-to-back clients all morning. I'd only just finished when I got your call. What's happened? You okay, Eva?' He bends down to give her a kiss and then looks at me, his forehead creasing. He puts a hand on my arm. 'Let's get inside. You're freezing.'

His key slides neatly into the lock and turns effortlessly. The door swings open and we fall gratefully into the hall. It seems like days since we were last home, rather than a few hours. My feet are now blistered and throbbing and I kick my shoes off, vowing never to wear them again.

'Did you forget your key?' he asks.

'No. I've got it, but it doesn't work.'

'Let me try.'

I hand it to my husband and tell Eva to go and have a warm shower and get into dry clothes.

'Am I in trouble?' Eva asks, her voice wobbling.

'Just go upstairs and get dry,' I say gently. 'We'll talk later.' On our walk back from school, Eva was subdued. I didn't push her to talk, mainly because of the storm, but also because I'm not even sure how I feel about her behaviour. She should never have hit her friend, but Lauren backed my daughter into a corner.

'You're right,' Robert says, coming back inside, wiping the rain from his face. 'It doesn't work.'

I give him a look.

'Sorry,' he says. 'I had to give it a try, just in case.'

'Let me see *your* key,' I say.

We hold our keys out to compare.

'They're different!' I note the configuration of the keys' teeth. 'Look, yours has two small ridges there, and mine has a single, larger one. How can that be?'

'Are you sure you used the right key?' Robert checks my other keys against his, but none of them match.

'That's impossible,' I say. 'How can my key have changed?' I stare down at the dull gold metal, wondering for a moment if I'm losing my grip.

'Are you sure you didn't pick up the wrong set?'

'No. All my other keys are here – my car key, work keys. It's just the front door that's different.'

'Weird,' Robert says.

I run the tip of my forefinger along the metal ridges, ignoring the water pooling at my feet from my dripping clothes. I didn't change the key – I would have remembered. So how could this have happened? Unless someone else swapped it out? Could someone have changed it on purpose… the same person who spray-painted my car?

'You're shivering, Gem. We can figure this out after you get dry, and then you can tell me what's going on with Eva.'

I nod and make my way upstairs, still trying to work out what could have happened.

After we're both finally warm and dry, Eva goes upstairs to make a start on her homework, and Robert and I sit at the kitchen table.

'So, what's been going on?' Robert asks. 'Why is Eva home early?'

I put the key issue to one side for the moment and start at the beginning of my day, when Katie went missing, and finish up with Eva's disastrous morning at school. I haven't yet mentioned the car graffiti, as it's too much all in one go. I want to concentrate on Eva's issue first.

'Bloody hell,' Robert says, taking my hands in his. 'What a crazy morning! I'm so sorry I wasn't here to help you sort it out. What can I do? Want me to speak to Miss Charming?'

I give a small smile at his nickname for Miss Chalmers. Charming she is not. 'No, it's okay. I'm pretty sure she didn't have a choice. I think we've just got to suck up Eva's punishment. But it does mean she's going to be at home for the next two days. Will you be okay to keep an eye on her? I've got to work.'

'I've got clients. Why don't I get Mum to look after her?' Robert suggests. 'She won't mind if it's just for a couple of days.'

I feel my shoulders getting heavier. Diane was a stay-at-home mum when Robert and James were young – as she's very fond of telling me – so every time we ask for her help with childcare I feel like I'm failing.

'Don't look like that,' Robert says with a smile. 'You know Mum loves having the girls over.'

I sigh. Diane doesn't approve of working mothers. The woman is like something out of the 1950s. I definitely am not what Diane imagined as a mother to her grandchildren. I'm an only child from a working-class background, brought up by my mum. I never knew my dad. Compared to me, Robert comes from serious money, so I'm sure Diane thought I was a gold digger. She was a little put out when my business started taking off, just after Eva was born, and my income soared. It didn't fit with her image of me.

When Diane's husband Terence was alive, he wouldn't let his sons have any handouts, which is why Robert started his personal-training business. But after his dad died a couple of years ago, Diane wanted to start paying him a monthly allowance to help with bringing up the children, even though my earnings mean we don't really need it. Robert said no to the allowance, much to Diane's disappointment. I'm sure she would have tried to use it as a way to exert more control over my family.

'So I'll give Mum a call about tomorrow and Friday?' Robert asks.

I don't really have any choice in the matter. 'Okay. But don't let her spoil Eva. She's off school because she walloped her friend, so she needs to do schoolwork, or at least read, not go online or watch TV.'

'Should we get her down and have a talk to her?' Robert asks, heading towards the door.

'Hang on, there's something else I need to tell you.' I explain about finding my car sprayed with the words 'bad mother', and his mouth drops open.

He pulls me to my feet and gives me a hug. 'What a crappy day you've had.'

'The thing is,' I say, trying to keep my voice from breaking, 'the thing is, maybe I am. Maybe I really am a terrible mother.'

'Don't be ridiculous. You're the best mother in the world.' His eyes soften and he puts a hand to my cheek.

'That's lovely of you to say, but we both know it's not true...' I sniff. 'I love the kids to death, but I spend most of my time working.' I pull away from my husband's arms and begin pacing the kitchen.

'Yes. You do. You work bloody hard. You're an amazing role model. A strong, working mum. There are all kinds of mothers – whether you stay at home or go out to work, as long as you love your kids, then no one has a right to judge or spray-paint horrible stuff on your car.'

'Thank you.' I stop pacing for a moment and lean back against the kitchen counter. 'You know, my mum worked hard all her life. She didn't have a choice. But I do. Maybe I'm making the wrong one?'

'Are you really going to let some cowardly vandal make you feel insecure about yourself?' Rob says, his head tilted to the side.

'I suppose not.'

'Good. Well then, we should report it to the police. Maybe they can find out who did it.'

I cringe at the thought of explaining it to them. 'Do we have to?'

'No, but—'

'It's humiliating.'

'Don't let some jerk make you feel bad. It's not humiliating.'

'Having to tell the police that someone thinks I'm a crap mum is definitely humiliating. I had a thought earlier… you don't think it could have been Rebecca, do you?'

Rob stares at me as though I'm crazy. 'Rebecca? You mean Lauren's mum?'

'She could have done it in retaliation for Eva hitting her daughter.'

'That's a bit extreme. You don't really believe that, do you?'

'No. I suppose not.'

But a part of me does believe it. Granted, it does seem a bit extreme, but it's a huge coincidence that it happened on precisely the same day that Eva hit Lauren. I mean, who else could it have been? Who else would do something like that? Unless… could it be something to do with Katie getting lost this morning? Could someone have seen her leaving the house, and then vandalised my car as a reaction? I don't know what to think. Unease ripples across my shoulders and trickles down my back. I shiver, wishing I could shake off these dark thoughts. But my mind is full of questions. And I have a feeling that finding the answers will be far from easy.

CHAPTER 9

I'm early. There's still ten minutes until the gates open for school pickup, but I wanted to get here in plenty of time. I need to see if Rebecca's here. Even though she took Lauren to A & E, she still has to pick up her youngest, Ethan, who's in Katie's class. I reverse into a tiny parking space and marvel at how much easier it is to park Robert's Golf than my huge CR-V. I couldn't face seeing that awful graffiti again, so my husband said he would pick up my car and take it to the body shop to be resprayed.

At least it's stopped raining. As I step onto the wet pavement and start walking around the corner to school, I realise my heart is pounding. Will everyone know what's happened? Will they all be judging me? Talking about me and Eva? Hopefully the news won't have travelled yet. Unless Rebecca has told everyone already.

'Gemma!'

I turn to see Suri jogging down the road behind me, dark curls bouncing around her shoulders. I wave and wait for her to catch up.

'I thought it was you,' she says. 'I was parked behind you, you know.'

'Sorry, I was in a world of my own.'

We start walking in step towards the school gates. 'Have you spoken to Rebecca yet, about… this morning?'

This confirms my suspicions that Rebecca has already been trigger happy with the school grapevine. 'I'm going to speak to her now – if she'll let me.' I follow Suri's gaze to see the usual huddle of school mums in the playground over by the fence. My insides churn, but the sooner I get this done, the sooner it'll be over. 'Wish me luck.'

Suri squeezes my arm and crosses her fingers. 'Don't worry, she'll have calmed down by now.'

'Hope you're right. I always feel so inadequate around that woman.'

'Inadequate? Psht.' Suri shakes her head. 'You're the perfect mother with the perfect family. You've got it all, Gemma.'

I look up at my friend, trying to work out if she's trying to be funny. But her expression is sympathetic. I sigh. 'It might look perfect from the outside, but some days it feels like I'm barely holding it together.'

'Well, you don't show it,' Suri says. 'Look, just hold your head up, apologise, and if she doesn't accept it, then she's not worth bothering with.'

Suri's right. Rebecca will get over it. They're just kids. And kids do stupid things all the time. No one's died. I'll apologise to her and that will be that.

But as I approach the school gates and see Rebecca holding court surrounded by all the other Year 6 mums, I seriously consider turning around and going back to the car. I could come back a bit later when everyone's left. Call the school and tell them I'm running five minutes late... For goodness sake, I'm a grown woman. I need to get a grip.

Rebecca catches my eye but pretends not to have seen me, resuming her conversation with Clarissa, Jodie's mum. I wonder how, as a reasonably successful businesswoman, I can feel so intimidated by a group of mothers, when I can stand up and give a speech in front of a roomful of professional business people without so much as a hand tremor. Again I can't help wondering if she's the person who vandalised my car. It seems extreme, but who else would have done such a thing?

I square my shoulders and approach the group, giving tentative smiles to some of the other parents. They smile back, but without too much warmth, and then turn their attention immediately back to Rebecca, nodding in my direction. Rebecca turns around to face me, beach-blonde waves framing her freckled face, like a lion's mane.

'What is it, Gemma?'

'Can I have a private word?' I ask quietly.

'You do know I had to take Lauren to accident and emergency this morning?' she says loudly.

So no private word then.

'I would have at least expected a call from you,' she says.

'I know. I wanted to come and apologise. See how she's doing. But Miss Chalmers said you were at the hospital, so I didn't want to disturb you. How is she?'

'We have to keep an eye on her overnight,' Rebecca says.

My heart sinks. 'They kept her in?'

'No. She's at home now. My sister's there, looking after her.'

'So she's okay?'

'No. She isn't okay. She's completely traumatised. There was blood everywhere.'

'I'm so, so, sorry. Eva is devastated about what happened. She never meant to—'

'Look, I'd really rather not talk to you right now, Gemma. It's been a really stressful day. So if you could just… leave me alone, I'd be grateful.' She puts a hand to her forehead and turns her back, leaving me on the outside of her circle. Everyone else's gaze slides away and I have no choice but to leave them all to gossip. The caretaker comes to unlock the gates and we all move into the playground. Suri is deep in conversation with one of the other mums and I don't want to interrupt them, so I stand on the other side today, staring resolutely ahead. I wonder what will happen when Eva returns to school next week. Will her friends give her the silent treatment too?

I can't let that happen. I have to make things right with Rebecca. I take a deep breath and cross back over to her group, feeling more determined this time. Clarissa nudges her and Rebecca turns to me, her jaw clenched. Without preamble, I launch straight into an apology that I hope will appease her. That I hope will make it easier for Eva when she returns to school.

'I just want you to know that both Eva and I are truly sorry about what happened. She's absolutely mortified and really wants to apologise to Lauren. We both value your friendship so much. What can we do to make things right?'

Rebecca's stern expression doesn't falter. Everyone else has turned away slightly, pretending not to listen, but they can obviously hear my grovelling apology. I'm not sure what else I can do or say.

'We really are sorry,' I repeat.

'It was such a shock,' Rebecca replies, touching her fingers to her cheek, multicoloured bracelets jangling. 'For someone to be so violent towards Lauren. You never imagine this sort of thing will happen to your child. Look, Gemma, I was thinking, you might want to consider getting Eva some professional help. You know' – she lowers her voice – 'psychological help… to manage her anger.'

I feel my protective mama-bear temper rising and I want to snap back that if her daughter hadn't been taunting and ridiculing Eva in the first place, she would never have lashed out. But that won't get any of us anywhere, so with Herculean effort, I bite back my retort. I have to admit that despite Lauren behaving like a little madam, Eva was still in the wrong. 'I'll have a think about it,' I reply, hoping this will appease her.

'Because if you don't nip these things in the bud, they can get really serious when kids become teenagers.' Her voice grows louder to ensure everyone nearby can hear. 'And if she does it again, Eva could end up being excluded permanently. And none of us want that.'

I'm wondering if maybe Eva inherited her violent outburst from me, because right now, I want to punch Rebecca in the face. I probably shouldn't have drunk so much caffeine today. Valium would have been a better option. 'I'm sure Eva's learnt her lesson,' I manage. 'She's so, so sorry. And it's pretty safe to say she'll never do anything like that again.'

'Well, I hope so,' Rebecca says. 'And she'll apologise to Lauren?'

'Of course.'

'Then let's say no more about it.'

Hallelujah. 'Thanks, Rebecca. For being so understanding.'

'I'm not one to hold a grudge.' She smiles and puts a hand to her batik-print scarf, fiddling with the fringe.

Again, my mind flits back to the graffiti on my car. My chest tightens. The school bell rings. 'So... are we good?'

'We are.' With Rebecca's forgiveness, it's as though the clouds have parted to reveal the sun. All the other mums stop pretending not to eavesdrop and turn back around, this time including me in their huddle.

Clarissa gives me a smile. 'We were all just talking about next year, going up to senior school. Eva's sitting the entrance exam in November, isn't she?'

I notice that Rebecca isn't very happy that Clarissa's talking to me so soon. But Clarissa doesn't seem to notice Rebecca's scowl.

'Entrance exam?' I ask, a prickle of worry inserting itself behind my breastbone.

'For the Grammar,' Clarissa says. 'Eva's going to the Grammar school, right?'

'I... I guess she is.'

'You know you have to apply by the end of the month?' Rebecca says, catching the eyes of everyone else, all of whom are trying not to look horrified at my lax parenting.

'Of course,' I reply, trying to style it out, but it's obvious I haven't got a clue. The problem is, Robert does most of the school runs, so I'm completely out of the loop. I remember getting a letter from school last term talking about senior schools, but I've been so busy that I haven't had time to look into it yet.

'Who's your tutor?' another of the mums asks. Clare, I think her name is. I can't remember.

'My tutor?'

'Eva needs a tutor if you're going to get her into the Grammar,' Rebecca says. 'No one except the super-braniacs like Kyle and Alice will pass the entrance exam without intensive tutoring. Lauren's been practising past papers since Year 4.'

Why am I only just now finding this out? Why didn't Rebecca think to mention this to me before now? I know why – because Eva is naturally more academic than Lauren and she didn't want Eva to do better in the exam. But that's unfair. It's not Rebecca's job to inform me about these things. I should have been paying more attention. I should have been taking Eva's education more seriously. Once again, I'm thinking about what a bad mother I am. Visualising those spray-painted words. Whoever did it really knows how to wound. I surreptitiously steal glances at Rebecca, wondering if it's her handiwork. She's so holier than thou. But I'm not sure when she would have had the opportunity.

'So, does anyone have the name of a good tutor?' I ask.

This is met by a wave of tutting and breath being sucked in through teeth.

'Sweetie,' Rebecca says. 'You'll never get a decent tutor now. They were all booked up months ago.'

'But surely—'

She bites her bottom lip and shakes her head. 'You'll have to… I don't know, tutor her yourself?'

I don't have the time or the skills to do that. 'What's so great about the Grammar anyway? What about Broad Heath Girl's School? Or Ethelstone Academy? They're decent schools, aren't they?'

The muted response tells me everything I need to know.

'Here they come!' Clarissa says.

I glance over to the school building to see the Year 2s coming out of their classroom. Catching sight of Katie's blonde head fills me with momentary happiness, before I remember my dilemma. Where am I going to find a tutor for Eva? And even if I do manage to find one, will I have left it too late for Eva to study for the entrance exams? When did life get so complicated?

CHAPTER 10

Dressed in a plain grey hoodie and sweatpants, I've left the hotel room for a brief evening run. I'm in some Midlands town with a name I can't remember. The houses are terraced and the shops are bland: hairdressers and off licenses, cafes and charity shops. It's all so uninspiring. Eventually, I check my watch and decide to head back to my hotel room. On the one hand, I wish I never had to return to its depressingly mint-green walls. But on the other hand, I'm anxious to check my messages. I still haven't replaced my discarded phone, so the laptop is my only means of communication at the moment.

Rounding the corner, the flaking rendered facade of the hotel comes into view, like a giant lump of mouldy clotted cream. There's a conference being held here at the moment. A black sign outside with those stick-on letters proclaiming the name of some company or other. People in cheap suits trying to sound important. Loud conversations. Power games. Name badges. Drinking. Flirting. I wish I didn't have to witness any of it. I push away the thought that this is simply jealousy talking. These are people who have normal lives. Careers. Families.

Head down, I slow to a walk and slip through the sliding doors into the foyer, avoiding eye contact with the guy on reception and heading straight up the stairs to room 16B. My room. Hopefully not for much longer.

Desperate to check my messages, I opt to prolong the agony by first having a shower.

Finally clean and dressed in my pyjamas, my hair still damp, hanging straight down my back, I open up my laptop and my heart gives a little leap. There are three unopened emails. I tell myself not to get my hopes up, but I can't help the flicker of excitement in my belly that one of these three messages could be the one to turn my fortune around.

I open the first message and delete it immediately, blocking the sender. The next one looks okay, but they want me part of the time in England and the rest of the time in France. I don't have a passport. I suppose I could procure one, but it would be risky. And the last thing I need is more risk.

Taking a deep breath, I open the final message. My heart begins to pound. This could be just what I need to put my previous nightmare behind me. I have a good feeling about this. This could be it. And I've always fancied living by the seaside…

CHAPTER 11

I pull into Diane's gravel driveway with Katie chattering non-stop in the back seat, telling me about her day at school. I'm only listening with one ear, as the rest of me is tied up thinking about Eva's entrance exam and about my presentation tomorrow. But Katie isn't pausing for breath, so I don't think she's too worried.

Diane lives in an enormous sprawling Edwardian villa opposite the golf course. It's the same family house where Robert and James grew up. An idyllic place with a half-acre garden that boasts fruit trees and a swimming pool. Diane always says it's far too big for her, but she couldn't countenance living anywhere else. She says they'll have to carry her out of the place in a coffin. That's her subtle-as-a-brick way of telling us that she will never downsize or be shifted into a granny annex, let alone any kind of nursing home. I admire her in a way. Diane Ballantine is a formidable woman.

Ideally, picking up Eva won't be a drawn-out exercise. Robert dropped her off this morning, so I haven't heard Diane's reaction to the event yet. This should be interesting…

'Are we having tea at Grandma's?' Katie asks, undoing her seatbelt.

'Not today.'

'Pleeease. Grandma does angel cake with the three colours. And she lets us use the posh plates.'

'I said, not today.'

'That's not fair. Eva's been here longer than me. I only get to come for one minute.'

'Come on, out you go, if you want to see Grandma.'

Before we make it to the front step, Eva throws open the wooden front door, her face alight. In her hands she's brandishing several carrier bags.

'Hi, Eva, how was your day?' I ask. 'What are those?'

'You'll never guess what!'

'What won't I guess?' I ask with a smile. 'You've been to the moon? You've grown a third leg? You've suddenly started liking broccoli?'

'Mu-um, no, listen.'

'You asked me to guess, so I'm guessing.'

Katie thinks this is hilarious and starts coming up with wild and crazy things that Eva might have done today. But I can see Eva is becoming irritated with our teasing.

Diane appears at the door. 'Come in. I've just put the kettle on.'

'Thanks, but we're not stopping, Diane.'

'Nonsense. Come in.' She turns away and walks across the vast hallway, which could probably accommodate the whole downstairs footprint of our home.

I sigh and follow her into the house, kissing Eva's cheek. 'Tell me, then, Eva. What's this thing I'll never guess?' I do a double take. 'Have you had your hair cut?'

'Yes!' she squeals. 'Just trimmed though. Grandma took me to her hair salon. Not a kids' place but a proper grown-up salon with magazines and fancy biscuits.'

'Very nice.' Eva's caramel hair has been styled and waved as though she's an eighteen-year-old debutante. It actually looks awful, but Eva is so pleased with herself that I daren't say what I really think.

'And we went shopping!' she cries, thrusting the carrier bags in my direction.

'That's not fair!' Katie wails.

I inhale and try to stay calm.

'Don't worry,' Eva says to her sister, 'we bought you some things too!'

Katie's eyes widen and the two of them go zooming off into the sitting room while I follow my mother-in-law into the kitchen.

'Thank you, Diane, but you really shouldn't spoil them like that.' I don't say what's really on my mind – that Eva has been excluded from school as a punishment, and shouldn't be given treats as though it's a special occasion. I'm worried that she'll go into school on Monday and start telling all her friends about her hair and new purchases. And I dread to think what will happen if it gets back to Rebecca. But I can't complain too forcefully; Diane is doing us a huge favour by having her.

'It's nothing,' Diane replies airily. 'I already had a hair appointment in town and I thought Eva would enjoy getting her hair styled too.' She fixes me with a stare. 'You'll have tea.' It's a statement rather than a question.

'Um, yes, that would be lovely.' I sit at the vast farmhouse table, conscious not to scrape my chair across the expensive slate floor.

'Now,' Diane says, spooning tea leaves into the pot, 'Eva tells me she was being teased for wearing another child's smelly PE kit, is this true?'

I permit myself an eye roll, as my mother-in-law's back is still turned. 'It wasn't smelly. It was perfectly clean. It was just taken from the spares box, that's all.'

'Perhaps you need to employ some help, dear.' Her gravelly voice grates on my nerves.

'We're okay,' I say evenly. 'It was just a one-off. Anyway, we already have Mandy, who comes in to clean once a week.'

'Yes, but the shopping, the cooking, the washing... You know, it's a full-time job. When the boys were younger, I had help and still I never stopped. There was always something to do. I don't know how you manage the house and the children while you're at work all day. It's impossible.'

'We manage between us. Robert's at home most of the day to sort out the girls, in between clients.'

'Yes, but he shouldn't really have to worry about shopping and washing the girls' clothes. It's a bit demeaning for him, don't you think? Emasculating, I think that's the word.'

I'm fairly used to Diane's old-fashioned attitude, but sometimes I really want to point out that we no longer live in the 1950s. 'Robert doesn't mind. We're a team.'

Diane sniffs and pours milk into a porcelain jug.

I think it's best if I change the subject. 'I was talking to some of the mums today and it looks like I'll have to get Eva a tutor.'

'Nonsense! That girl is as bright as a button.'

'I know she is, but apparently everyone tutors their children to get them into the grammar school.'

Diane raises an eyebrow. 'The boys got into the grammar without any tutoring.'

'Yes, but things have changed since then. There are fewer places. It's very competitive.' As I'm explaining all this to Diane, I'm realising that I've really taken my eye off the ball here. I should have sorted all this out a year ago.

'Hmm.' Diane's eyes narrow for a moment as she thinks. 'Leave it with me. I'm sure among all my friends at the golf club, I can come up with a good name for you.'

'Really?' I'll say one thing for Diane, she knows everybody who's anybody.

'Of course.'

'Thank you. That would be great.' With Diane's contacts, I just might get the opportunity to turn this around after all.

She places four slices of angel cake on a floral china plate and sets it on a tray next to the tea things. 'We'll have afternoon tea in the drawing room. Be a dear and take the tray through. I'll bring the biscuits.'

After a long evening at the office planning the rest of tomorrow's pitch for Mick, I'm finally home, sitting at the kitchen table with a cheese and mushroom omelette that Robert made me. I still have a little more finalising to do, but it shouldn't take more than an hour.

'Wine?' he asks.

'Better not. Big day tomorrow. This omelette is delish though. Thank you.'

Robert sits opposite me, sipping a cup of herbal tea while I give him a quick rundown of today's events, including Rebecca's delight in making me squirm before she finally accepted my apology. He's suitably sympathetic. I then go on to tell him that Eva needs a tutor. 'Your mum said she'll look into it for us.'

'Bet you any money she'll have a name for us by this time tomorrow.' Robert grins.

'You're probably right!'

He sighs. 'I'm annoyed with myself for not realising she needed a tutor. I should have been on top of it. When's the exam?'

'Sometime in November, I think. Thing is, one of us will have to be at home with the girls after school for the next couple of months while Eva studies. We'll need to be home to help her.' At the moment, both girls attend an after-school club most days, unless either of us are able to pick them up earlier.

Robert doesn't reply. He just nods slowly, gazing into his tea.

'Is there any way you could cancel your afternoon clients for a few weeks? Just until the exam's over.'

'I would if I could, Gem. But if I let my clients down, they'll go somewhere else. I know my career isn't as high-flying as yours, but I love what I do, and I'd miss it if —'

I hold out my hand to stop him talking. 'Of course. Sorry, it was unfair of me to ask.' I can feel this conversation has the potential to turn into an argument and I really don't want that to happen. As long as Robert and I are on an even keel, I can cope with everything else.

'Is there any way you can cut back your hours?' he asks.

I swallow the last piece of omelette and put my fork down. 'Cosgrove's on the verge of signing this contract, and two of my managers have just left. I'm stretched thin as it is.'

Rob runs a hand through his hair and sighs. 'Does she have to go to the grammar? There are other schools, surely?'

'Yeah, but apparently they all have awful reputations.'

'Can we afford private?'

'Maybe. But would we want to send her to private school? I mean, I'd much rather she mixed with kids from all backgrounds. And why would we waste the money when she could have a perfectly good state education at the grammar?'

'It's a minefield,' Robert says, shaking his head. 'I thought school was school. I mean, I know I went to the grammar, but I don't think things were so complicated back then. We just did the test and if we passed we got in, and if we failed we didn't. Pretty sure there wasn't any tutoring involved. Okay, so what about if we arranged some kind of childcare? Some kind of... au pair, or a nanny? Actually, Mum suggested a nanny a while back, but I didn't pay it too much attention. You know what Mum's like – always suggesting things. But now I'm thinking she might have actually been onto something.'

'Do we really want our children brought up by a stranger?' I reply, shuddering at the thought of someone else living in our house. 'It would be such an invasion of privacy. Imagine it. You and I would be in here having a late-night chat, and there'd be somebody else drifting around the house.'

'I suggested a nanny, not a ghost. But I take your point.'

'So…'

'I dunno, Gem. I've suggested everything I can think of. I suppose I could try to shuffle some of my clients around so I'm home by three. But it would probably mean you'd have to do all the school drop offs and a couple of the pick-ups.'

'I think I could manage that. Are you sure?'

'I can't promise. But I'll ask Selina and Karim if I can shift some timings around. They're self-employed, so it should be okay.'

'Amazing! Now all we need is a tutor.'

'Leave that to my mum. She'll be on the case.'

I nod, yawning. 'I just need to run over some figures before bed.'

'You look exhausted.' Robert comes round the table and starts massaging my shoulders.

'That feels amazing.'

He bends down and kisses my neck. 'Leave work for tonight and come to bed.'

I yawn again. 'I'd love to, but I really have to do this. After tomorrow, things shouldn't be so hectic.' Then again, if I end up winning this pitch, my workload will probably double. I don't mention that to Robert. I'll deal with that if and when it happens.

My husband's hands stop kneading my muscles. He pats both my shoulders and moves away. 'Right, well if you're not coming, I'm off to bed. I'm out at six a.m. tomorrow so I'll say good luck now.'

We kiss, and for a brief moment I'm tempted to blow off work. But eventually I pull away.

'Night,' he says.

'Goodnight.'

I watch my husband as he walks out of the door, wishing I could go up with him, but knowing that I have to get this pitch done. Although I'm not sure how I'm supposed to concentrate on work with so many other worries flying around my head. Ever since Katie went missing, I've had this anxious, crawling sensation in my belly. Like something terrible is about to happen. It's ridiculous, I know. I've never been one for believing in superstitious feelings or worrying over nothing, but too many odd things keep happening for me to keep ignoring them. The 'Bad Mother' graffiti wasn't random, I'm sure of it. And the swapped key – I can't make any sense of it. It must have been deliberate. And the thought of someone out there with a grudge or a vendetta against me and my family makes my skin go cold. I usually approach problems logically, working my way through them until I reach a solution. But there's absolutely nothing logical about any of this. The only explanation is that someone is targeting me. But who? And *why*?

CHAPTER 12

Out for my evening run, I am able to shift the past from my mind. Instead, I allow myself to daydream about the future. About how much better things are going to be. I need this to be the last time I'll check into a cheap hotel, or rent a crappy one-bed flat on the seedy side of town. I need this to work out.

My feet slap the green-grey pavement and my breaths come regular and heavy. Slap, slap. In, out. Slap, slap. In, out. Like a machine. I have to think of myself as an automaton getting the job done. No room for sentimentality or compassion. Just the steady rhythm of the job.

I'll plan it with military precision.

And then I'll execute it.

CHAPTER 13

Marco's is buzzing and this time I make sure to arrive fifteen minutes early, so there's no chance of keeping Mick Cosgrove waiting a second time. The waiter shows me to a table by the window overlooking the beach and sparkling sea beyond. This place is pricey, but it's worth splashing out to keep Mick sweet. The table is large and circular with plenty of space to work and eat.

With the lunchtime autumn sunshine blazing in, I'm now wondering if I should have reserved a table further away from the window. I remove my suit jacket and hang it over the back of my chair and decide that the view is worth it. Mick shows up five minutes early, and I let out a breath, relieved that I arrived before him this time. He's dressed more casually today, in chinos and a short-sleeved shirt. I feel a little overdressed by comparison in my cream suit. Getting to my feet, I hold out my hand to shake his, but – like last time – he leans in to kiss my cheek, and I get a waft of expensive cologne.

'Gemma, good to see you again. I'm impressed you managed to get a table here at such short notice.'

'Marco, the owner, is one of my husband's clients,' I reply.

'What does your husband do?'

'Robert's a personal trainer.'

'That's handy.'

'Very. Marco says he relies on Robert to help him burn off the calories from all the sample menu tastings.'

'I meant, it's handy having a personal trainer in the family. I noticed you look very... fit.'

Mick's eyes travel lazily over my body and to my irritation I feel my face flush. I'm not sure if he's flirting or not so I just give a quick smile and change the subject. 'Hope you got parked okay? As soon as the sun comes out, everyone seems to flock down here.'

'No worries, I got a cab.' He rubs his hands together. 'Looking forward to a glass of wine.' He holds up a hand and a waiter scurries over. 'Shall I get us a bottle? Red or white?'

'Thanks, but not for me. I'm driving.'

'Come on, Gemma, I'm not drinking alone. We can share a cab back. Red or white?'

I've never been one to give in to peer pressure, but this contract is important to me so I decide that half a glass won't hurt. I'll sip it slowly and make it last, then I'll still be okay to drive. 'Okay then, white.'

'Excellent.'

After a quick perusal of the wine list, Mick chooses a bottle of something I've never heard of. The waiter brings it over and pours. It's delicious – I'll have to be careful to stick to my self-imposed half a glass. We order our food – he orders pasta, I have my usual Caesar salad – and then we turn straight to business.

'Shall I walk you through the figures while we wait for lunch to arrive?' I ask, pulling my laptop out of my bag.

'Good idea.' Mick moves his chair around so he's sitting by my side. I suppose it's more practical this way as we can now look at the screen together. But I'm aware he's awfully close, and as he reaches for his wine glass, his bare arm brushes mine. I discreetly move my chair an inch to the left and launch into my pitch.

We're only ten minutes into my presentation when Mick lifts the wine out of the ice bucket and holds it out over my glass.

'Not for me, thank you.'

'You can't expect me to drink the whole lot on my own. I won't be able to concentrate.' I'm too late to cover the glass with my hand, and he pours despite my protests.

'I'll be giving you all the wrong figures!' I joke. 'You're a bad influence.'

'I hope so,' he chuckles. And then, bold as anything, he rests his hand on my thigh.

My instinct is to flinch and throw his hand off my leg. It's now pretty clear Mick Cosgrove is interested in more than just a business relationship. But I can't let him think of me this way. It will ruin everything that I've worked so hard for. I need to get this meeting back on track. Steer it round to something unsexy. Like cleaning contracts. To deal with his hand on my thigh, I close the laptop, and get to my feet to excuse myself. 'Just nipping to the bathroom, back in a minute.'

'Take your time,' he drawls.

Shit. I weave my way past the other diners, feeling more than a little unsteady on my feet. And it's not down to the wine. When I reach the ladies, the echoing chatter of the restaurant mutes as the door swings shut after me. I stare at myself in the mirror. My cheeks are flushed, and my breathing is shallow. Just because Mick Cosgrove is this hotshot businessman, I'm letting him get away with totally outrageous behaviour.

Splashing cool water on my face, I try to clear my head, to think about the best way to handle this without causing any offence, and without blowing this deal. I come to a swift decision. Mick Cosgrove is rich, successful and very good looking. But it doesn't give him the right to expect anything from me other than professional courtesy. I pat my face dry, take a breath and leave the bathroom, walking confidently back to the table. Once there, I move my chair a couple of feet away from his and pour myself a glass of water.

Thankfully, our food arrives and the conversation continues in a business vein.

'It's all sounding great,' Mick says. 'I really think I'm going to enjoy working with you.' His gaze rests on my face a little too long, and my chest tightens with disappointment. If he's going to insist on flirting so obviously, then this business relationship between us is not going to work.

'I'm pleased you think GB Facilities could be the right company for you,' I say, going for neutral corporate speak. 'I'll email you the presentation so you'll have all the information to mull over in your own time.'

'What about dessert?' he asks.

I pat my stomach, pretending I'm full up. 'Not for me. But do go ahead and order one, if you'd like.'

'I would like,' he says, shifting his chair closer again. 'But there's something else I'd like much more.'

I'm just about to stand when he slides his hand right up my skirt between my thighs. Instantly, I shove his hand away, jerk my chair back and get to my feet. He reaches out and tries to take hold of my hand, but I snatch it away.

'This is a business meeting and you just groped me!' I glance around the restaurant to see if anyone saw what just happened. But the place is busy and no one is paying us any attention.

'I'm married!' I snap. 'And I love my husband. And I don't appreciate being touched up like I'm a piece of meat.' I gather my things together with trembling hands.

'So what if you're married?' he says with a shrug. 'I won't tell if you won't.'

The man has skin as thick as a rhino. 'I'm leaving now,' I reply through gritted teeth.

'Look, Gemma. If you must know, I was never interested in your business. You're small fry. You're unprofessional, inexperienced and unfocused,' he says coolly. 'But I would have overlooked those issues if there was something else in it for me. End of the day, it's your loss.'

'You're unbelievable!' I flee the restaurant, trying not to give in to the threatening tears of fury. I need to get away from here as fast as I can. At least I'll never have to see his sexist face again. Not if I can help it anyway.

By the time I've collected Katie from school, and turned into Diane's drive to pick up Eva, I've managed to calm down a little. Katie's chatter in the car about school reminds me that business isn't what's most important. Family is everything to me. I realise I'm better off finding out now that Mick is a sleaze, rather than discovering the fact after we've signed a contract and I'm stuck with him. He's a predator. I should report him to the police.

I was hoping to collect Eva from Diane's with the minimum of fuss and then slink back home. But Diane ushers us through to the sitting room where my daughter is sitting on the sofa in between her Uncle James and Aunty Amelia. Usually I would love to see them, but right now I'm too shaken up for socialising.

'Gemma! How are you?' James booms, crossing the room to give me a hug.

Robert's older brother is an antiques dealer and the proverbial black sheep of the family. It's awful to say, but Diane heavily favours my husband over James. Robert is taller, more charming, more handsome. I often feel sorry for James; the brother who never quite measures up to Diane's exacting standards. But the funny thing is, James really doesn't seem to mind. The brothers have a great relationship and are always joking about Diane's favouritism. Her criticisms just seem to slide off James. Perhaps he's simply grown used to them. Witnessing Diane's constant cutting remarks towards James has made Robert and I doubly determined to show our girls absolutely no favouritism.

Whatever the situation between James and his mother, he's a lovely man, and has always treated me like a sister. His warm hug is threatening to undo me after the awful day I've had. I blink hard and clear my throat. 'Hi, James. I'm fine, thanks.'

'And what about this little lady?' James lets go of me and picks Katie up in his arms.

She flings her arms around her beloved uncle's neck. 'Uncle James, swing me round!'

'Not in here,' he replies. 'Grandma will have a conniption and feed us to the fishes if we break anything,' he jokes.

'Don't be ridiculous,' Diane replies.

'What's a *kernipshun*?' Katie asks.

James goes on to explain, making Katie giggle with other long words.

'Hi, Mum.' Eva gets up off the sofa and comes to give me a hug.

'How was your day with Grandma?' I ask, kissing the top of her head and wrapping my arms around her slight body. Her innocent smell grounds me for a brief, blissful moment.

'Fine,' she replies. 'I helped Grandma in the garden today.'

'Did you? Well done. Maybe we could do some gardening together at home over the weekend?'

'You don't do gardening,' Eva replies, staring at me like I've lost my mind.

'Well, maybe I could start.'

'Eva was very helpful,' Diane adds, making my daughter flush with pride.

'Hi, Gemma.' Amelia and I kiss one another on the cheek.

'Lovely to see you,' I say, meaning it. I get on well with my sister-in-law. She's a little showy – designer clothes, flash car, jewels – but I consider James's wife to be a good friend. Which is something of a turnaround, considering our shaky start.

Amelia is also Robert's ex-girlfriend. They had been together since high school. Robert's parents and her parents were old friends. They were practically betrothed at birth. But Robert broke things off with her. He said it was because they had grown to be more like brother and sister; the passion had gone – for him, anyway. And then, a year later, Robert and I met at a party and fell deeply in love. The kind of love where you can't breathe when you're away from the other person. Where you spend all day in bed because nothing else matters. Where you don't really think about other people's feelings. We were purely and wildly in love.

It was only some time afterwards that I realised Robert's childhood sweetheart was probably heartbroken. And I soon understood that Amelia would always be in our lives, at family gatherings and parties where she fitted in better. Diane treated her more like family than me, with my working-class background. And then, a few years after, Amelia ended up getting together with James.

It felt a bit weird at first, but Robert was genuinely happy for both of them, especially when they announced their engagement. I think he felt relieved that Amelia had finally found love again. So, there are no hard feelings any more. I admit, at the time, it felt awkward to have Robert's ex married to his brother. But now Amelia is extremely gracious about the past. After a few uncomfortable years, things have settled down to become normal and relaxed between the four of us.

'Are you okay, Gemma?' Amelia asks, her brow creasing. 'Hope you don't mind me saying, but you don't quite seem quite yourself.'

'I'm fine,' I reply, taking a breath and trying to shake off today's events. However, I can't get rid of Cosgrove's awful words, his sneering expression and his invasive hands. 'It's just work stuff on my mind,' I say, brushing away her concern, my voice sounding small and far away to my own ears. 'Nothing important. Anyway, look at you! Gorgeous as ever.' I take in Amelia's slim figure and salon-shiny chestnut hair, her perfectly made-up face and designer-casual clothes. I feel bland and businessy by contrast, my cream suit crumpled, my make-up faded. I'm too out of sorts to care. 'How are you doing? We haven't seen you guys in ages.'

'Amelia's been an absolute treasure,' Diane gushes. 'She's offered to help me organise the annual golf club charity dinner dance. I would have asked you, Gemma, but I know how busy you are with work.'

James shoots me a long-suffering look, out of view of his mother. Ordinarily, I'd give him a conspiratorial smile back, but I simply can't summon up the energy. And besides, Diane's beady gaze is still fixed on me.

'Oh, yes, no, that's fine. Of course.' Speaking to my mother-in-law always reduces me to a gibbering idiot. 'So, anyway, we won't keep you, if you're in the middle of organising things.'

'You're welcome to stay for afternoon tea again,' my mother-in-law says with a sniff. 'Amelia's right. You don't look yourself. Would you like to sit down?'

'Thank you, Diane, but no. Really. We'll leave you to it. You're busy, and the girls look tired. I'll get them home and fed and bathed.'

'I'm not tired,' Katie says, followed by a huge yawn.

Everyone laughs, even Diane. But my own laugh feels as though it could quite easily turn into a sob. Today's events have undone me and all I want is to climb into a bath myself and try to soak away the memory of Mick Cosgrove. My left hand has started shaking and I feel like I might be going into some kind of delayed shock. Did that man really grope me? I've never been in this situation before… and Mick can't get away with that type of behaviour. But right now I don't even want to think about it. I just want to put the whole tawdry episode to one side and get back to normality.

CHAPTER 14

Lying in bed with a cup of tea and the papers on Sunday mornings is our little luxury. So when the doorbell rings at 9.15 a.m. I tell Robert to ignore it.

'Have you got the financial section?' I ask.

He flips the pages, making a noisy rustling sound and getting the paper into a terrible mess. This makes me giggle and he pretends to be annoyed. 'You asked me to look, so I'm looking!'

'Yes, but now it's like an explosion at a printing press.'

The doorbell rings again.

'Mum!' Eva calls from downstairs. 'Someone's at the door! Shall I get it?'

'No!' Robert and I yell back.

'I'll go.' He sighs and pushes back the covers.

'And leave me with this newspaper mess?' I raise an eyebrow.

'You can go if you want?' he replies, tying his dressing gown. 'I'm happy to stay with the mess.'

'No. That's okay.' I shove the papers onto his side of the bed and sink down into the pillows. 'Tell whoever it is to bugger off.'

'Yes, boss.'

Robert leaves the bedroom, closing the door behind him, and I sigh. The spell of our Sunday ritual has been broken. It's probably someone selling something. Knowing Robert, he won't come back to bed now. He'll get sidetracked. And now that he's gone, my mind is drifting back to what happened on Friday with Cosgrove.

It's like a huge, dark blot on my brain. A cancerous lump that I can't get rid of. I didn't mention it to Robert because I'm trying to forget it, but maybe I should…

I'm also worrying about Eva going back to school tomorrow. It would have been sensible of me to have had another meeting with the head to make sure everything goes okay on her return. And I could have called Rebecca to arrange for Eva and Lauren to meet up this weekend. It would have given the girls space to smooth everything over before seeing one another at school again. I push my fingers into my temple. It's too late now. Hopefully I'm worrying about nothing.

I hear the creak of the front door opening downstairs. Muffled voices. I wish whoever it is had left us alone for half an hour longer. I mean, who the hell calls round before ten o'clock on a Sunday morning?

Thundering footsteps come up the stairs and our bedroom door opens. Robert pops his head in. 'Sorry, Gem. It's Mum.'

'Is she okay?' Concern replaces my irritation. Diane might not be my favourite person in the world, but she's family and I wouldn't want anything bad to befall her.

'She's fine, but she wants a word.'

'With me? *Now?*'

Robert nods and gives me an apologetic smile. 'Something to do with the tutor.'

'Oh. Okay, great.' I throw back the covers and shrug on my dressing gown. Hopefully she's found someone. 'Hang on, I'm coming.'

Diane is in the living room. She's immaculately turned out as usual in one of her trouser suits, hair coiffed, regulation pearls in her ears and around her neck. The girls are sitting either side of her having two simultaneous conversations.

'Hi, Diane.'

She looks up and tries to mask her disapproval of the fact I'm not yet dressed. 'Sorry to have woken you, Gemma. I've got a nine-thirty meeting at the club so I thought I'd pop in here on my way. But I can see I've disturbed your morning.'

'No, that's okay. Girls, can you go and get dressed?'

'*You're* not dressed,' Eva points out.

'I'm telling Grandma about my school play,' Katie says, folding her arms across her chest.

'Girls.' Robert says sternly.

At this, they peel themselves off the sofa and leave the room with scowls and mutters of 'it's not fair.'

'Can I get you a tea or coffee, Diane?' I offer.

'No thank you, I can't stay.' But she makes no move to get up from the sofa so I sit on the one opposite. 'Sit down, Robert,' she says. 'You're making me nervous hovering about like that.'

'Sorry, Mum.' He grins and perches on the arm of my sofa.

'Now,' Diane begins. 'I've been asking around at the club about tutors for Eva.'

'That's great. Thank you,' I reply.

She holds out a hand to quiet me. 'Well, don't thank me yet. Apparently, you've left it far too late. Although I think you already know that.' Her voice has an accusatory tone.

'It's not Gemma's fault,' Robert says.

'Did I say it was Gemma's fault?' She shifts her gaze back to me. 'As I was saying, all the decent tutors were booked up months ago. However, I've been given the name and number of a top-notch nanny who also tutors.'

'Thanks, Diane, but we don't really need a nanny.'

'Well, you should think about it. Like I said before, you could do with a helping hand around the house.'

'Mum!' Robert says.

'What's wrong with that?' Diane asks her son. 'With both of you working such long hours, it makes sense. And this particular girl also has impeccable teaching qualifications.'

'Would she consider doing the tutoring without the nannying?' I ask.

'No. I already asked. She's just come to the end of a contract and she'll move wherever her next job takes her.'

'That's a shame,' I reply. 'I'll have to try searching online for someone.'

'Well, I'll find out the details for you, just in case you change your mind.' Diane checks her watch and stands up. 'Anyway, I must dash.'

'Thanks, Diane. It's good of you to have asked.'

'It's my pleasure. I want the best for my granddaughters.'

Robert sees his mother out and I hear her tinkling laughter out on the drive. A sound I don't hear very often, as it's usually reserved for Robert alone.

Now that I'm up, I don't feel like going back to bed, so I retrieve my laptop from the sideboard in the dining room, which doubles up as a study and general dumping ground, and decide to start searching for tutors in Bournemouth and Poole. It's probably a waste of time, but maybe I'll find someone who has a spare couple of hours a week. I take my laptop back into the lounge and plonk myself on the sofa.

I type the word 'tutor' into Google, but when I try to type in the word 'Bournemouth' my keyboard doesn't respond. It seems to have frozen. *Bloody computers.* I tap the keys uselessly. Then I try to turn the whole thing off using the power button, but even that isn't responding. The front door slams. Robert must have come back inside, but there's no point asking him to help me – he's a total technophobe.

And then, just when I think I'll have to leave it for now and hope it unfreezes, Google shuts down. I tap the keys, but the keyboard is still not responding. A green loading bar suddenly appears in the middle of the screen. It's full, as though whatever was loading or updating is finished. But then I realise it has started running backwards. And now I see a line of text below the bar that says… 'Deleting Files'.

Deleting Files? Below this statement, fast-moving reams of text scroll and disappear, some of which I recognise as my work file names.

'Shit, shit, shit!' I stab uselessly at the keys, but the countdown continues and the files keep deleting. I put the laptop down on the sofa, stumble to my feet and unplug my mobile from the charger, waiting for it to boot up.

'Hey, Gems,' Robert says, coming into the lounge, 'what shall we do today…' His words tail off when he witnesses the sheer panic on my face. 'Gemma, what's the matter? What's happened?'

'My work! My laptop! It's deleting all my files. Everything's on there. What the hell am I going to do?'

CHAPTER 15

'What do you mean?' Robert says, going over to the sofa and picking up my laptop.

'Don't touch it!' I cry.

He sets it back down and raises his hands in surrender. 'Just trying to help.'

'Sorry,' I say, immediately contrite. 'I didn't mean to snap at you. It's just, it's deleting everything! I don't want to make it worse.' I start scrolling through my phone contacts and call Gary, my IT guy. I feel bad for calling him on a Sunday, but this is an emergency and he can bill me for the overtime. The phone rings and rings. He obviously doesn't believe in voicemail or something. The loading bar has reached the halfway mark on my laptop. I wonder which of my files have already been deleted. Finally, Gary answers.

'*Hi, Gemma. Everything okay? Hang on, let me take this outside.*' The sound of crying and screaming children is almost deafening down the phone line, so goodness knows how loud it is at Gary's end.

'Gary, I'm so sorry to call you at the weekend, but it's an emergency. My laptop is freaking out and deleting all my files.'

'*Deleting your files? Want me to come round?*'

'Would you?' I pause to exhale. 'I can come to you if it's easier?'

'*No, it's mayhem here.*' Gary has four children, including three-year-old twins. '*I'll come to you at the house, yeah?*'

'Thank you. I really appreciate it.'

'*Be there in ten.*'

Although it seems like aeons, Gary is as good as his word, arriving in just under ten minutes. I'm standing at the door to greet him as he revs up the driveway on his motorbike. Robert and the girls wave to him on their way out – my husband has offered to take Eva and Katie to the park to give us some peace and quiet.

'Thanks for coming, Gary,' I say as he undoes his helmet and follows me into the lounge.

'You did me a favour,' he says with a grin, putting his helmet on the coffee table with a clank. 'Got me out of the mad house.'

I'm too stressed to smile back. 'Do you think you'll be able to retrieve my files?' I hand him the laptop.

'I'll have a look. I'd love a coffee though.'

I nod and go off to make him one, then return to perch on the edge of the sofa next to him while he works on my laptop. He's typing in a bunch of code and I feel helpless, wondering if I'm going to lose everything.

'This will take me a while,' he says. 'At least an hour I should think. If you want to go and do something to take your mind off this, I'll call you when I'm done, okay?'

'Is it looking hopeful?'

'Too soon to tell. As soon as I find anything, I'll let you know.'

I take comfort from the fact that Gary is a computer genius. If anyone can sort this out, he can. I go into the kitchen and use Rob's laptop to continue my search for a tutor. I may as well take Gary's advice and do something to take my mind off this latest catastrophe. It takes me about half an hour to send five enquiries to various tutors who have advertised their success rates for coaching students through the grammar-school tests. I wish I could get a tutor sorted out today but I guess I'll just have to wait and see if anyone replies. I'm not the world's most patient person. All the while, I'm trying to remember how many of my files haven't been backed up. All the Cosgrove stuff for starters – not that I need it for *that* bastard. But the pitch could have been recycled for other potential clients.

Finally, after an hour or so, Gary calls me back into the lounge.

'Good news,' he says. 'I've restored your files.'

'Are you serious?' I press my palms to my eyes and let out a huge breath. 'You absolute star.' I walk over to the sofa and sit next to him, gazing at the laptop screen, at all the icons in their correct place. 'Did you manage to restore *all* of them?'

'Yep.'

'Thank you *so* much, Gary. You've just saved me hours of work.'

'Glad I could help.'

'I do feel guilty dragging you away from your family though.'

'Don't.' He raises his eyebrows.

'Poor Louise, though. It's my fault she's on her own with the children on a Sunday.'

'Don't feel bad. Her mother's over for lunch. She's very hands on. Louise is fine.'

'Okay, well that makes me feel better. Thank you so much again for saving everything. What on earth caused it to happen? Some kind of virus, do you think?'

'I know what caused it. But it's odd.'

'Odd? Why?'

'So,' he says, scratching his balding head with stubby fingers. 'You told me that the last thing you were doing on your laptop was searching for tutors, right?'

'I hadn't even started searching really. All I did was type in the word 'tutor' and then the screen froze and that deleting bar appeared.'

'Well, it's the weirdest thing.' Gary shakes his head.

'What's weird?'

'Watch…' he says.

I do as he asks and watch the screen as he types various words into the Google search bar. It all looks quite normal.

'*Now* look,' he says. Gary types in the word 'tutor' and then he tries to type in something else, but the keyboard has locked up.

My heart sinks as the loading bar appears. 'It's done it again!' I cry. 'I don't believe this.'

'Don't worry,' Gary says. 'I've saved all your files onto *this*.' He hands me an external drive.

'Good thinking! Thank you. Are you able to fix it again, or do I need a new laptop?'

'Your laptop will be fine. I made it happen again on purpose.'

'Okaaay. Why would you do that?'

'I'm about to remove the virus, but I just wanted to show you what happened. The file deletion only activated when I typed in the word "tutor". Before that, everything was fine.'

'So what are you saying? It doesn't like that particular word? That doesn't make any sense.'

'No. It doesn't. Unless someone has inserted a virus into your laptop to make it lock up when you type in the word "tutor".'

'What? Why would they do that?'

'You tell me.'

'And how would they do it? Wouldn't they need to physically have my laptop?'

'Not at all. They could have sent you an email with a link containing the virus. Can you think of any strange links you've opened recently? It might not even have been that recent. If this is the first time you've typed that word, then the virus could have been sitting dormant for ages.'

I link my hands behind my head and lean back into the sofa. 'I can't think of anything out of the ordinary. But I get all sorts of emails from all sorts of people – colleagues, friends, family.'

'Okay, so do you know anyone who might have done something like *this*?'

My mind scrolls through all the possibilities and lands on just one... *Rebecca*.

CHAPTER 16

Standing opposite the school with my mobile phone clamped to my ear, I pretend to listen to the imaginary person at the other end of the call. In reality, all my attention is focused on the school gates and the surrounding area. Watching. Waiting.

It only took a few hours to drive down to the coast this morning. I headed straight to the beach, stepped out of the car and sucked in lungful after lungful of sea air. Cleansing away the past few months. Everything feels fresher here. Warmer. But I mustn't get ahead of myself. I mustn't assume anything. That's how mistakes are made.

With my free hand, I slip out the photo from the back pocket of my jeans and study it once again. The father is handsome, relaxed in jeans and an open-neck shirt. He looks… perfect. The woman, on the other hand… she looks like a cold fish. Her blonde hair is short and stylish, elfin, not a single hair out of place. It might be hard to win her around. But I won't have to. If I can get the children on my side, then the parents should come on board quickly enough.

These kids are cute. Dressed in bright Boden colours. Catalogue pretty. Probably spoilt, though. But that can work in my favour. I can spoil them too. Win them over with treats and fun. I slide the photo back into my pocket. Feel it lying there like a living, breathing thing. A family captured forever on photographic paper. A record of a moment in time. But moments, by their very nature, never last.

The area in front of the school is growing busy now. The gates swing open and the horde of parents surges into the playground, gathering in their little cliques, or standing alone swiping at their mobile phones. Five more minutes tick past. Have I missed them? Did the mother or father go in without me noticing?

The school bell rings. A long, sharp sound that takes me back to my childhood. I shudder, relieved when the clanging finally comes to an end. Maybe I'll have to cross over and go into the playground itself. I don't want to do that. I don't want to make myself too conspicuous. At least I'm harmless looking – petite, slight, dark-haired. I could blend in quite well with the other mums.

My pulse quickens. Striding along the pavement comes a woman in a dark suit and heels. It's her. The mother. She's late. The woman's face is tense, strained. Not like the other mums. Anticipation tingles in my belly. My mind begins to race. I start making a mental note of all the things I'll need to do…

CHAPTER 17

I sit at my desk and stare out of the window at the distant indigo ocean, sipping my piping hot latte. Yesterday went surprisingly well. Eva slotted straight back into school with no trouble. And there was enough going on at work to keep me busy. To keep me from dwelling on Cosgrove. I brushed off Damien's enquiries about the pitch, saying that Cosgrove Properties' ethos didn't align with ours, or some such nonsense. Damien seemed to buy it. With any luck, I won't have to think about Mick Cosgrove ever again.

My PA appears at my open door, smart as always in a charcoal suit, his hair slicked back in an achingly cool quiff. 'Hey, Gemma, you've got an hour until the next one. We've just had someone drop out.'

'Oh, who was that? Not the girl from Manchester?' We've been interviewing for a new facilities manager, but so far the applicants have been dismal.

''Fraid so. But we still have four more this afternoon,' he says, trying to cheer me up.

'Do any of them sound promising?'

'Three of them are local with minimal experience, but one is coming from a respected company up north and says she's keen to move down to a seaside location.'

'Mm, sounds interesting. Okay, thanks. Let me know how you get on.'

Damien disappears off to his desk and I open up my personal emails. There are two more replies from the tutors I emailed. The first one I open is a gushing reply from a teacher called Louise Martin. She's apologising about being newly qualified, but says she's sure she can do a good job if I give her a chance. To be honest, she doesn't sound too promising. She has zero experience and comes across as a little unconfident. Today's second reply is a snooty guy who all but reprimands me for leaving it too late to book his 'extremely sought-after expertise at coaching bright young minds'. I'm tempted to type a sarcastic reply, but manage to restrain myself. However, his pomposity makes me look at Louise Martin's naivety in a new light. Everyone has to start somewhere, right?

I take the last few sips of my coffee, pick up the office phone and punch in her number. When it gets to the fourth ring, I think about hanging up. Everyone at school said I need someone experienced.

'*Hello?*' The voice on the end of the line is young, out of breath.

'Hi, is that Louise Martin?'

'*Speaking.*'

'It's Gemma Ballantine here. I sent you an email about—'

'*Oh, yes, Mrs Ballantine. Thank you so much for calling. Your daughter sounds lovely.*'

'Thank you.' I give a wry smile. Flattery is a good opener. 'Have you tutored anyone for the grammar-school test before?'

'*I haven't,*' she says carefully. '*But I know the papers inside out. All your daughter needs is someone to teach her the right techniques and guide her through what's expected. I can do that.*'

I decide I like the sound of her. 'How about we do a trial session, see how it goes?'

'*That would be wonderful! I'm free any time. Sorry, probably shouldn't have said that.*'

'It's fine. Let's say Thursday, four thirty?'

'*Fantastic. You won't regret it, Mrs Ballantine.*'

*

To try to build bridges, Eva's teacher has paired her up with Lauren for their school science project. Which is great, but the bad news is that they have to do it as part of their homework. So this afternoon, I have once again had to leave work early to have Rebecca, Lauren and her younger brother Ethan over after school. Robert offered to host it, but after last week's debacle, I need to re-bond with Rebecca anyway, so this afternoon is as good a time as any.

The other reason I want to have Rebecca over is to see if I can find out whether she has anything to do with the graffiti and the computer virus. She's the only person I can think of who could possibly want Eva to fail the grammar-school test, which would give her a motive to stop me finding a tutor. But it seems so… *extreme.* Anyway, maybe I can be proactive and find out if she is responsible.

So far, everything this afternoon is going well, apart from a few work calls I've had to take. Ethan and Katie are playing on the trampoline in the garden, while our kitchen table has turned into a scale model of Mount Vesuvius.

'I think it would be more realistic if you didn't paint the whole thing red,' Rebecca says to the girls, her blue eyes narrowed critically, head tilted. 'Maybe add some brown. And there would be grass at the base, so you can use green, too. Maybe we could get some real grass from the garden? Give it some texture.'

I would much rather let the girls get on with the project without our input. They're quite capable of following the YouTube instructions for creating a papier mâché volcano, but Rebecca is intent on managing every aspect of the process. In fact, I think she would rather do the whole thing herself without any child involvement. But I'm sure Mrs Slade can tell the difference between parent-made projects and our children's efforts, so I figuratively wrestle the paintbrush from Rebecca's hand and suggest letting the girls do it their way. The funny thing is, I'm usually quite a control freak myself, but Rebecca's discomfort at letting the girls make mistakes is pushing me further in the opposite direction.

'Come on, Rebecca. Let's leave them to it; take our tea into the lounge.' I pick my mug up off the table and take a step towards the door.

'Shouldn't we stay and keep an eye?' Rebecca says. 'You know, Miss Chalmers is going to pick the best ones to display in the hall during parents' evening.'

'Really?' Both girls look up.

'You can come and get us from the lounge if you need us, can't you, Eva?' I take another step away, but Rebecca hasn't moved.

'Is Miss Chalmers really going to pick the best ones?' Eva asks, blowing a loose strand of hair out of her eyes.

'She is,' Rebecca replies. 'So you need to make it extra-specially amazing.'

'We will,' Lauren says.

'What time's dinner?' asks Eva.

'Pizza will be here in' – I check my watch – 'half an hour.'

'Great, I'm starving,' Eva says dramatically.

'Pizza!' Lauren's eyes light up.

'I thought we'd stay with the Italian theme,' I explain.

Rebecca always cooks free-range organic everything, from scratch, but I didn't have time to shop and cook, so I decided to order in pizza as a treat. I'm hoping Rebecca won't judge. Thankfully, she doesn't comment one way or the other.

I eventually manage to coax Rebecca away from Mount Vesuvius and into the lounge where we sit and sip our tea. But away from our children, the atmosphere feels a little strained. I'm trying to think of a way to broach the subject of my laptop virus, but I can't think of a suitable opener. Rebecca seems ill at ease too. Perhaps it's a guilty conscience, or maybe we haven't quite got over last week's incident. I wonder if I need to apologise again, but bringing it up might make things worse. Luckily, Rebecca eventually brings up the subject I was hoping to talk about.

'Have you managed to find a tutor?' she asks.

'Funny you should ask that.'

'Really?' She frowns and then leans forward. 'You found someone?'

'Yes.'

'How on earth did you manage that?'

'Google,' I reply, watching her face for any telltale signs that she could be responsible for the virus.

'Word of mouth is better,' she says, her expression not giving anything away. Either she's a really good actress, or she's innocent.

'It was awful though,' I continue. 'I was searching online and my laptop must have got a bug, because it started deleting everything.'

'Don't you have antivirus software?' Rebecca asks, pulling her feet up onto the sofa and tucking them beneath her floaty skirt.

'Yes, but the virus managed to get around it.'

'Computers are a nightmare,' she says.

'Are you any good with them?' I ask.

'Useless. I have to get Charlie to format all my PTA spreadsheets for me.'

Charlie is her husband. I wonder if he could have created the virus at her request. But maybe I'm just being ridiculous and paranoid.

'So... who's this tutor then?' Rebecca steers me back onto the subject.

'Her name's Louise Martin.'

'*Who?* I've never heard of her. Is she local?'

'I think so. We've booked a trial session for Thursday. So we'll see how it goes.'

'Does she have a good track record?'

'She's newly qualified, so not yet. But she sounds lovely.' I realise I'm making excuses for our new tutor.

'Not being funny,' Rebecca says, 'but you're crazy to hire someone with no experience.'

It's no surprise that she isn't over the moon we've found someone, but I still can't work out whether she's annoyed we've managed to hire a tutor for Eva, or if she's genuinely worried that we've got someone who won't be any good. 'Surely it's better than having no one,' I say.

She purses her lips and widens her eyes like I've said something that doesn't even warrant an answer. Her attitude makes me want to forget the whole tutor thing completely and just see what happens. But another part of me is terrified that Eva won't get into the grammar and her life will be ruined, all because I didn't take my child's schooling seriously enough.

'I feel terrible that I didn't sort this out months ago,' I say. 'I feel like… I feel like a really bad mother.' As I say those last two words, I watch Rebecca's expression like a hawk. If it really was her who arranged for someone to vandalise my car, surely her eyes will widen at the phrase. But instead, they soften.

'You're not a bad mother, Gemma. We're all just trying our best.' And then she ruins it by saying, 'I know how important your work is to you. It's just a case of different priorities.'

'Actually,' I say, gritting my teeth, trying to ignore her passive-aggressive bullshit, 'my mother-in-law says she's found someone…'

'Oh?'

'Yes. She's been given the name of a highly sought-after tutor, who's also a nanny. So I'd have to hire her to look after the kids.'

'Your mother-in-law? You mean, Diane?'

'You know her?'

'Everyone knows Diane.'

Of course they do.

Rebecca fixes me with a serious stare. 'Listen, Gemma. I'm telling you as a friend. You'd be mad not to go for the best tutor – as long as you can afford it. If Diane's suggested this person then you know she'll be amazing.' Her lips tighten, and I know the competitive part of her is regretting encouraging me along these lines.

'Do you really think so?'

'It's up to you.' She shrugs. 'Of course, if you do hire the nanny, you better make sure she's not too pretty.' Rebecca laughs, and I still can't work out if she's simply being a competitive mother, or whether she has darker motives.

CHAPTER 18

I park my car almost opposite the house so I'm afforded a clear view of the driveway and front door. My navy Corsa is an inconspicuous vehicle; five years old, it's well maintained but not flashy. Almost invisible. I realise the husband will be harder to glimpse than the wife. He doesn't have a set routine, so I'll just have to sit here and wait. I know he's a fitness instructor; I've already examined his website forensically. It's professionally done with an up-to-date blog about healthy eating and various fitness tips, gushing testimonials – all the usual bollocks. I've dressed in my running gear, just in case.

After more than two hours of waiting, my backside going numb, I'm rewarded. A woman in a blue Mercedes SLK drives up to the house and pulls into the drive. She gets out of the car, goes up to the front door and rings the bell. She's wearing designer workout clothes, her sleek hair pulled back into a high pony. It's easy to deduce that this petite, dark-haired woman is a client. But is that all she is?

Using my long-lens camera, I study Ballantine's face as he and the woman leave the house, deep in conversation. He appears more laid-back than his wife was. He's handsome in real life, thank goodness. I smile. This might actually be fun.

They stretch together in the driveway and then jog out and off down the tree-lined road. I get out of the car and follow at a distance. Thankfully, I'm reasonably fit, due to my daily runs. There's probably no need to trail him as I have all I need for now, but I could do with the exercise after sitting around in my car for so long.

And I would also like to see just how flirty Robert Ballantine is with his clients.

CHAPTER 19

This is the second day in a row that I'm doing the school pickup. Yesterday was Mount Vesuvius with Rebecca and Lauren, and today Robert has to work again. I'm beginning to think a nanny might not be such a bad idea. It's not that I don't enjoy picking up my kids from school; I do. I love watching their faces light up when they see me in the playground. I love hearing their chattering excitement as they relay the day's news. It's just, I'm spreading myself too thin. My phone is constantly ringing and buzzing with questions to answer, problems to resolve, clients to mollify. I'm still no closer to hiring a new manager at work – the northern applicant has potential, but I'm in two minds as she doesn't quite have the experience needed. If I could just get some help at home as a stop-gap measure until I can sort out a new manager at work, then that would free up my time overall.

I'm about to step out of the car to walk to school when my mobile rings. I don't recognise the number, but that's not unusual. It might be a new client.

'Hello, this is Gemma Ballantine.'

The line is quiet.

'Hello?'

I'm sure I can hear someone breathing on the other end. Maybe someone's accidentally butt-dialled me. I end the call and slip the phone back into my bag, but as I do so, it rings again.

It's the same number.

'Hello?'

Silence.

More breathing.

I shiver. Is this an accidental call, or could it be some weirdo heavy breather? What if someone is trying to intimidate me? Harm me even? Am I being overly paranoid? It's just… there have been so many little, niggly things. Too many to brush under the carpet – the car graffiti, the laptop virus, the swapped key. What are the chances of it all happening at once?

'Hello?' I snap. 'Who is this?'

Whatever's going on, I don't have time for it right now. I end the call and shove the phone back into my bag, ignoring it as it starts to ring again. As I walk towards school, a cool breeze makes me hug my jacket tight to my body. I was already late before receiving those odd phone calls, and now I'm even later. But it suits me to arrive at the last minute – that way, I don't have to stand in the playground with all the other mums. I don't feel in the right frame of mind to socialise.

I realise I'm in an unsettled mood. Perhaps it's last week's dramas catching up with me. Perhaps those strange phone calls have unnerved me. Perhaps I'm simply tired. It's also the disappointment of losing the Cosgrove account. I'd been working on it for weeks, only to miss out because of his despicable behaviour. However, I grudgingly admit to myself that it might actually be for the best. After all, I do have a lot on my plate at the moment.

It starts to spot with rain. I check my watch and break into a jog – no easy task in a tight skirt and heels, but, judging by the flow of parents moving in the opposite direction to school, I might have misjudged how late I actually am.

In the playground, I see to my relief that there are still a few stragglers. I head over to Mrs Slade who's standing with three children, two of whom are mine.

'Sorry I'm late!'

'Hi, Mum,' Eva says. 'We thought you weren't coming.'

Katie throws herself at me. 'My teacher had to go, so I had to stay with Eva because you didn't come.'

'I'm only five minutes late, Katie.'

'It felt like hours,' Eva says. 'And it's raining.'

'A few drops, that's all,' I reply.

'Nothing like a bit of wanton exaggeration,' Mrs Slade says to me with a smile. 'It's fine. I'm still waiting for Thomas's parents anyway.'

'Sorry,' I say again. I put a hand on each of my children's backs. 'Come on then, you two, let's get you home.'

'Actually,' Mrs Slade says, 'before you go, Mrs Ballantine, can I have a quick word?'

I turn back. 'Sure.'

'Just wanted to check everything's okay after last week?'

I feel my face grow hot. I haven't spoken to Eva's teacher since the punching episode. 'Yes, everything's fine, thanks. Eva and Lauren have made up.'

'Good. Yes, they seem okay in class. It's just… I was wondering why you hadn't scheduled a slot for parents' evening. I hope you're able to come. It would be useful to have a chat about everything.'

'Oh. Yes, of course. I didn't realise parents' evening was on.'

'I gave the letter to Eva's grandmother when she picked up the children. It was supposed to have been returned by this Monday just gone.'

'Oh.' I think back to last week, but I can't recall Diane giving me any letter. 'She must have forgotten to give it to me. Or maybe she gave it to Robert and he forgot to tell me. Is it too late to arrange a time?'

'I do have a couple of later slots left.' She unfolds the sheet of paper in her hand and points to a couple of blank boxes on a spreadsheet. 'There – six thirty or six forty-five'

'Six forty-five would be great. Thank you.'

'No problem.'

In the car on the way home I use the hands-free to call Diane.

'*Hello, Gemma. What can I do for you?*'

'Hello, Grandma!' the girls call from the back seat.

I shush them. 'Hi, Diane. I just wondered about a letter that Eva's teacher gave you when you picked them up from school?'

'*The parents' evening letter?*'

'Yes!' At least she knows what I'm talking about. 'Do you still have it?'

'*I gave it to you, dear. Last week. Don't you remember? You got home from work and I told you all about it. You said you'd better get on and book an appointment because they fill up so quickly.*'

I actually have no recollection of that at all. 'Are you sure it was me and not Robert who you gave the letter to?'

'*Positive. I'm not quite senile yet.*'

No, she certainly isn't. But sometimes I wonder if maybe I am.

'*Everything all right, Gemma? You still there?*'

'Sorry, yes. It's just… I don't remember the letter, that's all.'

'*Well, I can assure you, I did give it to you.*'

'Yes, of course. I've just got so much on my mind.'

'*You're overdoing it, Gemma.*'

Damn, I shouldn't have said that. 'No, I'm fine.'

'*I gave Robert the name and number of that nanny. You should call her before she takes another job.*'

'Thanks. I'll, er, I'll speak to you soon, Diane.'

'*Of course. Goodbye, dear.*'

'Bye, Grandma!' the girls yell.

'*Bye, dears.*'

I'm preoccupied for the rest of our short journey home. How can I have forgotten a whole conversation? Diane's right – I have been overdoing it lately. For a moment, I allow myself to think about the possibility of a nanny. Could that be the answer? It's just that I've never seen myself as the type of person who would need to employ help with my children. I want to raise them myself – just me and Robert. I guess the only other possibility would be to ask Diane to help out more. But I certainly don't want that. Maybe all these awful things that have been happening to me are a result of trying to stretch myself too thin. I'm becoming forgetful, making mistakes, becoming paranoid about things that are simply coincidences or minor mishaps. I need to create some space in my life. And in order to do that, I need temporary help.

I pull into the driveway and stay seated for a moment while the kids spill out of the car with their bags and coats, which they never seem to actually wear, especially when it's raining.

'Come on, Mum!' Eva knocks on my window.

'Mummy, we're going to get soaked!' Katie says crossly, mimicking my tone exactly.

I give myself a shake, leave the car and we all tumble into the house, helped along by a violent gust of wind. The front door is whipped shut with a slam and I switch on the hall light.

'Shoes off, wash your hands!' I cry as the girls ignore me, charging into the kitchen shouting that they're hungry.

I follow them in and go straight to the pine dresser where the letter rack sits overflowing with 'important' to-do letters, including all the latest school correspondence. As the girls open the empty snack cupboard, I lift out the letters and begin rifling through the envelopes and sheets.

'What can we have to eat, Mum? These scones have gone mouldy.'

'I'll make you a sandwich in a minute,' I reply as my gaze lands on a letter from the school. Sure enough, it's the parents' evening letter. I put the other papers back and stare at the sheet. I need to apologise to Diane.

'Can we have chocolate spread?'

My phone buzzes in my bag and I know that will probably be Damien with more work questions that need answering.

Maybe… no, not maybe, definitely. I think I definitely need help looking after the house and the girls. I'm not sure why I've been resisting the idea for so long. Maybe it's because admitting that I need help feels like defeat. I've always prided myself on being able to do it all. The family, the career, the home – like my own mum did before she died. But lately, it's all been too much.

When Robert gets home, I'll tell him that maybe we should go ahead and interview the nanny. It doesn't mean we have to hire her. We can just… see what she's like. Maybe she'll be awful and that will make the decision for us.

Or maybe she'll be the answer to all our prayers.

CHAPTER 20

I much prefer this hotel to the previous one. It's not that it's any nicer — if anything, it's probably five points higher on the grotty scale. The walls are a dirty cream, the kettle is furred with limescale and the windows need a good clean. It's a shithole. But it's what it represents. This place actually feels like a stepping stone rather than yet another forced destination. I have a strong feeling I'll be out of here really soon and with any luck, I'll never have to stay in a place like this again.

Dumping the contents of my holdall onto the blue candlewick bedspread, I cast a critical eye over my 'capsule wardrobe', as I like to ironically call it. I know the type of thing I want to wear, but I can't overdo it. Subtlety is key.

First I pick out a cheap and nasty black polyester trouser suit. It has a horrible sheen to it which almost makes me want to gag. Next a hospital-blue, fitted cotton blouse. Finally, plain black low-heeled court shoes top off the ensemble. I peel off my jeans and sweatshirt and pull on my chosen outfit, eager to see the result. But there's no mirror.

I push open the bathroom door and wrinkle my nose against the faint smell of drains. There's a mirror above the sink so I stand on the loo seat to try to get a sense of what I look like. Hmm, not bad, but something's missing. I go back to the bedroom and dig out my washbag from the pile of stuff on the bed. Taking the quilted bag into the bathroom, I unzip it and rummage around until I find what I'm looking for — a small pot of Vaseline lip balm. I dip a finger into the pot and rub a glob of the stuff between my thumb and fingers. Then I slide my fingers through my dark hair. I keep going until my silky locks become dull and greasy. Then I tie the whole lot back in a low bun at the back of my head.

I should have cultivated a monobrow and let the dark, fine hair on my top lip grow back, but there was no time for such authenticity. This will have to do. I check myself in the mirror, and smile.

I am Sadie Lewis. Plain. Unremarkable. Perfect.

CHAPTER 21

She sits still and perfectly poised at the kitchen table. There is no nervous laughter or fidgety hands. Just polite responses to our questions. If only my facilities manager candidates came over as professionally as this woman does.

Her name is Sadie Lewis and she's here to meet with me and Robert with a view to becoming our nanny, and to tutor Eva. So far, I like her. She's young, reserved, and softly spoken. She's… nondescript and serious, her hair scraped back into a no-nonsense bun. I'm not a clothes snob, but Sadie's suit is truly hideous, with a shine that screams 'highly flammable'. I think back to Rebecca's warning about not hiring a pretty nanny and smile inwardly. There is nothing in the least bit provocative about Sadie.

'So, what made you become a nanny?' I ask.

'Actually, I got into it accidentally.' She gives a small smile. 'I'd just finished my A Levels and my parents had friends who were going skiing for a month and needed someone to look after the children while they hit the slopes. My mum recommended me to them, and they liked the idea as I was already a family friend. It worked out really well and I ended up staying with them for three years.'

'Wow!' Robert says. 'That's great. How many children did you take care of?'

'Three. Sam, Oliver and baby Maisie. I still miss them.'

'Yes, I can imagine that must be quite hard,' I say, 'bonding with them, being with them every day, and then leaving.'

She gives a small shrug. 'It's hard, but I've found the best way of dealing with it is to throw myself into my new job. Start bonding with my new children. And I still keep in touch with all my families, so it's not as though I never see them again.'

'That's so nice!' I say, relieved to hear it. If she keeps in touch, that means they parted on good terms. 'So, it says in your résumé…' I put my forefinger on the sheet of paper on the table, 'that you've worked for four previous families full-time, plus five temp jobs.'

'Yes.'

'Do you mind me asking why you left each of them?'

'Sure. Different reasons. A couple were fixed-term contracts so I was only required for a year or so. My first family moved abroad, and with my last job, the children grew up and the family no longer needed me.'

'How did you get your nannying qualifications if you went straight from A Levels to working?' I ask.

'I trained while working, getting my childcare and teaching qualifications, which are all listed on my résumé.'

'And you have experience of tutoring?'

'Plenty. I've coached children to get through school entrance exams, as well as GCSEs.'

'And what's your approach with children? I mean, are you strict or laid-back? Where do you stand in terms of discipline?' I realise I don't want some scary, strict person in our house. Although she doesn't look like she would be.

'To be honest, I always take my lead from the parents. But I would never want to be overly strict – that goes against my childcare ethos. I prefer the carrot approach.'

'Don't mind my wife,' Robert says, jokily, 'she's been inter-viewing for a manager at work so she's still in full-on business interview mode.'

I feign outrage and nudge him in the ribs. 'I'm not that bad, am I?'

'Just a little bit full-on,' he says.

'It's fine,' Sadie says, catching my eye and giving me a warm smile. 'They're your children. I'd be worried if you weren't asking probing questions.'

'See!' I say to Robert. 'It's normal to ask questions.'

'Is there anything you'd like to ask *us*?' Robert says.

'Can I meet them?' she asks.

'Oh. What, *now*?' The girls are currently upstairs watching a Disney movie to keep them occupied while we interview Sadie. I suppose it makes sense for her to meet them.

'If that's okay?' she says. 'I always find it's helpful to see how we get on before discussing anything else. I mean, if we're going to be spending every day together, it's better if we click.'

'You're right.' Robert turns to me. 'She's right, isn't she?'

I nod. 'I'll call them down.'

'That would be great. Maybe the girls and I could spend ten minutes or so together? Just getting to know each other a little bit.'

The more I hear Sadie talk, the more I think she would be absolutely perfect. I know it's very early days, but you tend to get a feeling about people when you meet them. And the feeling I'm getting from Sadie is that she could be a great addition to our family. Potentially even life changing.

We call the children downstairs and introduce them. They're shy, but Sadie takes charge and asks if the girls can show her their bedrooms. Eva hangs back and gives me a look that says she doesn't want to, but Katie immediately starts telling Sadie about her favourite cuddly toys.

'Do you like cuddly toys, too, Eva?' Sadie asks.

Eva shrugs. Katie is already halfway up the stairs.

'Eva likes music,' I say. 'Singing, dancing, that kind of thing.'

'Do you enjoy musicals?' Sadie asks her.

'We saw *Wicked* last year,' Eva says quietly.

'Oh, I'd love to see that show!' Sadie says. 'Will you tell me about it?'

Eva nods and follows her up the stairs. They're both chatting away to Sadie now. I turn to Robert and we smile at one another before heading back into the kitchen.

Fifteen minutes later, the girls bound back down the stairs, animated and laughing.

'Such lovely children,' Sadie says, following them down into the hall. 'We had fun, didn't we?'

Eva and Katie nod vigorously.

Once we've said our goodbyes, assuring Sadie we'll be in touch, I close the front door and turn to Robert.

'She was great, don't you think?'

'Yeah. Really nice.'

'And the girls absolutely loved her! I mean, I've never seen them so relaxed around a stranger before. She's a real Mary Poppins,' I add.

'Does this mean…' Robert begins.

'I think so.'

'Shall we offer her the job, then?'

'Yes. But we'll need to check out references.'

'Of course. But Mum recommended her and she's pretty much perfect – apart from being the woman that fashion forgot.'

I give him a light shove. 'Don't be so mean!'

He grins and pulls me towards him. 'Does this mean our lives are going to get easier from now on? Might we actually have some time to spend together?'

'That would be nice.'

'Although, knowing you, it'll just mean you're working longer hours.'

'Hey!'

He raises his hands in surrender. 'Sorry, sorry. Joke.'

But I know he's probably right. 'I'll try not to,' I say. 'I really will. We'll do more things as a family. With Sadie looking after the girls, I'll be able to get on with my work in the week, and then hopefully we can have more family time at the weekend.'

'Sounds good to me.'

'I hope she takes the job,' I say, suddenly feeling nervous. 'What if she's got other interviews? Other families who want her?'

'She'd be mad not to work for us. Our girls are the best.'

'You're right. Shall I call her now? Make sure we get in there before anyone else?'

'Maybe give the girl a chance to get home first.'

'Okay. I'll call in an hour.'

We're still standing by the front door when the bell rings, making us both jump.

'Do you think it's her again?' I ask in a whisper.

Robert shrugs and opens the door.

Diane stands on the doorstep.

'Hi, Mum!'

'Robert, darling!' She frowns and puts a hand to his cheek. 'You're looking a little thin and peaky. I'll have to make you some of my hotpot – feed you up a bit.'

Robert looks the furthest from thin and peaky a person could get, but this is Diane's subtle-as-a-brick way of saying that I don't look after my husband like I should.

'Hi, Diane. Come in. I'll put the kettle on.'

'Hello, Gemma. No tea for me, I won't stay. I just called in to see how the interview went.' Diane follows us into the lounge.

'Really brilliantly,' Robert says. 'Well done, Mum. She's a great find.'

'So you're going to employ her?'

Robert looks at me and I nod.

'Thanks, Diane,' I say. 'For recommending her. She seems perfect.'

To give her credit, Diane doesn't gloat or say I told you so. 'I wanted to come round and say that if you're serious about hiring this girl, then I'd like it to be my gift to you.'

'Gift?'

'Yes. I would like to pay her wages.'

'Oh, no, Diane, that's fine. We couldn't expect you to—'

She cuts me off. 'It's not a matter of expecting anything. They're my grandchildren, and if I didn't have my commitments at the club, I would look after them for you while you're both working. Instead, this will be my way of helping you both.'

'But—'

'Thank you, Mum. That's incredibly generous,' Robert says, giving me a look.

I'm not sure what to think about this. Robert's right – it is incredibly generous – but I don't like taking handouts and normally, neither does Robert. I wonder what got him to change his mind.

CHAPTER 22

It has all happened so quickly. From interviewing Sadie, to offering her the job and then checking her references. And now, today, she's actually moving in. On the phone, she said she was available to start as soon as it was convenient, and Robert and I saw no reason to delay as the grammar entrance exam is only two months away, and we're both still crazily busy at work.

Unfortunately, I had to call Louise Martin, the tutor I found online, to tell her we no longer needed her services. It was awful. She actually started to cry on the phone. She told me all she needed was a chance to prove herself. Practically begged me to give her the job. I was kind but firm and told her we would bear her in mind if our situation changed. But I feel bad for having raised her hopes only to dash them again.

When the doorbell rings, I try to quell the nerves in my stomach. Tell myself not to be so silly. But it's the speed of everything. Even though I've come round to the idea of a nanny, I haven't really had time to get used to it yet. This time last week, I had no intention of hiring any help. Now, here we are, about to invite this relative stranger into our home.

'Is that Sadie?' Katie cries, rushing down the stairs.

'Wait for me!' Eva cries, following her. 'Mum! Don't open the door without me!'

Robert and I laugh at their excitement. At least the children are thrilled.

'Calm down, girls,' I say, quietly. 'Sadie will be here every day, so there's no need to worry about being left out of anything. You'll both get plenty of time with her.'

Robert opens the front door, and Sadie is standing there with a large holdall by her side. She's wearing unfashionable jeans and a baggy, salmon-pink fleece with white piping, her hair pulled back into a low ponytail. She looks considerably younger than I remember, and quite, quite nervous.

'Sadie, hi. Come in,' I say, trying to be as welcoming as I can. 'We're all excited to have you here.'

'Hello Mrs Ballantine, Mr Ballantine.'

'Please, call us Robert and Gemma,' my husband says. 'Here, let me get that.' He reaches forward and picks up her bag. 'Come in. It's nippy out there.'

From being boisterous and excited all morning, the girls have suddenly turned incredibly shy, hanging back behind me, Katie with her arms around one of my legs, so I can't move properly.

'Hello, Eva,' Sadie says, peering behind me. 'Katie, is that you hiding behind your mum?'

The girls nod shyly and mumble their hellos.

'I'm looking forward to you showing me your rooms again,' Sadie says.

'You can play in my room first, if you like,' Katie says, stepping out from behind me.

'She'll probably prefer to hang out in mine,' Eva replies. 'It's more grown-up.'

'No it's not!'

'I'm sure I'll love spending time in both your rooms,' Sadie says with a smile.

'Before the girls drag you away, shall I show you *your* room?' I ask. 'And then you can come down and have a cup of tea with all of us.'

'That sounds lovely. Thanks.'

'Robert, do you want to stick the kettle on, while I show Sadie upstairs?'

I persuade the girls to stay downstairs with the promise of chocolate cake when we return.

Sadie follows me up. We're lucky that the house has had a loft conversion so she can have her own floor at the top, giving us all a bit of privacy. There are two bedrooms and a bathroom up here. It's one of the reasons we fell in love with the house – we thought that when the girls are older, they'll be able to have more space and privacy. It made the extra mortgage money worth it. And if times ever get tight, we can even rent out the rooms.

Yesterday Robert helped me to turn the larger of the two bedrooms into a makeshift lounge with an Ikea sofa, a small dining table and a TV. We put a mini fridge and kettle up here, too, so Sadie has her own little guest suite. We also cleaned the house from top to bottom, paying special attention to the girls' rooms, which were an embarrassing mess. It's ironic that we've employed someone to free up some more time, but then we've spent hours tidying and scrubbing the place before her arrival. My shoulders are still aching today. But it will be worth it, I tell myself.

'It's lovely,' Sadie says, taking in the homely space. 'Really nice. I didn't expect to have all this to myself. In my last jobs, I've just had a bedroom and en suite shower.'

'I'm so pleased you like it.' It surprised me that she took the job without wanting to see her accommodation first, but I did describe it to her on the phone, and I guess some people aren't that fussy about where they lay their head. 'Tell, you what, why don't I leave you up here to get settled, then you just come down when you're ready. We'll be in the kitchen.'

'Perfect,' Sadie replies. 'Thank you for giving me the job. I think I'm going to love living here.'

I give her arm a squeeze. 'And we're going to love having you.'

As I walk back down the narrow stairs, I must admit I do feel strange having someone else in our house. But I tell myself that it will be worth it not to feel so frazzled about everything. I haven't been coping with my work–life balance, but now things should hopefully start getting easier. I wonder how I'll feel about asking Sadie to do things. I'm used to telling people what to do at work, but it will feel odd to treat Sadie like an employee when she's living in our home. I suppose I'll just have to get used to it.

Once we've all had tea and cake, the girls drag Sadie upstairs to show off their newly tidied rooms. Robert and I stare at one another across the kitchen table and break out into giggles.

'Weird, isn't it,' he says.

'I know. She's nice though. And if it gets too weird we can always ask her to leave.'

'I think it'll be fine,' Robert says.

We both cock our ears, listening for sounds from above. But all is quiet.

Half an hour later, Sadie comes back down the stairs. Robert is watching TV in the lounge and I'm in the kitchen pricing up a job on my laptop.

'Sorry to disturb you,' Sadie says. 'I know it's Sunday evening, and I'm not sure how you want to do things, but I've started them off on their homework, and checked their schoolbags for notes. Katie has to take in some recycling things to school tomorrow for a project, so I was wondering where your recycling—'

'Recycling bin is in the utility room through here.' I start to get up, but Sadie stops me.

'No, it's okay. Sit back down. This is what you employed me for. I may have to keep asking questions for the first few days, but soon you won't even notice I'm here. I'll come back down in half an hour to make a start on the girls' supper. I'll eat with them, if that's okay?'

'Erm, yes. That's great.' I'm pretty certain that if Sadie wasn't here, the letter about the recycling would have remained unread in

Katie's bag until the end of term. Already, I'm feeling like a weight is being lifted. 'I'll go into the lounge, get out of your way,' I say. 'And please do help yourself to any food in the fridge or cupboards.'

'Thanks.' She goes into the utility room and I take myself and my laptop into the lounge where Robert is watching the football. No problem; background noise doesn't bother me.

'Everything okay?' Robert asks.

'Yes,' I reply. 'Everything's fine. I think Sadie is going to work out brilliantly.'

CHAPTER 23

The house is quiet. Still. Just the settling of pipes and the odd rattling window pane. I wipe down the last of the kitchen counters and exhale. My shoulders drop – a relief of sorts. I'm here. As jobs go, this one is pretty good. I have my own comfortable space, the mother is out for most of the day, and the kids aren't too brattish.

I think back to last night when Gemma showed me the nanny accommodation, how proud she seemed of the space, like she was giving me the keys to a five-star hotel, rather than the servants' quarters in the attic. Well, I'll show her. Although I admit I did lay it on quite thickly – the whole unworldly, innocent act. I was so quietly spoken and serene, I'd forgive them for thinking I was fresh out of a nunnery. I really played up the whole I'm-happy-to-put-my-life-on-the-backburner-so-I-can-propel-your-offspring-into-greatness act. Does she truly believe I'm grateful? Swallowing down the rising bile in my gullet, I remember why I'm here. And it's not for Gemma Ballantine.

I walk over to the dresser, where a letter rack sits overflowing with correspondence. I pick up the letters and take them to the kitchen table. Start flicking through them to see if there's anything of interest. It's mainly boring school stuff. There's also an invitation to a charity dinner dance at the local golf club – that's interesting. I file the information away in my brain as a possibility to use later.

For a supposed business woman, Gemma is very trusting. Sure, she did her due diligence by emailing her new nanny's previous two 'employers', receiving glowing references from both the Hamilton family and the De Sousa family regarding their fantastic nanny, Sadie Lewis: 'We loved her like she was part of the family.' But neither the Hamiltons nor the De Sousas even exist. The email addresses were fake. I wrote the references myself. It's laughable how simple it was to fool my new family. It's scary how some people take everything at face value.

I think the Ballantines must be mad to allow a stranger into their home.

Especially a stranger like me.

CHAPTER 24

As I drive home from work, instead of panicking about a half-finished task, or about running late, I realise that my mind is uncluttered. Today felt freeing. For the first time in ages I was able to concentrate on work without guilt. Without being pulled in two directions. Without worrying that I was going to have to leave early to do the school run because Robert has a client, or that one of the girls has left her PE kit at home. Instead, I was able to throw myself into my job, and it was a luxury. Knowing that Sadie is at home picking up the slack has taken a weight off my shoulders. I hate to admit it, but Diane was right. I was stretching myself too thin.

I turn on one of my music playlists – an upbeat one that I created a while ago. Sister Sledge's 'We Are Family' comes on and I smile at the memory of dancing with the girls at a summer barbecue we hosted a few years ago. We used to have impromptu barbecues and parties several times a year, but recently, there just hasn't been any time for socialising. Maybe that can all change. But I'm probably getting ahead of myself. Sadie has only just arrived in our lives. It's still early days.

I sail through all the green lights and reach home with a nervous anticipation in my chest to see how the girls have got on with Sadie. I may even cook something from scratch this evening, rather than shoving a ready meal in the microwave. Robert won't be home until after eight, so I'll have plenty of time to cobble something together.

I put my key in the lock and walk into the hallway. I note the girls' coats and schoolbags hanging on their pegs, rather than dumped on the bench. Their sports bags packed ready for PE tomorrow. A delicious smell of cooking hits me. I go straight through to the kitchen but it's empty. It's also spotless, the counters gleaming, the dishwasher grumbling through a cycle. A large covered oven dish sits on the hob. I lift the lid to see some kind of filling topped with lightly browned mashed potato. My mouth waters.

'Mummy!'

I replaced the lid and turn as footsteps clatter down the stairs and Katie thunders into the kitchen, hurling herself into my arms.

'Hello, darling. How are you? How was your day? Goodness I missed you so much.' I scoop my daughter up into my arms, even though she's far too heavy to be carried. She's warm and clean, already in her pyjamas, smelling of bubble bath and shampoo.

'Good. It was good. Sadie picked us up from school. And we got ice creams on the way home and we had a competition where we counted car colours. But Eva won because she chose silver cars. And it's not really fair because everyone knows that there are more silver cars. I chose red ones. But Sadie chose yellow, so she came last.'

'Where are Eva and Sadie?' I ask, sitting down heavily on a kitchen chair, Katie still clinging on to me, limpet-like.

'Upstairs. Sadie's doing Eva's hair. She said she'll be finished in two minutes.'

'Did you have supper yet?'

'We had cottage pie that Sadie made. It was really nice.'

That explains the dish on the cooker. 'I thought you hated cottage pie?'

'No, Mummy.' She rolls her eyes. 'I love it. It's actually my favourite dinner now.'

If Sadie can get my kids to eat new things then she truly is a miracle worker. I plonk Katie on another chair and put the kettle on, letting my daughter prattle on about school, enjoying the fact that I feel so relaxed, and that she seems so happy. A few minutes later, Eva comes down in her dressing gown, her hair in immaculate French braids.

'Hi, Mum.'

I hold my arms out and she lets me give her a quick squeeze. I kiss the top of her head but she jerks away.

'Careful of my hair. Sadie braided it so when I take them out tomorrow it will be all wavy.'

'Lovely. Where is Sadie anyway?'

'She's just tidying stuff upstairs. Said she'll be down in a minute.'

'Let me go up and say hello, then I'll come back and you can tell me all about your day. Did you have a good one?'

'It was all right.' She shrugs.

'Just all right?'

'Lauren was mean.'

'I thought you two made up.' *Ugh, I can't cope with any more tween drama.* Please don't let this turn into another disaster.

'We are friends, kind of.' Eva scowls. 'But she was saying stuff to Lucy behind my back.'

'You can come and play with us, Eva,' Katie says. 'Me and my friends won't be mean to you.'

'That's very kind, Katie,' I say. 'Thank you. Do you think you can go and brush your teeth?'

'Done it.'

'Okay, well, do you think you can pop upstairs while I talk to Eva for a minute?' I need to get to the bottom of what's going on with Lauren. Try to nip it in the bud before it flares up again.

'It's okay,' Eva says airily. 'I already spoke to Sadie, and she told me what I should do.'

'Well that's nice of her. What did she say?' I look up to see Sadie coming into the kitchen dressed in sweat pants and a hoodie. She was so quiet on the stairs I didn't hear her approaching. 'Hi, Sadie! How are you? I'm just about to make tea. Want some?'

'Hi, Gemma. No thanks, I'm okay.'

'It's so lovely to come home and find the girls fed and bathed. Thank you!' I find myself speaking to Sadie in overly bright exclamation marks. I need to calm down and speak normally. It's just, I'm trying to make her feel welcome; we haven't really established our relationship yet. Hopefully it will all start to feel more normal soon.

'They're such lovely children,' Sadie says. 'We've had fun today, haven't we?'

My daughters nod enthusiastically.

'We also worked through an English past paper this afternoon. Eva's a bright girl. I think she'll do well in the entrance test.'

'Really? I mean I know she's bright, but it's great to hear you think she'll do okay.'

'More than okay, I think.' She winks at Eva, whose cheeks turn pink. 'Well, I'll go up to my room now and leave the girls with you for a while, if you like? Then I can come back in an hour to put them to bed and read them a story.'

'No, that's okay,' I reply. 'I'll do it. You go and relax for the evening.'

'Are you sure? I don't mind.'

'Absolutely.' It's great to have Sadie take care of all the minutiae – the household chores and practicalities – but I want to be the one to tuck them up and read their bedtime stories. Having Sadie here will enable me to do that. It will allow me to concentrate on spending quality time with my children.

'Have you eaten yet?' I ask Sadie. 'Do you want to have dinner with me and Robert later?'

'It's okay, I ate with the girls.'

'I saw the cottage pie. Very nice.'

'There's enough left over for you and Robert, if you'd like?' she says. 'I've left it to cool, but you can heat it up in the microwave and have it with the salad I made. It's in the fridge.'

'Wow! Really?'

'Sure. I love cooking. Katie helped me while Eva was doing her English paper at the table. Katie and I can make something different each night, and if you want I'll make enough for you and Robert, too. Then you don't have to worry about what to cook when you get in from work.'

'That sounds wonderful. Let me know what ingredients you need and I'll make sure to add them to the weekly shop.'

'I can do the shop,' Sadie says. 'Just let me know anything that you and Robert don't like to eat and I'll make sure I don't cook it.'

'Fantastic.'

'Mummy hates olives,' Katie says.

'And mushrooms,' Eva adds. 'And Daddy only likes healthy food, because of his job. But he does drink wine.'

Sadie and I laugh, and the kids join in.

'Great,' Sadie says. 'I'll work out a nice, healthy meal plan with no olives and no mushrooms.'

'And lots of wine!' Katie cries, breaking out into more peals of laughter.

'That's settled,' Sadie says. 'Okay, I'll go on up. Shout if you need anything, Gemma. Night, girls.'

'Night, Sadie!' they chorus.

'We're glad you're here,' I add.

'So am I,' Sadie replies with a grateful smile.

CHAPTER 25

I stare out the window of my attic lounge, sipping my coffee, feeling like a student in a bedsit. Another place, another view. The garden below is covered with a sprinkling of autumn leaves, and the sky is a uniform pale grey. Gemma is at work, Robert is out with a client, and the girls are at school. It's nice to have the whole house to myself. I can wander around and imagine it belongs to me. Of course, if it was mine, I would never have let it get into such a state. It wouldn't take much to give this place a lick of paint, update the kitchen, revamp the garden and sort out the windows. The house has good bones, it just needs some TLC. But Gemma Ballantine seems more concerned with looking after her clients than looking after her home.

I already feel pretty good about how things are progressing. The kids love me and Gemma is almost falling over herself with gratitude. What else does the woman expect? I'm not skivvying and nannying for the pleasure of it. I'm doing it for a pay cheque. But then, maybe that's unfair. If Gemma wasn't acting all grateful, then I would think she was an entitled bitch. Basically, Gemma can't win. And that's okay. It helps if I can loathe Gemma. Makes things easier. Robert, on the other hand... I smile to myself.

Checking my watch, I see it's ten o'clock already. Robert said he'd be back at lunchtime so that gives me at least two hours. I drain my cup and set it on the windowsill, turn around and head down to the first-floor landing. There are three double bedrooms and a family bathroom on this floor. The only room I haven't seen yet is Robert and

Gemma's. *Their bedroom door is firmly closed. I put a hand on the doorknob and turn it clockwise, pushing it open.*

The room is large and square, but it's a shabby mess like the rest of the house. The furniture is mismatched, the bed unmade, piles of clothes lie discarded on the floor and the door to the en suite is open, revealing more mess beyond.

I walk in, a thrill in my chest knowing I'm doing something taboo. I pull open the drawer of the bedside table nearest to me. I'm guessing this is Robert's side as there's an action-thriller paperback on the floor next to a pair of discarded sports socks. The drawer contains an empty packet of ibuprofen tablets, a hardback notebook with a picture of the ocean on the front, a pen and a strip of condoms. My fingers close around the notebook. I open it and flick through the creamy white pages. It's empty. I slip it back where I found it and slide the drawer closed.

So what's in Gemma's bedside drawer? Making my way around the bed, my heart begins to beat in anticipation. Why is snooping always such a buzz? It must be the fear of getting caught. The danger. This feeling is primal. It's why we watch horror films and go on roller coasters. But something makes me stop before I open Gemma's drawer. I cock my ear at a noise from downstairs. A muted thud. Could one of the Ballantines have come home while I was up in my attic room?

I step away from the bed and head back towards the door, but before I get there, I hear the sound of footsteps on the stairs, slow and laboured. What should I do? Hide? No. It would be awful if I was discovered hiding. Better to brazen it out. I can't believe I've let myself get caught out like this. Such a stupid thing to have done.

Taking a breath, I step out of the bedroom onto the landing, where I come face to face with an older woman in a tabard, carrying a plastic tray full of cleaning products. The woman freezes and puts a hand to her chest, almost dropping the tray.

'Who are you?' she barks, visibly shaken by my appearance from the bedroom.

'I was about to ask you the same question,' I say with as much authority as I can muster. At least it isn't one of the Ballantines.

'I'm Mandy, I clean for Gemma and Robert on Tuesday mornings. Who are you?'

'I'm the nanny.'

'Nanny?'

'Yes. I just started working for them.'

'They never told me.'

'Call them if you like.'

Mandy raises a thinly plucked eyebrow. 'So if you're the nanny, what were you doing in their bedroom?'

I grit my teeth and clench my fists by my side. 'If you must know, I'm allergic to feather pillows so I was looking for a hypoallergenic one.'

'The spare bedding's in the airing cupboard,' Mandy says, nodding her head towards a door on the landing.

I can tell that the cleaner doesn't believe my story about pillows. To be fair, I wouldn't have believed me either. I wonder just how much of a problem that's going to be.

I realise I'm going to have to fix this.

CHAPTER 26

The coffee shop is crowded with mums, sticky-fingered toddlers and fractious babies. Pushchairs line the steamed-up windows like Formula 1 cars ready to race. This isn't exactly the relaxed vibe I was after when I asked Sadie if she'd like to go out for a coffee.

Sadie has been with us for over a week now, but we haven't had a proper moment to chat together, so I thought it might be nice if we bonded for an hour or two over lattes and cake. She seemed pleased to be asked and, touchingly, it looks as though she's made a real effort with her appearance today, wearing a skirt and blouse and a faint dab of lip gloss. Even her hair is shiny, pulled off her face in a half-up ponytail. She might be a bit frumpily dressed, but actually, her face is really pretty.

'There's a spare table at the back.' Sadie points to a table strewn with empty plates and coffee cups.

'Is this okay? We could always go somewhere else? It's a bit messy and… noisy.' I give an apologetic smile.

'No, it'll be fine.' She heads over to claim the spare table. 'I'll just get rid of these things.'

I help her clear the table and we sit opposite one another as a very young, stressed-out looking waitress comes up to us and wipes down the table.

'Sorry about the mess,' the waitress says. 'It's always busy at this time of the morning, after the pre-school singalong at the library round the corner.'

'No problem,' I reply. 'Sadie, what would you like?'

'A flat white would be great, and…' She looks up at the waitress. 'I don't suppose you have any red velvet cake?'

'Umm, yes, I think so. Would you like a slice?'

'Ooh, make that two slices,' I add. 'Red velvet is my favourite.'

'Really?' Sadie replies. 'Mine too!'

'You've obviously got good taste.' We smile at one another.

Once the waitress has left the table, there are a few moments of awkward silence. Sadie smiles shyly and It's apparent we're both thinking of what to say next.

'So,' I begin, 'are you settling in okay? The girls already love you!'

'They're so sweet. I'm really enjoying spending time with them.'

'That's great to hear.'

'I hope everything's okay?' she says, twisting her fingers in front of her on the table.

'Yes, everything's fine,' I reply. 'Why wouldn't it be?'

'It's just… you inviting me out for a coffee. Is it to tell me I've done something wrong?' Her eyes have grown large and filled with worry.

'No, no, not at all,' I reassure. 'It's just the opposite. I wanted us to get to know one another a bit better. We haven't had much of a chance to chat since you started.'

Her shoulders relax. 'Oh, that's a relief.'

I now feel bad that she was worrying about this morning. Our drinks and cakes arrive and we both take sips of our coffees.

'I'm so glad we've got you to help out with the girls,' I say. 'Especially since our cleaner's let us down. She was my little lifesaver. Keeping the mess under control.'

'She's left?' Sadie takes a forkful of cake. 'Wow, this is delicious!'

I smile, and then frown, remembering Mandy's short message giving me her resignation. 'She sent an email saying she had a family emergency and wouldn't be able to work for us any more.'

'That's a shame,' Sadie replies.

'I know. I hope she's okay. She hasn't replied to any of my messages since.'

'Maybe she's in the middle of something. I'm sure she'll message back once she's able to.'

'You're probably right.' I take a sip of my drink. 'But now I have to find another cleaner. I don't suppose you know anyone?'

'Um…' Sadie starts to say something, but then goes red and stops.

'What is it?' I prompt.

'Well, it's just, I'd be more than happy to do the cleaning for you. If you like?'

'Really? No, I couldn't ask you to do that.'

'Why not? I mean, I'm at the house while the children are at school anyway. And I actually enjoy cleaning – weird, I know.' She gives a small laugh.

'Gosh, well, if you're sure… that would be brilliant. I'd pay you the going rate, of course.'

'Okay, great. That's sorted then.'

I can't believe my luck. Although I am still worried about Mandy. She's been with us for years. I hope everything's okay with her and her family.

Sadie tilts her head. 'What's your job, if you don't mind me asking? I know Robert's a personal trainer, and I know you work really hard, but I never actually asked what it is you do.'

'I own a facilities management firm.' I'm about to go on to explain what that is, as no one ever usually knows, but Sadie interrupts me.

'Oh, yes, my uncle was a director at Stathams in London.'

'Stathams? That's one of the biggest FM companies in the UK. I'm impressed. What's your uncle's name?'

'He's actually my great uncle, and he's retired now. Has been for years. But he used to work crazy long hours.'

'Comes with the territory, I'm afraid. It's one of the reasons I need you to help out with the girls! How are you liking Bournemouth so far?'

'It's gorgeous. I've already been out for a few runs on the beach.'

'I didn't know you were a runner?'

'I love it. Keeps me sane,' Sadie replies with a laugh.

'I should visit the beach more often,' I say.

'Come running with me, if you like?' Sadie offers.

'I might just take you up on that. Especially after eating this huge slab of cake!'

'You've got a great figure,' she says.

'Thank you. We should definitely make coffee and cake a regular thing. We can catch up on the week's events, and you can tell me how it's going with the girls. I mean, of course we'll chat during the week, but it'll be good to set aside time to talk about everything properly.'

'Okay. Sounds lovely.'

This is exactly how I'd pictured things with Sadie. Us having cosy chats and bonding over our love of the children. Her becoming more like a friend than an employee. Okay, I know it's too soon to be certain, and we're still a little awkward around one another, but I'm sure things will soon feel more relaxed. I hope this is the start of something great. A fresh new beginning for our family.

CHAPTER 27

Katie is upstairs reading a book on her bed, while I'm in the kitchen 'helping' Eva with a maths paper. Luckily Eva is a smart girl, so all that's really required is to sit her down with a past paper each evening and let her get on with it. If there's a query, I tell Eva we'll go over it the following day. This gives me plenty of time to find the answer on BBC Bitesize. I'm not a qualified teacher but my professionally typed résumé says otherwise. Plus, I speak nicely, with authority, and carry myself with confidence, so the Ballantines have bought into my educational persona. Confidence is the key to ninety-five per cent of everything.

I'm pacing myself. I have all these things I want to implement, but it won't work if I rush them, so I'm moving slowly, methodically. I have to get the whole family to trust me. To rely on me. To love me. Bonding over coffee with Gemma was a great start. The stupid cow got so overexcited when she discovered we share the same favourite cake, when in actual fact, a quick scan of Facebook showed a photo of her shoving a huge slice of red velvet cake into her smug mouth, with the caption 'best cake ever'. So I used that information. The truth is I hate red velvet cake – it's too sickly. People are so easy to impress. Of course I already knew what Gemma does for a living. I googled her and then made up some fake uncle who worked at a well-known company in the same industry. These are the types of things that get people to like you, to feel connected with you. Honestly, people are so easy to play.

But not everything has gone exactly to plan. My run in with Mandy, the cleaner, was unfortunate. I'm not thrilled at adding cleaning to my list of duties, but I needed Mandy gone because I had a sense that she might be my undoing. She looked at me as though she could see who I really was. Who I really am. I give myself a shake and bring myself back to the present. To Eva.

'How are things at school with Lauren?' I ask.

Eva's head is bent over her work. She straightens up at the question. Puts her pen down. 'Are you still timing me?' she asks.

'I'll stop the timer for a few minutes, if you like? So we can have a little chat.' I sit opposite the girl. She's too conscientious for her own good. A bit of a swot. No wonder the other girls tease her. Katie's more of a free spirit. More fun. I really believe Eva should loosen up a bit. Especially as Gemma would hate it. I smile to myself.

'What's funny?' Eva asks.

'Oh, nothing. Just thinking back to when I was your age.'

'What were you like?'

'I was fun. More fun than I am now.'

'Why?' Eva's eyes light up. 'What did you do when you were my age?'

'I shouldn't really tell you.'

'Oh pleeease. I won't tell anyone.'

I lean across the table and lower my voice conspiratorially. 'I know it might be hard to believe, looking at me, now that I'm old and boring—'

'You're not old! Or boring.'

'That's sweet of you to say. But anyway, at school I was pretty popular. Everybody wanted to be my friend.' This is a blatant lie. But if I had my time again, I know without a doubt I would be the most popular girl at school. Everyone would love and fear me.

'I wish I was popular,' Eva says, slumping over her test paper.

'I'm sure you are.'

Eva's mouth turns down and her eyes brighten with unshed tears.

'What's the matter, Eva? You know you can tell me anything. I'm here for you like a best friend or a second mum.' I know adding that last bit was somewhat of a risk, but Eva doesn't seem to mind.

'It's just, Lauren and Emily are always saying mean stuff to me.'
'Did you tell your mum about them?'
'Yes. She just told me to play with someone else. But it's not like that. If they want to be mean to you, then they just follow you around.'
'I know,' I say, sticking out my lower lip in a sympathetic pout. 'They just won't leave you alone, will they? It's not fair.'
'Yeah. It's not. I hate them.'
'Maybe that's your problem,' I say, as if I've only just thought of it.
'What do you mean?'
'Well, maybe instead of hating them, you should be more like them.'
'But they're mean.'
'I'm not saying you should be mean, I'm just saying that if you want them to like you, you should do what they're doing, but you should do it much better, with more style and confidence.' I flash my eyes and flick my hair dramatically. Then I laugh to get Eva to cheer up.
The girl gives a grudging smile. 'I don't know how to do all that.'
'Don't worry. I'll teach you.'
Eva picks up her pen and starts twirling it through her fingers.
'Don't you believe me?' I ask gently.
Eva shrugs. But I persist. I'm dropping little seeds here and there which will eventually sprout fruit. Fruit that will hopefully prove to be highly toxic.
'If you do what I tell you, pretty soon you'll be the most popular girl in the school.'
Eva looks up at me, her eyes tinged with doubt. 'Really?'
I reach across the table and link my little finger with Eva's. 'Pinky promise.'

CHAPTER 28

Putting on the back of my earring as I walk down the stairs, I think about how things have changed over the past ten days. It's parents' evening tonight, and if we didn't have Sadie, I would have been racing around yelling at everyone to get ready, while not even having attempted to get ready myself. Instead, I got home from work to find Sadie cooking dinner while the girls were playing in the lounge without TV or devices – which is a miracle in itself. Although maybe I spoke too soon, because I can hear raised voices coming from behind the living-room door.

'But I look more like her, so it should be me,' Eva cries.

'No you don't. And anyway, we're supposed to take turns.'

I push open the door and go in to see both girls standing in the centre of the room, scowling at one another.

'What's going on in here?' I ask.

Katie opens her mouth to speak, but Eva glares at her so she clamps her mouth shut.

'Girls,' I say with a warning note in my voice.

'Nothing,' Eva replies.

'Well, Daddy and I are going out in a minute, so I'd like you both to get along while we're gone. Eva, you're the eldest, so be nice.'

'I am!'

'No she's not,' Katie says. 'She's being bossy and mean.'

'Are you going to tell me why you're arguing?'

Silence.

I realise my best bet is to get Katie to spill the beans, so I fix her with my crossest stare.

She finally crumbles. 'Eva won't let me be Sadie!'

Eva glares at her sister again, but Katie doesn't let her sister intimidate her this time.

'We're playing "families",' Katie explains, 'and one of us has to be you and one us has to be Sadie.'

'And you both want to be Sadie,' I say, realising why Eva was trying to keep Katie quiet – she didn't want to hurt my feelings. Stupidly, it *has* hurt my feelings, but of course I would never let my children know that.

'No, it's okay, Mum,' Eva says. 'I actually want to be you, because you're nice too.'

'Yes!' Katie cries, oblivious. 'That means I can be Sadie!'

Eva scowls and nudges her sister in the ribs.

I try to shake off the silly knot of jealousy that has lodged in my chest. Of course they both want to be Sadie. She's new and interesting and exciting. And she's giving them all her attention. Unlike me. I make a mental note to do something fun with them at the weekend. Something that will make me the centre of their universe again.

Robert comes down the stairs and pops his head around the door. 'You ready? It's almost half six.'

We hug the girls and say goodbye to Sadie before getting into Robert's car.

'It's good, isn't it?' Robert says, pulling out of the driveway.

'What's good?'

'You know, having Sadie here. Being able to go out like this.'

'What, to parents' evening?' I laugh.

'You know what I mean.' He grins. 'Why don't we go for a drink afterwards?'

I think about all the work waiting for me at home on my laptop. Then I look across at my handsome husband and think that actually he's right. 'Okay, I'll text Sadie, let her know we'll be late back.'

Robert puts a hand on my leg and strokes it with his thumb. 'I love you, Gemma.'

'Love you too.' I lean back in my seat and think about how life is pretty perfect at the moment.

Mrs Slade is running half an hour late, so Robert and I wait outside the classroom flicking through Eva's work books. It all looks fairly impressive. Her writing is imaginative, and her maths book is neatly laid out with lots of ticks and good-work stickers. Through the window, I see that my friend Suri and her husband Steve are in there, talking intently to Mrs Slade. Maya isn't in with them, but they also have a teenage daughter, Jade, so they've probably left them both at home.

Five minutes later, Suri comes out, her eyes red. Steve's arm is wrapped around his wife's shoulder. I try to catch her eye to say hello, but she bows her head and they leave quickly. I don't have time to speculate with Robert because Mrs Slade is beckoning us in. Robert and I park our backsides carefully in the child-sized chairs and wait for Mrs Slade to start talking. Up until recently with the Lauren incident, Eva has always been a model child – never getting into trouble and always working hard, so these evenings typically go well. But I'm a little anxious about tonight's meeting.

'So,' Mrs Slade says, 'some good news for you both.'

Robert and I lean forward in our chairs, eager to hear what she's going to say.

'Eva's standard of work has really leapt up a gear. She's focused, she's engaged and her homework last week was really excellent.'

'That's great news,' Robert says. He glances across at me and I know what he's thinking – Sadie. Her input is probably already having a positive effect.

'I'm expecting that she'll do brilliantly in the SATs next May, as long as she keeps up this level of enthusiasm and commitment to her schoolwork.'

'I'm so pleased,' I say, feeling a little tearful. Perhaps this is the reason Suri was emotional when she came out of the classroom. There's nothing like hearing your kids are doing well for bringing a tear to the eye.

'Now,' Mrs Slade says, chewing the side of her lip. 'Unfortunately, I also have some less positive news to give you.'

My heart dips and I frown, wondering what on earth she's about to say. Robert gives my hand a quick squeeze.

'Eva has recently developed quite a lot of new-found confidence,' Mrs Slade says.

'That's good news, surely,' Robert says.

'Ordinarily, yes. But this last week she's been buddying up with some of the more forceful characters. And, well, I've had a couple of parents contact me to say that their child is being… now I hesitate to use the word bullied… but…'

It takes a moment for Mrs Slade's words to sink in. 'You think Eva is being a *bully*?' I just can't imagine it. There's no way my daughter would behave like that. 'Are you sure it isn't the other way round? I mean, that time she hit Lauren, you know it was purely in retaliation for being bullied herself. All the girls were ganging up on her. Maybe that's what's been happening again—'

'Please, Mr and Mrs Ballantine, I really don't think it's anything to get too worried about. Like I said, it's only been happening in the last week. And it's very out of character.'

'What *has* actually been happening?' I snap. 'Can you give me specific examples?' Somehow, this feels even worse than when

Eva was the victim. 'I really cannot believe she would be mean to another child!'

Robert places a calming hand on my shoulder.

'Okay, well, for example…' Mrs Slade's voice is maddeningly measured and calm, making me sound like a deranged banshee. 'Eva and a couple of the other girls were saying things to Maya earlier today about her size.'

'What! No way. No way would Eva ever say anything like that.'

'Look, Mrs Ballantine, I didn't hear it first hand, but a few of the other children did. And it's not something we can tolerate.'

'Of course not. But was it Eva who actually said it? Or was it the other children she was hanging around with?'

'Apparently it was all three of them. They were chanting it.'

No wonder Suri was upset. No wonder she didn't catch my eye coming out of the classroom earlier. I'll have to call her. Apologise. Get Eva to apologise. What a horrible, horrible situation.

'Who were the other children doing the chanting?' Robert asks.

'It doesn't actually matter, about those children,' Mrs Slade says. 'Let's keep the conversation about Eva.'

'I'm so sorry,' I say. 'You know this is totally out of character for her. She's usually a sweet, kind girl.'

'I know,' Mrs Slade replies, nodding sympathetically. 'Sometimes they get carried away trying to show off in front of their friends. I've spoken to her and she assures me she's sorry and won't do it again. We would have called you about it, but I knew you were coming in this evening, so thought it best to wait and speak to you both face to face.'

Finally, Robert and I leave the classroom and make our way out of the school and back to the car. We don't speak, shell-shocked by what we've just heard.

'I don't think I'm in the mood to go for a drink now,' I say to Robert once we're inside the car, my shoulders slumping.

'Me neither. We're going to have to go home and have a serious chat with Eva before she goes to bed.'

'Do you think Sadie knows about it?' I ask.

'No. She'd have said something to us.' Robert turns on the engine.

'I suppose so…' I stare unseeing out of the window. 'Do you think we should tell Sadie about it?'

'Not sure. It might put her off.'

'Maybe we could just say Eva's been a bit mean to another girl. Get Sadie to – I don't know – talk to her about being kind.'

'Yeah. Sounds like a good plan. But the truth will probably come out anyway. These things always do.' Robert's voice is flat. I guess we both assumed that today's parents' evening would be like all the others – glowing praise for our wonderful daughter. It's Katie's turn next week. I hope hers goes better than Eva's.

I still can't believe our daughter was being so mean to Maya. What on earth could have prompted such awful behaviour?

CHAPTER 29

Breakfast this morning is subdued. Eva's behaviour went far beyond what I hoped for when I told her to buddy up with Lauren and Emily. Possibly a little too far with the size issue; I'll have to tell her to rein it back a bit, teach her the art of subtlety. But my little protégé has all the makings of a first-class mean girl. Gemma is distraught. And that's the point. That's a result.

While the girls are upstairs brushing their teeth, I start to clear away the breakfast things. As I load the dishwasher, I ask Gemma if I can take the children to a Shakespeare play that's showing at the Pavilion Theatre in town next week.

'Normally, I'd say that's a lovely idea,' Gemma replies, passing me her mug to put in the dishwasher, 'but I'm not very happy with Eva at the moment. I don't want to hand out treats today. Not after what I learnt at parents' evening. I had to call and apologise to my friend, Suri. She was very gracious but I felt awful.'

I put on a sympathetic expression. 'I know you're not happy with Eva, but children do these things without thinking. I can tell Eva's upset with herself. Probably more upset about what she's done than you are.'

'Hmm.' Gemma looks unconvinced.

'The play isn't until next week,' I persist, 'and to be honest, seeing a play like this would really help with her grammar-school test preparation.' I'm hoping that my use of the 'G' word will sway Gemma. 'If you want her to be inspired, there really is no substitute for watching a live play.'

'Gemma folds her arms across her chest. 'Shakespeare, you said? Which one?'

'A Midsummer Night's Dream.'

'Oh, I love that play. Robert took me to an open-air version at Regent's Park when we first started going out. Maybe you're right.' She stares out of the window for a moment. 'Okay, yes, book the tickets, but don't tell the girls yet. I want Eva to know she's being punished this week with no screen time or treats. We'll tell them at the weekend.'

'Shall I book you a ticket too?' I ask. 'If you loved that play, then it seems only fitting you should share it with your girls.'

Gemma's face lights up. 'What a wonderful idea, but which night is it showing? I'm so busy next week.'

'It's running for the whole week, Monday to Friday, so if you give me the dates of the nights you're free, I can book it. Or if you'd rather go without me, then that's absolutely fine…'

'No, no, I'd love us all to go. It can be a girls evening out. Fantastic. Let me check my diary. I'm sure there are a couple of dates I'm free.' She scrolls through her phone and shows me that she's free next Thursday evening.

'Okay, I'll book tickets,' I say, feeling a judder of excitement at the prospect.

'Great! Okay, I'm off. Have a lovely day. And if you get a chance to talk to Eva about being kind to others, I'd appreciate it! We've already spoken to her, but it can't hurt for her to have another perspective on it.'

'Don't worry,' I say. 'Eva and I will have a nice long chat on the way to school.'

'You're an angel.'

Unfortunately, it won't be the kind of chat Gemma's hoping for.

CHAPTER 30

Sitting at my desk, I end the conference call with one of my top clients. He isn't happy with our cleaners. Something about smeary windows. I've managed to smooth things over with him, but I'll have to get Joan to give her cleaners a talking to. I can't have sub-standard work. If I let one thing slide, the client will look for other issues, and before I know it, I'll have lost a contract.

The past few days at work have gone by in a crazy blur. We're still interviewing for the new manager's position, but I haven't found anyone suitable yet. We've had a lot of impressive résumés, but once the candidates get to interview stage, they seem hopelessly lacking in charisma. I need managers who get on with people, not just box tickers. I guess the problem is that the job doesn't sound very sexy. Facilities Manager sounds boring as hell, but it's actually not. It's varied and interesting. Well, it is to me, anyway.

I'm the only one left in the office, but I've got a long night ahead of me and so I order a delivery from the local Thai restaurant. As soon as I end the call, my phone buzzes again. It's Sadie. She's never needed to call me at work before. I hope the girls are all right.

'Hi, Sadie. Everything okay? Hope you've had a good day.'

'*Yes, fine thanks.*' There's a pause. '*I was just wondering if you'll be back soon.*'

'Erm, no. I'm working late tonight. I've got back-to-back client meetings on Skype all evening.'

'*Oh.*' There's silence on the end of the line.

'Sadie? Is everything all right?' I tense up, starting to get a little worried now. 'Is Robert there?'

'*Yes, he's here. It's just… the play starts in forty-five minutes and we need to leave now if we're going to get parked in time to make the show.*'

'The play?' I scratch my cheek. 'You mean *A Midsummer Night's Dream*? But that's tomorrow. It's Wednesday today. I said I was free on Thursday.'

'*Oh.*' She sounds thrown by this.

'Didn't I? I'm sure I said Thursday.'

'*I… thought you said Wednesday.*' Her voice is panicked.

'Okay, look, don't worry.'

'*We can meet you there if it's easier,*' Sadie says. '*Or if you want to come home first, we can afford to be a little late – although, I don't think they let you in once the curtain's gone up, so we'd have to miss the first act…*'

'No,' I say. 'You go without me.'

'*Are you sure?*'

'Absolutely.' I didn't realise I would feel so disappointed at missing out. I've been looking forward to the play all week. Although, come to think of it, the girls seemed to assume we were going to the play tomorrow as well. 'Are you absolutely sure you've got the date right?' I ask. 'Maybe just double check.'

'*I'm so sorry, but yes. I'm looking at the tickets right now.*'

'*Is Mummy coming?*' I hear Katie's voice in the background and it breaks my heart.

'Tell the girls I'm sorry.'

'*I feel terrible about this,*' Sadie says.

'These things happen. It can't be helped. I'll let you go – I don't want you all to be late.'

'*All right. Maybe we could plan another show?*'

'Great, yes, of course. Get Robert to give you money for ice creams and programmes.'

'*Okay. See you later, Gemma.*'

'Bye.' I end the call with a sudden feeling of heaviness. The girls will think I've put my job above them. I do work hard, but I always make a point to keep my word. If I say I'm going to do something with my children, I try to stick to my promises. And I really wanted to go. It was going to be the perfect way to reconnect with my girls after a few weeks of change. This was going to be my chance to be a 'fun' mum again.

Did I give Sadie the wrong day? I suppose it's possible. I should have double checked. But I could have sworn I said to her this morning that I was looking forward to the show tomorrow. I check my online calendar and see that I did put in the correct date originally, but then changed it for some reason. Oh well, it can't be helped now. Like I said to Sadie, these things happen.

And right now I somehow have to summon up the enthusiasm to talk to my clients. Normally I enjoy this part of my job. Now, I just wish I could cancel all my meetings and go to the theatre. *Come on Gemma, pull yourself together.* But I keep hearing Katie's little voice asking if I'm coming.

When I finally pull into the driveway and turn off the car engine, it's after ten and the whole house is sitting in darkness. Even the hall and porch lights are off, which is unusual. There's just a faint glow from the street lamps beyond the hedge. I also realise Robert's car is missing from the drive.

Inside, it's clear no one is home. They must still be at the theatre. But I wonder where Robert is? I switch on the hall light and walk through to the kitchen. There's a note propped up on the kitchen table. Must be from Sadie.

Hi Gemma,
Robert decided to come with us!

I suppose it makes sense that he went. There was a spare ticket after all. And it's perfectly reasonable that he would have wanted to go to the play with his children. I didn't ask him to come because I thought it might be odd for the five of us to go together. I thought it might make Sadie feel a little gooseberryish. Anyway, it's fine. They'll be home soon.

I make myself a cup of herbal tea and sit at the kitchen table, waiting. I haven't seen the girls since breakfast. Seems like days ago.

It's almost ten thirty when I finally hear the sound of Robert's car come up the driveway, his headlights sweeping through the stained-glass porch windows. A beat of silence as the engine turns off, then the thunk of the car doors and my noisy girls laughing and chattering. I smile at the sound and get to my feet.

Eva and Katie slip past Sadie and tumble through the hall into the kitchen, full of excitement and laughter, wearing their best dresses and faux fur coats like mini princesses. They have little handbags over their shoulders and they're clutching programmes between their nail-polished fingers.

'Mummy! Mum! It was brilliant!' Katie cries.

'You should've come, Mum,' Eva says. 'You would have really liked it.'

'Sorry we're so late,' Sadie says, her blue eyes shining.

I do a double take. Sadie looks really pretty tonight, wearing a plain black dress, simple heels and a jade wrap, her raven hair swept up in a stylish chignon. Her make-up is sparse – pale plum lips and a lick of eyeliner. She really seems to be coming out of her shell.

Robert walks in last, looking devastatingly handsome in a dark suit and open-neck shirt. As he stands next to Sadie, I push away the jealous thought that they look like a beautiful couple.

'Hey, Gems.' Robert comes over and kisses me on the lips.

'Hi,' I say, putting a hand to his cheek. 'How was it?'

The girls start talking all at once, squeezing their bodies between me and Robert.

'Look!' Eva cries, thrusting her programme under my nose.

'What's this?' I ask, sitting down and patting the chair next to me.

Eva sits and lays the programme on the table, opening it at the first page.

'We queued up and they wrote in our books!' Katie says, shoving her programme on top of Eva's.

'Hey! *I* was telling Mum.' She shifts Katie's programme off hers.

'You can both tell me,' I say.

'We went to the stage door,' Eva says, 'and waited for the cast to come out. They gave us their autographs. It was brilliant.'

'There was someone called Bottom,' Katie says, dissolving into giggles.

Eva joins in and soon we're all laughing.

'So you enjoyed it?' I ask.

'It was the best night ever!' Eva says.

'Fantastic,' I reply. But although I'm happy they had a wonderful time, there's still a part of me that feels sad I wasn't there with them.

'Right!' Robert claps his hands. 'Time for bed, monsters!'

'O-oh,' they groan in unison.

'You promised,' Sadie says. 'We had a deal – we said you could queue up for autographs if you went straight to bed when we got home. Remember?'

The girls' shoulders droop. They nod and get to their feet, yawning.

'And we have to take that nail polish off before school tomorrow,' Sadie adds. 'Come on, let's go, lickety split.'

'I'll be up in a moment to put them to bed, Sadie.'

She nods and I watch them shuffle off upstairs, their exuberance vanishing with every step as tiredness kicks in.

'It's a shame you couldn't come tonight,' Robert says, pulling me to my feet and wrapping me in his arms.

'It was a mix-up with the dates,' I say.

'Sadie told me. She felt really bad.'

'I don't think it was her fault. There were a few mix-ups on my calendar at work where dates had been changed.'

'That's annoying.'

'These things happen,' I say for the second time this evening. But an awful lot of 'these things' seem to be happening to me at the moment. Perhaps most of them are simply a case of bad luck and crossed wires, but I can't help thinking that someone out there has got it in for me. That I'm being targeted for some reason. None of the incidents have been major, or life-threatening – apart from when Katie went missing. It's just… when you add them all together, they feel calculated, personal, dangerous. I take a breath and try to relax my shoulders. It would be nice if I could have one week that's straightforward and uncomplicated. Where my children aren't getting into trouble, or going missing. Where my laptop doesn't start deleting my files and I'm not the subject of sexual harassment or vandalism. Where I can simply have a nice evening out with my family. Is that too much to ask?

CHAPTER 31

I'm sitting at the kitchen table eating toast, going through my emails. I like to get up early, sit in silence as dawn glows through the windows. It's almost seven. Robert is usually out with his first client of the day by now, but he has a rare morning off and I left him upstairs in bed, fast asleep. Sadie will be getting the girls up soon and everything will go into fast-forward mode. Noise, mess, drama. I love it as much as I enjoy the peace beforehand. Especially now that I have Sadie to lighten the load.

'Hey.'

I look up to see my husband, showered and dressed. 'I thought you were having a lie in,' I say.

'I did,' he replies. 'Hungry. Need breakfast.'

The front door opens and Sadie comes into the kitchen, her cheeks flushed.

'Morning!' she says. 'Just been for a run. It's gorgeous out there. Chilly, but the sky is so clear.' Instead of her usual baggy joggers, she's wearing navy Lycra leggings and a crop top. Her hair is tied up in a swinging ponytail and her skin is glistening with a light sheen of sweat, like gold glitter. I wish I could look that good after exercising. When I run, I go bright red and the sweat drips off me.

I also notice, for the first time, that Sadie actually has an incredible figure – petite and toned. I glance at Robert to see that he's noticing too, his eyes darting swiftly down her body. But maybe I imagined it. He's busying himself with the kettle now.

'Anyone for tea?' he asks.

'I'll have mine a little later,' Sadie replies. 'Just going to wake the girls and get showered.'

Maybe I need to start paying more attention to my own body. I've let myself go a little over the past year – nothing drastic, but I could certainly afford to lose a few pounds and tone up. Because of Robert's job, his body is always at the peak of physical fitness. But he never pushes me to work out – and for that I love him – but surely he must compare my body to those of his clients. I think I'll ask my husband to schedule me in for a couple of mornings training a week. I don't really have the time, but I need this for my self-esteem. And it would be good to spend some time together.

Another thing I really want to do is plan another outing with the girls. I think I'll do something without Sadie. Maybe just the four of us. After my error with the Shakespeare play, I need to make it up to them. Do something to make them remember that I am their mother. That I love them. It's daft that I should suddenly feel so insecure around my own children. It's all very well having help with the practical things, but I didn't expect to have to share their affection with a stranger. But then, that's not entirely fair. Sadie isn't a stranger any more. I should be grateful to her that she's so lovely with the girls. That they're happy to spend time with her. It would be ten times worse if they hated her. If she was mean to them, or too strict.

'Just nipping upstairs to see how the girls are getting on.'

'Okay,' Robert replies absent-mindedly, looking at his phone while pouring milk onto his cereal.

Leaving the kitchen, I decide that *I'm* going to get the girls ready this morning. I'll also ask them what they want to do this weekend. I jog up the stairs, excited to spend a few precious minutes with them. Keen to show that I'm here for them. On the landing, Katie comes out of the bathroom. She's already in her school uniform, but her hair is sticking up all over the place.

'Morning, KitKat,' I say holding out my arms for a hug.

'Hi, Mummy.'

'Did you sleep well?'

'Yep.'

'How about… you come into my room and sit at my dressing table while I braid your hair?' This is one of Katie's favourite things for us to do, but I'm usually too busy and end up just tying it back in a ponytail while she's having her breakfast.

'That's okay, Mummy. Sadie does my hair now.' My chest constricts at my daughter's casually wounding words.

'Oh, okay. Well, it's great to have Sadie to do your hair, but I can do it today.'

Katie pulls a face. 'She's doing Dutch braids today. Can you do Dutch braids?'

'How about French ones?' I offer.

'Hmm, no thank you. You can do Eva's hair.'

That's me told. 'Okay, you go and have your Dutch braids. Show me when they're done.'

'Okay!' She skips off to her room.

The door to Eva's bedroom flies open. She's dressed too. It's a miracle how Sadie can get the girls to wash and dress without all the usual chivvying along that I have to do.

'Morning, darling. How are you?' I ask my eldest daughter, kissing her forehead.

'Tired.'

'Well, you had a late night. Shall I do your hair?'

'Sadie's doing Dutch braids today.'

My shoulders slump but I manage a weak smile. 'Okay.' I rest my hand on top of her head for a moment, contemplating how an easier life also comes with its downsides. This woman I hardly know is braiding the girls' hair and getting them ready for school like she's the one who's their mother. I feel a stab of guilt mingled with fear. The girls are so relaxed around Sadie. I feel almost redundant. But whose fault is that?

'Mu-um. I've got to go and brush my teeth.' Eva ducks out from beneath my hand and slips into the bathroom. The lock slides across. I sigh and go back downstairs.

I've arranged to meet my sister-in-law at Marco's for lunch. After what happened there with Cosgrove, I almost suggested somewhere different, but I'm not going to let that man put me off my favourite restaurant. I want to put the whole nasty episode behind me, even though I'm still contemplating taking action against him. I walk in to see Amelia already sitting at a window table, a glass of white wine in front of her. She stands to greet me and we hug and kiss. As always, she's looking immaculate, in dark jeans, a cotton-knit Lurex top and vertiginous crocodile heels, her chestnut hair shot through with new caramel highlights.

'Gemma, you're looking gorge,' she says.

'Frazzled, more like. But you certainly are. Love the hair.'

'Thanks. Just had it done this morning. And thank you for meeting up. I know how busy you are. But when I saw you at Diane's, it reminded me how little we've seen of you guys recently.'

I hang my bag on the back of the chair, slip off my jacket and sit opposite her. 'Totally my fault. Things have been so busy recently. And not just the usual brand of crazy, but a whole other level of madness.' I catch the waiter's eye and point to Amelia's glass of wine and then to myself. He nods.

'Sounds interesting,' she says.

'Give me boring any day.' I roll my eyes.

The waiter comes over with my wine. I order the Caesar salad again – because I know I'll enjoy it, and I can't be bothered to look at the menu – and Amelia orders a salade niçoise.

'So?' Amelia prompts. 'What's been happening?'

I launch into the past few weeks' dramas while Amelia stares, wide-eyed and disbelieving. I also tell her about my suspicions that Rebecca could be behind some of it. The only thing I don't tell her is the Cosgrove incident, because I don't want to relive that day, plus I haven't told Robert.

Amelia leans back in her chair. 'Your head must be spinning.'

'To be honest, I'm trying to forget about it all. Move on. Surely that's my quota of bad luck for a while.'

'And you think this Rebecca woman is behind it?' Amelia leans forward. 'The computer virus and the spray paint?'

'I really have no idea. But she's the only person I can think of. She's like this passive-aggressive earth mother who rules the playground.'

'Sounds awful.'

'I know!' I give a little laugh. 'Anyway, how are things with you?'

James and Amelia have been going through IVF but I don't want to ask her about it specifically, in case she doesn't want to talk about it. I'm wary of mentioning the children in front of her for the same reason, although she always loves seeing them and hearing about their latest antics.

'Well, James and I are stopping the IVF for now. Hence the wine.' She gives me a sad smile. 'We'll try again next year, but I think James needs a break from it. Plus it's so expensive and the antiques business isn't doing great at the moment. Too much online competition, you know how it is.'

I nod, wishing I could help them out in the quest to have a baby. I decide to have a word with Robert – see if he can speak to his brother. Perhaps there's something we could do to help them out financially. 'Maybe a break will be good,' I say. 'Give you a chance to relax for a bit.'

Amelia shrugs and looks out of the window at the sea beyond.

'If there's anything I can do…' I say.

'Oh, ignore me,' she says, turning back to face me. 'Shouldn't be drinking wine at lunchtime on an empty stomach. It's making me maudlin.'

I reach across the table and give her hand a squeeze.

'Anyway,' she says, recovering her composure, 'how are my lovely nieces?'

'They're fine. Always talking about their Aunty Amelia.'

'Has everything settled down now?'

I stare at her blankly for a moment.

'With Eva, at school? Diane told me about the suspension – her friends teasing her, and then her lashing out.'

'It was awful,' I reply with a small shudder. 'So unlike Eva to do something like that.' I can't bring myself to mention that Eva was also involved in mean behaviour herself.

'But she was provoked…'

'I know, but the school doesn't see it like that. Anyway, hopefully it's all behind us now.' I change the subject. 'You and James will have to come over for dinner soon.'

'Lovely. Just say the word. Diane told me you've got a new nanny. How's that working out?'

'Really well, actually.' I hadn't wanted to talk about Sadie as I'm not sure if Amelia and James know that Diane is paying her wages. It feels a bit awkward.

'The kids like her then?'

'They love her. Actually, I'm beginning to think they love her more than they love me.'

'Never!'

'It's true. She's so good, I'm becoming redundant.'

'But you were running yourself ragged before. I think it's great you've got someone to help out.'

'Yeah, I know. I definitely have more time now. I mean, look at me, I'm actually having a social lunch rather than a business one!'

'Ha! Careful. If you have too much free time, Diane will rope you into helping organise the golf club dinner dance.' Amelia grins.

'How's all that going?'

'Don't ask.'

'Oh. Like that, is it?'

'No, it's fine. I don't mind. Although the closer we get to the big day, the more like a Sergeant Major she's becoming.'

'Oh dear. I shouldn't laugh.'

'That's another reason why I'm drinking. This afternoon I have to go and sort out table decorations.'

'Sounds okay.'

'It would be if I could just get on with it by myself. But I have to run everything past Diane twenty million times.'

'Poor you.'

'I mean I love her, she's like a second mum, but she does drive me loopy some days.'

I smile, but I don't comment. I never feel like I can criticise Diane in front of my in-laws. Amelia has known Diane since she was a kid, so it comes off as affectionate. But if I was to bad-mouth her, it would sound too critical. I just nod and laugh instead.

'So, this nanny?' Amelia says, her eyes flashing. 'What's she like? Is she young and pretty?'

'Why does everyone want to know if she's pretty?' I ask, suddenly feeling irritable.

'Well, it's that old cliché, isn't it? Where the husband gets a crush on the hot nanny. Not that Robert would have his head turned while he's got you as a wife.'

'Thank you, I think!' I feel a little bit uncomfortable with the way this conversation is going. Especially as Amelia used to go out with Robert.

'So, what's she like? Hot or not?' she teases.

'Sadie is quite pretty, yes.' I think back to Robert's eyes on Sadie's Lycra-clad body this morning. 'But she's not like that. She's... straight-laced, unflirty. Like I said before, she's purely focused on the kids.'

'It's the straight-laced ones you have to watch,' Amelia says, tapping the side of her nose.

I know she's joking, but nevertheless her words chill me.

CHAPTER 32

While we wait for the school gates to open, Eva chats to Lauren and Emily. Their giggles sound cute. But I'm guessing their laughter isn't innocent. I'm guessing it's at the expense of another less popular child. Katie holds my hand, chattering non-stop about last night's play, but I'm only half listening. I have most of my attention trained on Lauren's mother. With her honey-blonde waves and ethnic-bright clothes, she's a multicoloured butterfly surrounded by moths.

I make my way over to her, making myself appear less confident, getting into character.

'Excuse me,' I say timidly. 'Are you Rebecca Taylor?'

She turns around, her bracelets jangling. Her gaze sweeps over my dowdy clothes, my hunched, obsequious posture. 'Hello... um... yes, I'm Rebecca.' She gives me a not-quite-smile.

'Hi, my name's Sadie. I'm Eva and Katie's nanny.'

Her eyes widen a fraction. 'Oh, well, it's nice to meet you.' The woman drips condescension.

'I just wanted to check if I'm allowed to come to the next PTA meeting? I know I'm not a parent, but I'm very involved in the children's lives and if there's anything you need help with, I'm more than happy to—'

'You want to help out?' She gives me a puzzled smile.

'If that's okay?'

'Um, yes, I don't see why not. As far as I'm concerned, the more volunteers we have, the better.'

'*Great. So…*'

'*Our next meeting is actually being held tonight at the Holly Tree in Charminster. Do you know it?*'

'*I'm sure I can find it.*'

'*Seven thirty in the lounge bar. Oh, look, the gates are opening. See you later!*' *She turns away and I'm once again left in the shade. The woman is magnetic. If the daughter is anything like the mother, Eva will have a hard time trying to outshine her. I already knew the PTA meeting was tonight – I found the letters in the girls' school bags and threw them away so Gemma wouldn't see them. Not that she's a PTA mum, but I didn't want to take the chance. My heart starts thumping with excitement at what's next.*

Back at the Ballantines', I whizz around the kitchen tidying up. Robert has a free morning and is in the front room with the door closed so I don't disturb him. Instead, I finish cleaning the kitchen, then take myself up to the attic where I spend the rest of the day beautifying myself. I treat my body to the works – manicure, pedicure, deep-conditioning hair treatment, waxing, moisturising… it feels quite decadent. Stopping for a quick bite to eat – a Waitrose chicken salad from my mini-fridge – I then paint my nails and relax on the sofa bed while they're drying.

As three o'clock rolls around, I pick up the children from school, help with their homework, go through an English paper with Eva and then, finally, get the girls off to bed super-early, with the excuse that they had a late night the night before and need to catch up on their sleep.

Gemma will be home soon. I need to set the scene.

With the girls now tucked up in bed, I strip off my clothes, spritz myself with perfume and throw on a fluffy pink robe. I select two incredibly frumpy dresses from my wardrobe and bring them down-stairs, carrying them on their hangers.

Robert is in the kitchen listening to some music and surfing the net on his phone. I walk in timidly and clear my throat. Luckily, my theatre visit with Robert means that we've already bonded a little. My accidental screw-up with the theatre dates wasn't quite as accidental as Gemma thought. It was a lovely evening with the four of us. Almost like we were a proper family. Maybe not as cosy as I was hoping for, but these things take time... and effort. Lots of effort.

'Robert?'

He looks up from his screen and smiles. Sets his phone down on the table. 'Hi, Sadie. What's up?'

'It's a bit embarrassing,' I say. 'I wanted to ask Gemma's opinion on something, but she's not home yet.'

'She won't be long. Maybe half an hour.'

'Or maybe you *can help?'*

'I will if I can.' He taps his fingers together.

'Thank you!' I give him a grateful smile and go on to explain. 'Would you mind giving me your opinion?'

'Sure. On what?'

'Okay, so which of these two dresses do you prefer?' I hold them out timidly, laughing internally at his facial expression. I can tell he hates both of them and is trying to work out how to spare my feelings.

'Can I ask what the occasion is?' he says tactfully.

'I've made friends with a couple of the mums from school and we've arranged to go out for a drink tonight, but I really can't decide what to wear. They're quite glamorous women, and, well, you can probably tell from my clothes, I'm not very up on fashion.' I give a sad laugh. 'Anyway, I've whittled my choices down to these two dresses. To be honest, I don't think either of them is up to it. The mums are all so fashionable and I'm afraid I don't have a clue.' I swallow and stare at a spot on the floor. 'They're probably all going to laugh at me.'

'Of course they won't!' Robert reaches forward to touch one of the dresses. 'What material is this?' he asks.

'Not sure.' I make a pretence of looking at the label. 'Nylon and polyester.'

Neither of us speak for a moment. Robert shifts in his seat and I break the silence.

'It's okay, you don't have to say it – the dresses are hopeless.'

'No,' he protests, 'not at all. I'm just deciding which one would... be best.'

Sighing, I pretend to examine the dresses along with him. 'I wish I had half of Gemma's style. She always looks amazing.'

'Well... why don't you borrow something of hers?' he suggests. 'You're roughly the same size – maybe you're a little smaller. But I'm sure she'll have something suitable. And Gems won't mind.'

I bite my lip and widen my eyes. 'Are you sure? She's not here for me to ask and I don't want to overstep the mark.'

'It's no problem at all. Come on, let's go up and have a look in her wardrobe. I'm sure we'll find something to impress those mums.'

'Wow. That would be brilliant. Thank you so much.'

I smile to myself and follow Robert up the stairs and into his bedroom.

CHAPTER 33

On my way home from the office, the traffic is light and I let my mind wander over the day's events. Work was uneventful, everything ticking along pretty smoothly. Now that we have a nanny, I don't feel quite so stressed about juggling everything. That's good, surely. So why do I have this little finger of doubt tapping away at my chest?

I came away from my lunch with Amelia worrying about Robert being attracted to Sadie. But I realise how silly I was to let Amelia spook me. My sister-in-law had a bad experience with Robert and so she's naturally suspicious, but Robert and I are soulmates. We've never had cause to doubt or mistrust one another. I've never been jealous of another woman taking his attention. And Sadie is... well, she's certainly a lot prettier than I first thought, but she's also homely and serious. She seems young for her age. I'm really not worried.

I turn into our driveway at exactly seven o'clock. As I step out of the car into the autumn evening air, I smile, excited at the prospect of seeing Eva and Katie, of reading them a bedtime story. Missing out on last night's trip to the theatre has made me appreciate my daughters even more than usual. And I've been thinking about them all day. I think sadly of Amelia and James, and their quest to have a family. I hope they get their wish soon.

Stepping into the hall out of the chilly wind, I'm expecting the girls to come running up to me with tales of their day, as usual.

But the hallway is quiet. A strong scent of perfume hangs in the air – musky, with tones of vanilla, making my nose twitch. Ahead of me, the kitchen door is closed, yellow light spilling through the gap at the bottom. Snatches of adult laughter filter through the door. Has Robert got friends over? I can't remember him saying anything about it. I check my reflection in the hall mirror, just in case. Check my teeth for lipstick. I'm fine. I'll do.

I open the kitchen door and am confronted with an unexpected scene of domestic cosiness. Sadie and Robert are sitting at the kitchen table having a glass of wine together. For a second, I feel as though I'm intruding. Like I've interrupted something private. The smell of perfume is stronger in here. It must be Sadie's. It catches in the back of my throat and I swallow.

'Hi, Gemma!' Robert says. 'Shall I pour you a glass?'

'Hi, guys,' I say, feigning breeziness to cover my discomfort. 'How are you? Where are the girls?'

'I put them to bed early,' Sadie says. 'Hope you don't mind. They were shattered after last night.'

'Ah, that's a shame. I was hoping to read them a story.'

'Don't worry, I already read to them. I should think they'll be fast asleep by now.' Sadie scrapes her chair back and stands up. 'Right, thanks for the drink, Robert. I should get going.'

I take in Sadie's appearance. Far from being the plain little mouse she was when she first came to us, the woman standing before me is a vamp. A sexy seductress. Her face has been artfully made up and her hair is a curtain of black silk. Her curves are astounding – she must be wearing a new bra, although from this angle I wouldn't rule out the possibility of breast-enhancement surgery. Her dress is gorgeous – a grey sheath that is stunning in its simplicity. In fact, it looks very similar to... I frown. 'Is that...? Are you wearing one of my...?'

Sadie looks at Robert, her eyes slightly panicked.

'Huh?' Robert says. And then, 'Oh, yeah.' He turns to me. 'Gems, I said Sadie could borrow one of your dresses, that's okay, isn't it?' He says it as though it's no big deal.

But my gut reaction is saying otherwise. Seeing her look so good in a dress that no longer fits me is not my idea of 'no big deal'. I wonder if he picked it out for her. Or if he took her into our bedroom and opened my wardrobe so she could choose.

Sadie turns to face me. 'Rob said you didn't wear this dress any more so you wouldn't mind if I borrowed it. I hope that's okay, but if not, that's fine – I can put it back.'

Rob? She called him *Rob.* That's a bit too familiar. And that dress has particular nostalgic value – Robert bought it as a gift for my thirtieth birthday. It's my favourite item of clothing. But it's become a little too tight so I haven't worn it for a while. I won't be able to – not until I lose a little weight. I'm furious with my husband for letting Sadie borrow it. For letting her stretch out the bust area with her uplifted boobs. For letting her drench the material in her cloying perfume. But I can't tell Sadie to take it off. Not without sounding like a real bitch. 'Of course you can wear it. It really suits you.'

'Told you she wouldn't mind,' Robert adds, making me want to throttle him.

'Well, if you're sure,' Sadie says uncertainly. 'Thank you so much. My clothes are so plain. I really need to go shopping. Are you absolutely sure you don't mind, Gemma?'

'Of course not.' What else can I say? I know she hasn't really done anything wrong. It's my husband who was being insensitive. 'Are you going out somewhere nice?' I ask, trying to dispel the bitterness lodged in my throat.

'I'm meeting some of the mums from school for a drink,' she says. 'They're all so lovely, aren't they? They've really taken me under their wing. Rebecca especially.'

'Rebecca?' I snap. I take a breath and try to calm my breathing. To speak more evenly. 'You mean Rebecca Taylor. Lauren's mum?'

'Yes, that's her. We're all going down to the Holly Tree tonight. Fancy coming along?'

I shake my head, unable to trust myself to speak. Those are *my* friends she's going out with. Okay, I know I'm not a major part of the clique, but for them to invite Sadie and not me – it's such a snub. It's humiliating. 'I think I'll just stay in and have a glass of wine with my husband.' I realise I sound dismissive and condescending, but I can't help it. 'You have fun, though, and say hi to the gang from me.'

'Aw, they'll miss you, I'm sure. Okay, well, see you later.' She turns to Robert. 'Thanks for all the fashion advice! I think you could have a second career as a personal shopper.'

Robert laughs. 'I'll bear it in mind. Actually, it was quite good fun.'

Amelia was right at lunch today. Sadie is getting too comfortable around my family. She's overstepping her bounds. What's more, she's looking decidedly more beautiful. Not that it should matter. But it does. When there's another woman living in your house, you don't want that woman to be as stunning as Sadie looks tonight. Especially as I'm at work full-time and Robert is often home during the day. I trust Robert implicitly. I do. But should I trust Sadie? The situation is starting to make me feel uncomfortable, like there's a piece of food trapped between my teeth that I can't work loose. I'm annoyed with myself for even having these thoughts. But I can't help the cold jealousy that is beginning to snake down my back and coil itself around my chest.

My husband is clearly enamoured with the woman. My children can't stop talking about 'Sadie this' and 'Sadie that'. Even my friends are embracing her. Sadie said Rebecca had taken her under her wing. Is this Rebecca's way of getting back at me, after what happened between Eva and Lauren? Or am I reading too much into their friendship? I wanted a nanny who would fit in with the family and make my life easier, but I can't help feeling that she is becoming much more than that.

I can't help thinking that Sadie Lewis is not who I first thought she was.

CHAPTER 34

The rain bounces off my umbrella as I walk to school to pick up the kids. But my mind isn't focused on the weather, I'm running through the events of last night. Events that I would class as a resounding success. The look on Gemma's face when she saw me was priceless. The poor cow was devastated by how good I looked in her dress. And Robert didn't have a clue about the huge faux pas he'd made letting me wear it. Of course, I was way too overdressed for a PTA meeting, so before I arrived at the pub, I spent a few minutes in the car wiping off my make-up and changing into skinny jeans and a designer sweatshirt. The dress was purely for Gemma and Robert's benefit – to make Gemma jealous, and to show off my hidden curves to Robert.

I could tell Gemma wasn't happy about me meeting her school-mum friends either. I may have exaggerated just how pally we'd become. In fact, Rebecca hardly paid me any attention at the meeting, aside from a cursory hello, and the rest of the women were deadly boring, talking about cake sales, raffle tickets and the Christmas fete like they were discussing the European political landscape. I faked enthusiasm for the whole three mind-numbing hours, finally volunteering to man the bottle stall with someone called Leanne – yippee.

I need to be a little bit careful at this stage, though. I don't want to give Gemma a reason to fire me. I need her to realise that I'm good for her children. That the benefits of employing me outweigh the negatives. Which is why I'm going to have a little talk to Eva this afternoon. Plant a little seed in her impressionable young brain.

The teachers rush out into the damp playground, huddling under umbrellas and desperately peering through the huddled mass of parents so they can finally palm off the children, get home and make a start on their mountains of planning and marking. Katie comes out first, splashing through puddles and hurling herself against me with the unbridled affection of a wet puppy. Next comes Eva, deep in conversation with her friends, picking her way across the playground towards us.

'Did you bring the car?' she asks.

'No, but I brought you both umbrellas. Zip up your coats and pull up your hoods.'

Eva grumblingly does as she's asked while Katie dances around in her own little world, singing a song. I feel a small pang of affection for them both, wondering what it would be like if they were my children. How would I raise them if I didn't have Gemma breathing down my neck?

I hand Katie her plastic ladybird umbrella and pull up her hood. 'Okay, little miss, come on, let's go.' She puts her cold, wet hand in mine and the three of us leave the school.

'Shall we go to our little café for hot chocolate on the way home?' I ask.

'Yes please!' Katie says.

'Okay,' Eva says.

'Great. Shall we jog there? Get out of this rain?'

A few minutes later, we're sitting at a table in Crumbs by a steamed-up window having ordered a couple of hot chocolates and a coffee for me. We've been here a few times after school. I like having a place besides the house where we can go. Somewhere where it feels like they're mine. Where they'll tell me their secrets and worries.

Eva is quiet while Katie chatters about this and that. After our drinks arrive, I ask Eva how her day was.

'Good,' she replies.

'Are you still friends with Lauren?'

'Yes. We're not best friends though. She's best friends with Emily. Everyone has a best friend except me.'

'My best friend is Maisie!' Katie says, dunking her teaspoon into her hot chocolate and stirring it noisily. 'No, actually my best friend is Zac. Or Eliza. I don't really know. I've got lots of best friends.'

'Why do you think you haven't got a best friend?' I ask Eva.

'Dunno.' She blows on her drink.

'Maybe it's because their mums are good friends?' I suggest.

She doesn't reply.

'Or maybe because they meet up after school a lot, and at the weekends.'

'Maybe.' She brightens. 'Can Lauren come round to our house? It was great when we had to do that project. Lauren thought I was brilliant because we ordered pizza and her mum doesn't normally let her have it. Maybe she could come round and we could have pizza again?'

'Sounds like a great idea,' I reply. 'Lauren's mum and I are starting to be really good friends now so I could arrange that for you.'

'Really?'

'And can my friends come round, too?' Katie asks.

'Yes,' I reply. I turn back to Eva. 'It's a shame you don't have a phone yet.'

'Mum won't let me have one until I start senior school. She said she'll buy me one if I work hard for the test.'

'Do your friends have phones?' I ask.

'Nearly all of them do.'

'Even Lauren?' I ask, remembering Rebecca spouting off last night about the dangers of children being online. I doubt she would let her daughter have a phone if she feels so strongly about it.

'Lauren's got the latest iPhone,' Eva says, dispelling my preconceptions. 'She's had a phone since Year 3.'

'Gosh, she's lucky,' I say, thinking the opposite. 'Her mum's very generous. So, are you the only one without a phone?'

'I don't think Maya has one either,' Eva says.

'Does Maya have a best friend?' I ask.

'No. Maya doesn't really have any friends.'

'Well I think you're very grown-up not to mind feeling left out when Lauren and everyone are chatting away every evening on Instagram and Snapchat. Don't worry though. Once your mum lets you have a phone, you'll be popular too.'

Eva doesn't reply.

Perfect. She's falling for my plan, just like I knew she would.

CHAPTER 35

After much deliberation and changing of minds, the girls finally decided that the thing they would like to do most this weekend is to make fairy cakes for the school cake sale. Ordinarily, I would have run out to the shops and bought some, but with my new resolution to do more fun things with the girls, this gives us the perfect opportunity for some mother–daughter bonding time. Rob is out getting some shopping for tonight's dinner, but he promised to be back by eleven so we could all sample the cakes with a cup of tea.

It's Sadie's day off, and she's out somewhere, so we have the house to ourselves. It feels blissfully decadent, relaxing without her here. I was surprised that the girls chose something as simple as making cakes. I offered to take them to the cinema, bowling, rock-wall climbing or to the paint-a-plate café. But this was what they wanted. So this is what we're doing.

I'm no chef, so we're following a simple recipe on YouTube. The kitchen is already an absolute mess, but we're all having a great time. I made sure the girls each had their own baking trays and icing bags so there's no rivalry or arguments. So far so good.

'Mum, you need to ice one too,' Eva says.

'Ooh, am I allowed?'

'You can do one of mine and one of Katie's.' She passes me a cupcake.

'Brilliant. Thanks, Eva.'

She smiles. 'You're welcome.'

'Do you think four trays of cakes will be enough?' Katie asks. 'Maybe we should make some more, because there are loads of people at our school.'

'Yeah, but we're not the only ones making cakes,' Eva says. 'Lots of people are.'

'Ours are the best though,' Katie says.

'I bet Lauren's will be better.' Eva's shoulders drop.

'No way,' I say. 'Our cupcakes are the best cupcakes in Bournemouth.'

'The best in England!' Katie cries.

'The best in the world!' I yell, thrusting a cupcake into the air. 'Come on, Eva.' I give her a nudge with my elbow.

'The best in the universe,' she mumbles.

'Sorry, what was that?' I ask.

'In the universe,' she says a little louder.

'Can't he-ear yo-ou!' Katie sings.

'The best in the universe!' Eva yells, making Katie and I jump, and then collapse into helpless giggles.

Eva gives us both a grin. Then she turns serious. 'Mu-um?' she says.

'Yes?'

'Do you think… am I… would I be allowed to have a phone?'

'We've already talked about this, Eva. Dad and I agreed that you can have a phone when you start senior school.'

'But everyone else has got one.'

'Does Maya have one?' I ask, knowing the answer is no.

Eva shakes her head. 'But she's the only other person.'

'I'm sure she can't be the only one. And even if she was, it doesn't change anything. We agreed we would wait.'

'I've got that birthday money Grandma gave me. You wouldn't have to pay for it. I could buy it myself.'

'It's not about the money, Eva.'

'Then why aren't I allowed one?' Her expression clouds over and I can see this morning's easy atmosphere rapidly evaporating.

'Dad and I feel that, until you're old enough to go off on your own, you don't really need a phone. Once you start getting the bus with your friends it will be useful, but until then…'

'Okay, so can I go to town with my friends? Lots of them get the bus, and—'

I can already see where this conversation is heading and I need to nip it in the bud. 'You're not having a phone, and you're not old enough to get the bus into town without an adult.'

'It's not fair!' She folds her arms across her chest.

My heart sinks. I can't give in to her, but I don't want our weekend to turn into a massive sulk-fest. 'Right,' I say, changing the subject and picking up Katie's icing bag. What shall I pipe onto this cupcake? A butterfly? A flower?'

'A butterfly!' Katie says.

'Who cares,' Eva mutters.

'I beg your pardon?' I turn to my daughter. 'What did you just say?'

'Nothing,' she says, her face turning red.

'Don't be rude, young lady.' I realise, with a pang, that I sound like my mum.

'I'm not being rude. I just want to get a phone like all my friends. But you don't care that I'm left out because I'm the only one who can't join in on Snapchat. You're turning me into a loser, like Maya.'

'Right! That's enough! Don't talk about your friend like that.'

'She's not my friend.'

'Go to your room!'

'Fine! I'd rather be there than here with YOU!' Eva marches out of the kitchen, slams the door and stomps up the stairs.

I realise my hands are trembling. I have never had a conversation like that with my daughter before. She's always been so gentle. I've never heard her say mean things about anyone. I have no idea what's got into her or how to make things better. Is this a taste of the teen years ahead of us?

'Does Eva hate you, Mummy?' Katie asks in a small voice.

'No, sweetie. She's just a bit cross at the moment. We'll leave her to calm down and then she'll say sorry and everything will go back to normal.'

'I hope so. She was really angry. Her face went red and her eyes were mean.'

Katie and I finish icing the cakes, but our joyful morning is ruined. I resist the temptation to go upstairs and see how Eva's doing. She needs time to think about her behaviour. I'll clean up the kitchen and then go and see if we can mend fences.

Half an hour later, once the cakes are iced and the kitchen is tidy, I can bear it no longer. 'Right, KitKat, you stay here a minute while I just go and see if your sister's any happier.'

'Can I come with you?'

'Maybe in a while. Let me speak to her first, okay? You watch out the window for Daddy coming back. But no going out the front door without me!'

'I won't.'

I take a breath and make my way upstairs to Eva's room. Her bedroom door is closed and so I give a little knock. There's no reply.

'Eva?'

I knock once more.

'Eva? I'm coming in, okay?'

I open the door, but my eldest daughter isn't in her room. My eye lands on an envelope propped up on her chest of drawers. It has 'Mum' written on the front. My heart begins to thump. I snatch up the envelope and tear it open:

You don't love me so I'm leaving home. Don't bother trying to find me. I don't believe this! Has she run away? 'Eva!' I race around the house, throwing open every door, but she's not in any of the rooms. I'm getting flashbacks to when Katie went missing a few weeks ago. But this time, Eva has chosen to leave. Why? What's got into her lately? She must have snuck out while we were in the kitchen. How is this happening again?

I run down the stairs as the front door opens.

'Eva?' I cry out, breathless.

But it's Robert, laden down with about four bags of groceries in each hand.

'What's the matter?' he asks, seeing the expression on my face.

'It's Eva. She's run away.'

'What are you talking about, run away? I thought you were baking?'

'We were, but we had an argument and she stropped off to her room. I just went up to see if she'd calmed down, and found this note.' I hand him the piece of paper that's still in my hand.

'Daddy!' Katie runs into the hall. 'Eva shouted at Mummy.'

Robert dumps the shopping bags on the floor. 'How long's she been missing?'

'Can't be more than half an hour. Maybe less.'

'I'll go out in the car and look. You call my mum and James.'

'And her friends…' I add. 'Maybe she's gone to one of their houses?'

'Call Sadie too,' Robert suggests. 'She'll want to help look.'

'It's her day off.'

'She'll still want to help. Call her.'

'Okay, okay, I'll call her. Go! Call me as soon as you find her.'

The irony isn't lost on me that if Eva had a phone we'd probably have been able to track her down in no time. I sink to my knees for a moment wondering how the hell things have gone from happy to horrendous in such a short space of time. But I don't have the luxury of wondering.

I need to find my child.

CHAPTER 36

I'm in the park, sitting on a damp swing, when I receive a garbled phone call from Gemma telling me that Eva has run away from home. Honestly, I have one day off, and this is what happens. Gemma is losing control of her kids. Of herself. I get up off the swing and walk a little way away, over by the park fence where no one can hear our conversation.

'Slow down,' I say calmly, injecting as much concern into my voice as I can muster. 'Tell me what happened.'

'Eva and I had an argument,' *Gemma says.* 'She left me a note saying she was leaving home. I know it's over-dramatic. But I'm so worried. Robert's gone out in the car looking. I know it's your day off and I'm sorry to call, but I just wondered if you knew where she might have gone.'

'I don't. But I'll start looking,' I say.

'Would you?'

'Of course!'

'Thank you so much, Sadie. And you'll message me the moment you hear anything, or if you find her.'

'The very instant,' I reply.

'Okay, I'd better get off the line in case Robert's trying to get through.'

'Okay. And Gemma…'

'What?'

'Try not to worry.'

'Thanks.'

Gemma ends the call and I walk back to the swings.

'Was that my mum?' Eva asks, half-heartedly swinging back and forth, and then kicking at the squidgy playground surface with the toe of her trainer.

'Yes, it was. She's very worried. We should tell her you're safe and sound. It's been almost an hour since you came and got me. What would you have done if I wasn't in the coffee shop?'

'Don't know. Waited for you outside I s'pose.'

'Well, it's a good job I was there, isn't it?'

I'd been sitting in Crumbs when Eva burst in, her face colourless, her eyes bloodshot. She told me she'd had an argument with her mum and never wanted to go home again. We sat in the café for a while until she eventually said that maybe she should go home. So we left. But as we got closer to the house, she changed her mind and asked to go to the park instead. So, here we are, hanging around in the cold drizzle.

'Do you think it's unfair that I'm the only one without a phone?' Eva asks.

'I understand it's not fair, but it's less than a year until you start senior school. Not that long to wait. And running away isn't going to solve anything, is it? If I could change your mum's mind I would try. But I can't. She's made up her mind and that's that.'

'I wish you were my mum,' Eva says.

My heart swells, and I look across at her, at her pale, tear-streaked face, her long brown hair. I suppose people might assume we were mother and daughter. Our colouring is very similar. 'Your mum loves you, Eva. We need to take you home.'

'No! I don't want to go home. I'll run away again if you take me back. Can't we stay in the park?'

I sigh.

'Just for ten minutes?'

'Okay. But only if you promise to come back home with me after that.'

I think about Gemma back at the house, going insane with worry over her missing daughter. About Robert combing the streets, hoping to catch a glimpse of his little girl. One phone call could put them out of their misery. But I think I'll leave it a little longer. After all, it's not like Eva is actually in any danger. She's perfectly safe with me.

CHAPTER 37

The park isn't far from our house, just a ten-minute walk, but it will be quicker to drive so I grab my phone and keys and jump into the car with Katie. Sadie just left me a message saying she's there with Eva. *Thank you, God. Thank you, thank you, thank you.* Before leaving home I fired off a hasty WhatsApp message to Diane, James, Amelia and Robert, letting them know Eva's safe.

'Is Eva okay?' Katie asks as she does up her seatbelt.

'Yes. She's with Sadie.'

'Is she in trouble?'

'She shouldn't have gone out of the house on her own.' I almost wheelspin out of the driveway, then I force myself to slow down. The last thing I need is to have a car accident. I drive the two minutes up the road to our local park, stop at an awkward angle and wait for Katie to get out, before taking her hand and running across the muddy field to the playground at the other side.

'Gemma!' I turn to see Robert behind me with his brother and Amelia. They must have arrived seconds after me.

'They're in the playground,' I cry without stopping.

'Daddy!' Katie cries, letting go of my hand and running back towards Robert. I let her go to him. On the phone, Sadie said that she'd looked everywhere she could think of, and finally found her in the park. I can see them now, side by side on the swings. Sadie stands and waves. Eva remains on the swing, her shoulders hunched. Apart from Sadie and Eva, there are only a couple of other families here with their kids. No one else wants to spend a wet Saturday at the park.

I barge through the wooden gate and let it fall back with a clatter.

'Eva!' I say, rushing over to her. 'Are you all right? I was worried sick.'

She's still staring at the ground. Sadie murmurs something to her and she looks up, her eyes red from crying. 'Sorry,' she mumbles.

'Oh, Eva!' I cry. 'You're okay!' I crouch down to give her a hug, but she pulls back and stares past me.

'Dad!' She jumps to her feet, slips around me and goes over to Robert, who crushes her against him.

'We were so worried about you, Eva,' he says. 'We've had everyone out looking.'

'Sorry,' she says, burying her head in his sweatshirt.

'Sadie…' I turn to where she's standing, a little awkward amidst our family drama. 'I can't thank you enough for finding her.'

'Hi, I'm Amelia. Eva and Katie's auntie.' Amelia comes over and introduces herself to Sadie. 'That's my husband, James. Well done for finding Eva!'

Sadie's cheeks flush. 'It was a fluke… I just—'

'Doesn't matter if it was a fluke or not,' I interrupt. 'You found her and that's what matters. Shall we all go back to ours for a cup of tea? Or lunch, maybe? Eva, you must be hungry.'

'Hi, Diane!' Sadie says warmly.

I turn to see my mother-in-law has now arrived. She's wearing a stylish mac and carrying a golf umbrella.

'Hello, Sadie, dear. Well done for finding Eva. Come and stand under my umbrella, you're soaking.'

'Yes, I don't know what would have happened if you hadn't found her,' Robert adds. 'Thank you so much.'

'This girl is an absolute godsend,' Diane says. 'How did you two manage before she came along?'

'Do you know each other?' I ask, turning from Diane to Sadie.

'Of course,' Diane says. 'Sadie brings the girls over for afternoon tea from time to time. I must say, she's got a wonderful way with them.'

It disturbs me a little to know that Sadie has been spending time at Diane's house. 'How did you end up going to Diane's?' I ask Sadie.

'Do the girls need permission to visit their grandmother?' Diane answers.

'Of course not,' I reply. 'I'm just surprised, that's all.'

'I popped in to your house one afternoon and invited them round,' Diane explains a little huffily.

I wonder why Sadie didn't tell me she'd been to my mother-in-law's.

'We were very happy to be invited,' Sadie says. 'My grandparents died when I was very young, and I always wished I'd known them. I told Eva and Katie they need to cherish their grandma. The girls are lucky to have you, Diane.'

My mother-in-law simpers. She actually *simpers*. Why can't I evoke that response in her? The most I get is a sniff. But then, I guess I've never flattered and fawned around her the way Sadie's doing right now.

'Tell you what,' Robert announces in a loud voice. 'If Eva had a phone, we'd never have lost track of her. Why don't we go into town and buy you girls an iPhone each?'

'Really?' Eva looks from her dad to me.

I try to keep my face neutral, but inside I'm absolutely seething. What the hell does Robert think he's playing at? When it comes to parenting the girls, we normally make these sorts of decisions together. He doesn't know the reason why Eva went off in a huff in the first place. If he'd waited for me to explain, he would know that buying her a phone now is the absolute worst decision he could have made.

'And one for me too?' Katie squeals. 'Did you say one for both of us, Daddy?'

'I did, KitKat.' Robert looks at me with shining eyes, expecting me to be thrilled with his announcement. I throw him an icy glare before feigning excitement for everyone else. What choice do I have if I don't want to end up being the hard-arsed bad parent once again?

None whatsoever.

After a celebratory lunch with everyone at our house, my in-laws finally leave and it's just us and Sadie left. She tactfully takes herself up to her rooms. Eva's sulk has vanished and she seems to be talking to me again. Katie is leaping around the kitchen telling Robert and me all the things she's going to do once she gets her iPhone. I won't take out my frustration on either of the girls. It's not their fault – of course they're going to be excited to get phones. What child wouldn't be?

'Okay, can you two go up to your rooms for a quiet half hour?'

'Are we still going to town this afternoon?' Eva asks.

'Yes, we are,' I reply with a smile.

Eva gives me a shy smile in return. 'I'm sorry about this morning,' she says.

'Can we have a hug?' I ask.

Eva nods and melts into my body. I give her a squeeze, waiting for her to immediately let go like she always does. But she only hugs me harder. I kiss the top of her head and realise she's crying.

'Hey, why are you upset?' I ask. 'We're going to have a nice afternoon later, aren't we?'

She nods but still doesn't let go of me.

'Eva?'

'I just feel really bad for shouting at you and running off. I didn't want to, but I just did it and it felt awful, but I couldn't help it.' Her body is shuddering with sobs now and I lead her over to the kitchen table and pull her onto my lap.

'Hey,' I say. 'Everyone has days like that now and again.'

'Even you?' she asks.

'Especially me.'

'And Daddy?' Katie asks.

'I'm the worst one of all,' Robert says, pulling a face. 'I slam doors and cry and go storming off. Mummy has to put me in time out.' He catches my eye and I know he's trying to figure out what he's done wrong as I've been giving him the silent treatment all through lunch.

The girls start giggling. 'Do you really give Daddy time out?' Katie asks.

'All the time,' I say dryly, refusing his attempts to win me round.

'Okay, girls,' Robert says, turning serious, 'so Mum and I need half an hour's peace and quiet. Go on upstairs now.'

'Are you all right?' I ask Eva.

She nods.

'Let's forget this morning ever happened, okay?' I say. 'I know you're sorry, and that's what counts. As long as you promise to never ever run off like that again.'

She nods and slides off my lap. 'I promise.'

My two girls go upstairs, and now I have to speak to Robert.

I pick up a dinner plate and start scraping the leftovers into the bin.

'Leave that for a minute,' Robert says, 'and tell me why you're so angry with me.'

I put the plate on the draining board and pick up another, scraping more food into the bin. 'The reason Eva stormed off this morning,' I begin, my voice cold, 'is because I said she couldn't have a phone until next year. And so what do you go and do? Offer to buy her and her six-year-old sister a phone.'

Robert's face darkens. He gets to his feet and takes the plate out of my hand. Places it back on the table, to my annoyance. 'Well I didn't know all that. If I'd known I wouldn't have offered to get them.'

'But we should have talked about it first, before you made a grand gesture and gave in to her emotional blackmail.'

'That's a bit harsh!'

'Well it's true.'

'Okay, you're right, we should have talked about it first. But we didn't, and I made a mistake. I'm sorry, okay?'

He doesn't sound sorry. He sounds annoyed.

'The thing is,' I say, stacking the empty plates, 'I don't want them turning into spoilt brats, thinking they can have tantrums and we'll cave in. And I also hate the fact that I look like the bad guy.'

'You don't look like the bad guy.' Robert frowns.

'Yes, I do.' I straighten up and face him. 'You know I do. You and Sadie are the lovely ones who let them have fun and treats, and I'm the evil, witchy mother.'

'Now you're being ridiculous.'

'Am I?' I fold my arms across my chest, staring at my husband across the kitchen table, willing him to understand how I'm feeling.

'Eva was all over you just now, apologising to you and hugging you,' Robert says, trying to appease me.

'Yes, but she's changed lately. She's not the gentle little girl she's always been.' I lower my voice. 'And I don't think it helps having Sadie here.'

'What? What's this got to do with Sadie? Anyway, she was the one who found Eva today. If it wasn't for her, we'd probably still be out searching.'

I shake my head, angry at my husband's stubborn refusal to see that something else might be going on here. 'I don't know. There's something off about her. I can't put my finger on it. And calling you "Rob" the other day – what was all that about?' My mind flashes back to them sitting at the kitchen table together, sharing a bottle of wine.

Robert's eyes widen. 'I didn't even notice. Anyway, lots of people call me Rob. I don't mind.'

'It just feels weird, when I don't call you that, but *she* does.' I try to damp down the corrosive burn of jealousy in my chest, but it won't go away.

'Now you're being silly.'

I know what I'm saying sounds petty and silly, but it doesn't make it any less true. I don't know how to get Robert to see what I'm seeing. As I voice the worries that have been bubbling under the surface for days, they seem to become more real, more urgent. 'I think we're relying on her too much. We should cut back on her hours.'

'Sorry, Gem, but if you didn't work such long hours we wouldn't have needed Sadie in the first place.'

I grit my teeth and yank out a chair from beneath the table, sitting down heavily. 'Okay, so now we're getting to it.'

'Sorry.' He raises his hands. 'I shouldn't have said that.'

'But it's what you think?'

'No. No, it's not.' He sits opposite me and steeples his fingers. 'I just think we've had a stressful morning and we should probably not talk about stuff like this when we're so… emotional.'

'You mean when *I'm* so emotional?' He's not wrong though. My heart is racing and the blood is hot in my veins.

'No, that's not what I mean. Jeez, you're impossible to talk to sometimes!' He gets to his feet once more, paces the room, running a hand through his hair.

I know Robert hasn't done anything malicious. He hasn't purposely undermined me. But I wish he would see things from my point of view sometimes. That it's bloody hard work being the breadwinner and the perfect mother and the perfect wife. That sometimes it takes its toll and sucks my energy reserves dry. That seeing Sadie and Robert being so wonderful and laid-back about everything highlights all my inadequacies.

'Once the entry test is over, we need to ask Sadie to leave,' I say. 'Go back to how we were before.'

'That's a bit drastic!' Robert says. 'And I think it would be a mistake. She takes the pressure off you, Gemma. She's good for our family. I thought you felt the same way?'

I shake my head, suddenly emotionally drained, and decide to drop it for now. But I'm not happy. I've decided – I don't want Sadie Lewis in my home any more.

CHAPTER 38

Everyone is out at school and work this morning and I'm sipping my morning coffee in the kitchen. It's been almost a week since Eva ran away, but everything's settled down again. Gemma was quite snippy with me last weekend, but she seems to have recovered from whatever it was she had her knickers in a twist about – probably Robert's grand gesture of buying the girls phones. I couldn't have planned that one better myself. I almost snorted with laughter at Gemma's face when he announced that in front of everyone.

I finish my coffee and leave my mug on the kitchen table. I'll come back and tidy up later. I have something else I need to do. Something important.

Things are going well with the Ballantines, but I need to up my game. They're used to me now. Eva is doing well in her studies and I think Gemma is pleased with her daughter's progress. I'm proving my worth. And I've been super helpful and lovely to Gemma all week. I haven't let her see me anywhere near Robert. So I think I can afford to move things up a gear.

Robert will be home soon. I sashay up the stairs, revelling in what I'm about to do next. Luxuriating in the knowledge that this will most definitely throw the cat amongst the pigeons.

CHAPTER 39

Tonight is the night of Diane's charity dinner dance at the golf club. The one she's spent the last six months organising. I leave work early, but the Friday traffic is a nightmare. Diane will kill us if we're late. Or rather, she'll kill *me*. She'll assume I left work late; that I wasn't organised enough. I'm sure this dinner dance is just an excuse to put her family on display. She loves to show Robert off to her golf-club buddies. Although she'd hate me referring to them as her *buddies*. Diane doesn't have buddies. She has family friends or acquaintances. I sigh. I need to stop thinking like this, it'll only make the evening worse. I'll make an effort to be extra nice to her tonight.

Home at last, and I have less than half an hour to get ready. I fly inside, say hello to Sadie, plant kisses on the children's cheeks, promising them we'll catch up properly tomorrow morning, and I run upstairs. Robert is in the bedroom wearing nothing but his boxers, about to put on his shirt and dinner jacket, which are hanging on the back of the door.

'Hello!' I say. 'Looking good, Mr Ballantine.'

He grins and flexes his muscles in the parody of a bodybuilder. 'I was worried you were going to be late,' he says.

'Me? Late? Never.'

He snorts.

'Traffic was crap,' I add, stripping off my work clothes.

'Friday night mayhem?'

'Yep. Well, I'm here now. Thought I'd wear my green dress – the one with the diamante clasp.'

'Good choice. But, then again, you look good in everything,' he says.

'Aww, thank you.'

He kisses my bare shoulder. 'Can you hurry though? Mum made me promise we'd be there right on the dot of half seven.'

'Sure. I'll be ready in ten... no, maybe fifteen minutes.'

'Perfect.'

While Robert finishes getting dressed, I jump into the shower. As the warm water washes the day away, I realise I'm quite looking forward to tonight. We'll be sitting at the same table as James and Amelia, so the evening will definitely be fun. We'll drive there and get a taxi back, or maybe we'll even walk back. I could quite easily spend another ten minutes under this blissful hot water, but I turn the dial off after a two-minute blast. I get dried in record time and head back into the bedroom, the towel wrapped around me. Robert's not here so I guess he's already dressed and has gone downstairs.

Rebecca and Charlie are going too, so I'll have a chance to chat to her away from the children. I asked Suri if she and Steve wanted to come, but she said they were busy. I hope that wasn't an excuse. I made Eva apologise to Maya after the name-calling incident, but things have been strained between us since then. I don't suppose I can blame her. Hopefully the girls will make up and Suri will find it easier to talk to me again.

I slap on some body lotion, then put on my underwear before sitting on my side of the bed to pull up my stockings. Sadie must have tidied up the house today. I notice the bed has been made. I wrinkle my nose. I can smell her perfume in here. It's so strong. Maybe I could ask her not to wear it. Say I'm allergic to it or something. But I can't do that. That's probably not an acceptable thing to ask. I'll just have to put up with it while she's here. And I must admit, after my doubts, she's been fantastic this week. Really sweet and helpful.

I open the wardrobe and locate my emerald-green dress, praying it's not creased or stained. I should have checked beforehand. Holding it under the light, I run my eyes across the crepe material. Luckily, it appears crease- and stain-free, so I slide it over my head. Then, from the jewellery box on my dressing table, I select a diamante cuff and wear it on the opposite wrist to the art-nouveau shoulder-clasp on my dress. In the mirror, I eye myself critically. Just hair and make-up left to do now. Should take me five-ish minutes.

I sit at my dressing table and blast my blonde locks with the dryer. That's the beauty of having a short style – it doesn't take long to dry. Next, I slick some product through it and apply my make-up. Lastly, I spritz some perfume onto my wrists and throat. I'm impressed with how quickly I managed to make myself presentable. I'll put my shoes on once I'm downstairs. I get to my feet and turn to pick up my discarded towel from the bed when something catches my eye.

A hair.

A long, dark hair stuck to my side of the bed, near my pillow. I walk over to the bed and pick it up between my thumb and forefinger. Sadie was in here tidying today, so it's entirely feasible that one of her hairs ended up on my pillow. But I realise the smell of her perfume is stronger right here, overpowering my own subtle perfume. I bend down to sniff my pillow and rear back in shock. My pillow absolutely stinks of Sadie's perfume. It's almost as though… as though she's lain here.

I pull back the duvet and press my nose to my sheet. The smell is even stronger in my bed. And then I see another long, dark hair stuck to the underside of the duvet.

My heart begins to race. Surely this doesn't mean anything. It can't mean what I think it means. But how else can it be explained?

I walk round to Robert's side of the bed, my legs unsteady, my insides twisting. I can smell it here too, not as strong, but it's still here. What should I do? Should I say something to my husband? Ask him about it? Accuse him?

I straighten up as I hear footsteps on the stairs. The bedroom door opens.

'Are you nearly ready, Gems? Wow! You look stunning.'

I stare at him as though he's an alien creature. Not my gorgeous, familiar husband. Surely he would never betray me like this. I trust him. But that scent... her hair...

'Weird thing...' I begin, my voice unsteady.

'What?' He's still standing in the doorway. 'We've really got to go, Gemma.'

'Our bed... it smells like Sadie's perfume.'

'Sorry, what?'

'Our bed smells like Sadie's perfume. And I found one of her hairs. Well, two hairs actually – one on my pillow and one under the duvet.' The words tumble out of my mouth before I realise what I'm saying.

'What are you talking about?' Robert glances at his watch.

I take a breath, realising that I have to follow this through. 'I'm telling you that Sadie has been in our bed.'

'Why would she...' He breaks off when he sees my stony expression. 'You don't think... You're not suggesting...'

'I don't know what to think, or to suggest. I'm just telling you what I found.' It's weird. I don't feel angry, or upset. I just feel numb. Like I'm in shock or something.

'Gemma.' He gives a disbelieving laugh and takes a step towards me. 'Show me this hair.'

I realise it's still pinched between my fingers. I hold it out for him to see.

'Sadie cleans in here, doesn't she?'

I pick up my pillow. 'Smell that.' I hand it to him.

He does as I ask, wrinkling his nose a little. 'That's strong!'

'So?' I wait for him to give me an explanation. To admit something to me, but his face is darkening, his eyebrows knitting together.

'For goodness sake, Gemma! You think I've… been in our bed with Sadie, is that it?'

'No! I don't know. But it's pretty bloody odd, don't you think? The perfume and the hair?'

'Maybe it's odd, or maybe there's a perfectly innocent explanation. But I don't know what it is, because I've got nothing to do with it! Okay? Why don't we go and ask Sadie?' He glances at his watch again. 'And now we're going to be late.'

'You're worried about being late for a golf-club dinner when I've just told you the nanny has been in our bed? Don't you think this is a little more important?'

'Actually, no, I don't,' Robert says, snapping. 'Whatever you've found in our bed, it has nothing to do with me. Are you telling me you don't trust me, is that it?'

'Of course I trust you. But…' I don't know what to say next. Do I really believe Robert would sleep with Sadie? I sit down heavily on the bed. 'I'll have to change the bedding.'

'Look, Gemma…' Robert's voice is soft. He comes and sits next to me on the bed. 'I haven't been in here with Sadie. You're my wife and I love you. I don't want to be with anyone else. And to be honest, it pisses me off that you could even think I would do that. Especially in our bed!' His jaw clenches. 'Now, can we please get going? My name is going to be mud all night if we don't leave soon.'

'Fine,' I say, not sure what to think any more. Have I overreacted? Or have I not reacted *enough*? I don't want to have a shouting match with my husband if he's innocent, but I'm also not going to be taken for a fool. And if Robert is denying it, I don't want to then go and accuse Sadie. My thoughts are too jumbled to think straight. The evidence is there. It's clear. But my husband is a good man. He would never cheat on me. Not like this. Would he?

As I retrieve my satin shoes from the bottom of the wardrobe and follow Robert down the stairs, I try to swallow the lump in my throat. To even out my shallow breaths. To sniff back the threatening tears. I realise that it's not just in my bedroom – Sadie's perfume pervades the house. It's everywhere, strong and sickly, stinging the back of my eyes and sticking in the back of my throat. She's chipping away at my life, taking away its familiar shape bit by bit. Carving something new. Something unrecognisable. Something horrible…

CHAPTER 40

We're half an hour late to the dinner dance. It's heaving inside the clubhouse, the normally sedate room now alive with silk dresses and black ties. The swing band is already playing and a few couples are standing around the dance floor deciding whether or not they're drunk enough to dance yet. Diane lowers her thickly made-up eyelids across the room at me and Robert. Her frosty gaze telling us she's not amused at our tardiness. But right now, I couldn't give a shit about Diane's offended sense of propriety. My mind is still churning over what I found in our bedroom. Robert is by my side, holding himself stiffly. His growing anger – or is it guilt? – radiating off him in almost visible waves. Far from the enjoyable and relaxing evening I was anticipating, tonight is going to be excruciating. But I'm just going to have to get through it. I can talk to Robert properly afterwards.

I go through the motions of greeting everyone, smiling, making small talk. Robert doesn't even try. His responses are terse, unsmiling, and Diane keeps shooting me daggers as though I'm to blame for our lateness.

'I'm getting a drink,' Robert says, leaving my side and heading to the bar.

'I'll get my own then, shall I?' I mumble. His initial reaction of confusion and denial has morphed into outrage at my veiled accusation. But what else was I supposed to do? Ignore the hairs and perfume? Pretend they didn't exist?

'Hi, Gemma.'

I turn to see James and Amelia standing behind me. James in a slightly too-tight dinner jacket, and Amelia almost blinding me in a floor-length silver sequined dress.

'Wow! You look amazing,' I say.

'Thank you,' Amelia replies. 'You too. I love that dress. The colour looks fab with your hair.'

'Hi Gemma, lovely to see you. Is Robert here?' James asks.

'At the bar.'

'I'll go and find him. You two okay for drinks?'

'I ordered a bottle of champagne for our table,' Amelia says.

'Great. I'd love a gin and tonic though.' The urge to get drunk is strong, even though I know that's possibly not the best idea.

'I'll get you a G & T.' James goes off to find his brother and Amelia leads me over to our table. 'You okay?' she asks. 'You seem a bit distracted.'

'I had a row with Robert.'

She sits down and pulls a sympathetic face, takes a sip of champagne and then pours me a glass. 'That's bad timing. I was looking forward to the four of us having a laugh tonight.'

'I know,' I reply, sitting next to her. 'Let's talk about something else though. The clubhouse looks amazing. You and Diane have done an incredible job pulling all this together.'

'It was actually pretty enjoyable in the end. I'll miss all the rushing around and organising.'

'You should set up your own events business,' I suggest.

'Ooh, maybe I should!' Her face lights up for a moment.

Although she and James aren't great with money, so on second thoughts it's probably not the best idea. Amelia is fonder of spending it than making it.

The evening rolls by with me and Robert managing not to say a single word to one another. I talk to other people in a daze, having bright conversations on the surface, while a gnawing fear chews at my thoughts.

Rebecca and Charlie are at a table with a group of school mums and dads. If my mind wasn't elsewhere, I would probably feel a little snubbed. Rebecca never asked if I wanted to join their table. But then again, I don't socialise with any of them, so why should she have asked me? I think my argument with Robert has clouded everything. I pull myself together and go over to say hi to them. If nothing else, it will help take my mind off everything.

'Gemma,' she cries exuberantly, leading me to believe that she must have had quite a bit to drink, as normally she's quite cool with me. 'I meant to come and say hello earlier, but I kept getting sidetracked!'

'Same here,' I reply. 'Are you having a good evening?'

'Lovely, lovely. Had a few too many glasses of champagne, but we don't go out that often, so we may as well enjoy ourselves, right, Gemma? How's everything with you? Things okay with the lovely Sadie?'

I inhale, trying not to blurt out anything inappropriate. 'Yes, fine thanks.'

'She's a bit of a sex kitten, that one.'

I freeze at her words. 'What do you mean?'

I realise Rebecca is more than just a little drunk, the pitch of her laughter boring into my skull like a dentist's drill. 'You know,' she says.

'What are you talking about?' My heart is hammering uncomfortably and my cheeks heat up. Is she about to reveal something awful about Robert and Sadie? Is she going to confirm my worst suspicions?

Rebecca gets up out of her chair and leans in to whisper in my ear. I think she's about to reveal something important. 'Got to go to the ladies,' she hisses loudly. 'Bit pissed. Need a wee.'

I exhale. 'Rebecca, what were you going to say about Sadie?'

'Nothing, nothing.' She puts her fingers to her lips. 'Shhh. Don't tell Gemma.' She staggers off in the direction of the ladies and I try to keep pace.

'Don't tell Gemma *what*?'

'Ha! Trying to trick me.' She puts a finger on the tip of her nose and points at me. 'You're Gemma.'

'Yes, I'm Gemma. Rebecca, you're friends with Sadie, aren't you?'

'Gotta go to the loo,' she replies, pushing open the door and walking into the cubicle. 'See you later!' She slams the door on me and slides the bolt across.

Did she mean anything by what she said? Or was it just a lot of drunken nonsense? Does she know something about Sadie? I clench my fists and tell myself to relax. I could drive myself crazy thinking about all this. Second guessing myself.

Over the loudspeaker, the MC asks everyone to take their seats as dinner is about to be served. I want to wait for Rebecca to emerge, but I know I'd be better off talking to her when she's more clear-headed. I turn and make my way back to our table, butterflies kicking in at the thought of having to sit next to Robert with so much unsaid between us.

During the main course – which consists of some kind of chicken in a sauce with spiralised vegetables – even Diane remarks on Robert's grumpiness.

'You haven't been looking after your wife this evening, Robert,' she chides. 'You need to pay Gemma some attention.'

I'm taken aback by Diane's comments. Normally *I'm* the one who comes in for all the criticism, while Robert can do no wrong. Perhaps it doesn't look good for her, having a miserable son and daughter-in-law. She wants the world to see her perfect, glowing family. I realise I'm now quite drunk, but I'm sober enough to know that opening my mouth here is a bad idea. Robert doesn't reply either; he just grunts into his wine glass.

'Robert, did you hear me?' Diane persists.

'Yes, Mother, I heard you.'

Diane purses her lips and starts talking to James, but she continues to dart glances at the two of us while I studiously try to avoid catching her eye.

Instead, I continue drinking; alternating gin and tonics with the champagne that Amelia keeps pouring into my other glass. But I can't seem to reach the state of dull oblivion that I'm aiming for. Instead, sadness and anxiety mingle in my bloodstream, sloshing around with the alcohol. Lately, Robert and I seem to have lost our easy relationship. Our lives these past months have been nothing but peaks and troughs, irritations and misunderstandings. I hope this isn't some midlife precursor to a divorce. Is he bored with me? Does he still love me? Could he actually be having an affair with Sadie? Does Rebecca know more than she was letting on?

Truly, I don't think Robert *is* having an affair. Maybe… maybe Sadie fell asleep on our bed today. Maybe she even brought a man home and slept with him in our bed. Why she would do this when she has her own bed upstairs is beyond me. Although, she does only have a single bed up there, so maybe that's why. But to bring a stranger into our house is out of order. And to sleep in our bed with him is crossing way over the line. Although it's far more preferable to her sleeping with my husband. I want to go home and tell Sadie that we don't need her any more. I want her to pack her bags and leave.

The evening is endless. After the main course – of which I ate about two mouthfuls – has been cleared away, the charity auction begins. A cheesy guy with a microphone is up on a makeshift stage at the end of the room. Next to him, a table of offerings up for auction: cases of wine, a day at the races, a night at a four-star hotel, lunch with a local celebrity, a ghastly watercolour by a local artist, and more. Every time a new item comes up, Diane nods at Robert and James, encouraging them to raise their paddles and bid.

'We can't bid on everything, Mum,' James says, rolling his eyes. 'People will realise we're doing it to get the prices up. It's getting embarrassing.'

'It's for charity,' Diane retorts. 'No one will mind. Girls, you can bid too, if you like.'

Amelia catches my eye, trying not to laugh at Diane's blatant sexism. I force out a smile, annoyed that I'm unable to enjoy tonight. That it's all going over my head while I stew in a cloud of agitation.

Finally, the auction ends. Robert and I are now the proud owners of the ghastly watercolour as well as a wine-tasting afternoon at a north Dorset vineyard. If indeed we actually are still 'Robert and I'.

Once we've had dessert and coffee, the band starts playing again and the dance floor fills up. I go over to Diane – who's talking to the auctioneer – to congratulate her on a wonderful evening.

'It has been rather wonderful, hasn't it?' Her words are ever-so-slightly slurred. She takes my hand for a moment. 'You need to kiss and make up with Robert,' she says. 'Whatever he's done, it's not worth arguing over.'

'Whatever he's done?' I repeat.

'Yes. Whatever he's done. Terence wasn't a saint, you know. Far from it. But he was my husband and the boys' father and I loved him. I didn't love everything he did, but we were married and back then we didn't make a fuss about things the way people make a fuss of things these days.'

'You mean we don't roll over and take it?'

She lets go of my hand in disgust. 'You have a family, Gemma. Don't ruin their lives to soothe your ego.'

I love how she thinks *I'm* the one who's doing the ruining. 'Thanks for a lovely evening, Diane. I'll see you soon.'

'You should listen to me, Gemma. I know what I'm talking about.'

I consider leaving the golf club without telling Robert, but that would make things worse, so I go over to the bar where he's laughing with some old school friends. He senses me at his side and turns away from his friends, towards me, a tumbler of whisky in his hand.

'I'm going now,' I say quietly to him. 'You stay if you like.'

'You're not going home on your own,' he replies, putting an arm around my waist and drawing me close. 'I'll come with you.' His tie is undone, his shirtsleeves rolled up. Robert is easily the most handsome man in the room. *Did he sleep with Sadie?*

'I don't mind if you want to stay,' I reply evenly, scared of the conversation that lies ahead of us. I take two steps away from him so his arm is no longer around my waist.

'I'm coming.' He downs the rest of his drink and says his good-byes. We collect our coats and make for the exit. 'I'll call a taxi.'

'Let's walk,' I say. 'I need to clear my head.'

'Are you okay to walk so far in your heels?'

That's the thing about my husband – he's considerate. 'To be honest, I can't even feel my feet any more. We can walk slowly.'

'Okay.'

We exit the warmth of the clubhouse and step out into the cold night-scented air – pine trees and woodsmoke tinged with exhaust fumes and the distant salt-tang of the sea. Crossing the gravel car park, we head out onto the wide pavement in silence. Not touching any more. Our footsteps loud on the pavement, our shoes clipping along in the quiet night.

'Gemma…' he stops walking for a moment, but I keep going, so he's forced to catch up. 'I didn't do anything with Sadie. I wouldn't do that. I thought you knew I would never do that.'

I want to say, *But what about her perfume, and her hair?* But I don't. Instead I say, 'I think we should get rid of her.'

'Because you think I did something?'

'No. Because… I don't know. Because I think that since she's come into our lives I haven't been able to relax.'

'What about Eva's entrance exams? They're in a few weeks. She needs Sadie to help her through it or she might not get in. And look at our work situation – unless you can cut back on your hours at the office, we need her. She's giving us more time in our lives. Don't you remember what it was like before she was here? Everything was so chaotic. No time to breathe – Katie going missing, Eva getting into trouble at school because we didn't have time to even wash her PE kit. It wasn't all roses before Sadie.'

'And you think it's all roses now?'

'Life isn't roses, Gemma. We just have to do what we can to make it okay. And I think it's better *with* her than without her – I mean, in a practical way.'

I know Robert is right, but I can't stand the thought of that woman in our house any more. I'm stuck between a rock and a hard place. If I confront Sadie, either she'll leave or I'll end up firing her and then Eva will be left with no tutor to get her through the exam. And I'll be back to square one trying to juggle running a business with managing my home life. We won't be able to find a replacement in time.

For the sake of Eva, I need to stick it out a few weeks longer. I can do that. I can hold on until then, can't I? In the meantime, I'll rework my business schedule and make more of an effort to find a new manager so I can spend more time at home.

It'll be fine.

I hope.

CHAPTER 41

This weekend has been tense to say the least.

Gemma and Robert are awkward around one another. Perfectly polite, but their easy banter has disappeared. They're acting like strangers. I breeze through the house as though entirely oblivious. But in reality, I'm paying close attention. Picking up on every nuance of their floundering relationship. Of course, I would have preferred for them to have a blazing row with yelling and screaming and things being thrown across the room. But their relationship doesn't appear to be rooted in passion. It's boring and staid. Drab. Perhaps this civilised ignoring of one another is their version of a fight.

Did they even talk about the intrusion into their bedroom? Did Gemma bring up the question of why my scent was all over her bedding? Did she accuse Robert in her calm, rational way? Or is she stewing over it, letting her suspicions eat her up from the inside? It's so frustrating not knowing what she's thinking. The only inkling I have that she noticed is the fact that she stripped off their bedding on Friday night and replaced it with clean sheets.

In the meantime, I'm nice as pie, sweet as honey, innocent as a new day. I won't let her find fault with my work. I won't let her kick me out.

If anyone does the kicking out, it will be me.

CHAPTER 42

I'm at my desk in the office on Monday afternoon when I have an epiphany. I should probably give myself a few days to think about this epiphany. Take time to consider my new idea. But I can't see any downsides and I actually think this could be the perfect solution. Eva's education is important to me, but I'm not prepared to put my family at risk. After Friday night's argument, Robert and I are back on an even-ish keel, but things could be better. I need to spend more time at home.

I get up and pop my head round my office door. 'Damien, can you come in here for a second?'

'Sure.' He follows me into my office, where I gesture for him to take a seat. He does so with his notepad and pen in his hand – always prepared.

'How are we doing with the next batch of interview candidates?' I ask.

'I'm sorting through them now.'

'Anyone stand out?'

He screws up his face. 'Maybe a couple who could be trained up. But no one who really stands out, no.'

'How long have you been with me, Damien?'

'Coming up to three and a half years.'

'Is it that long? Already? And do you like your job? I mean, is it where you want to be, career wise?'

His eyes widen for a moment. I've surprised him with my question. 'Honestly, I don't know. I mean, I do love my job. You're a great boss…'

'Thank you.' I smile.

'But, is it where I want to be? I don't honestly know where I want to be. I was talking to Josh the other day about it.' Josh is Damien's boyfriend. They've just moved in together. 'You know, he's just been offered a promotion to head chef at the Ocean View.'

'That's fantastic. Send him my congratulations.'

'I will. He's over the moon about it.'

'So that's kind of what I wanted to talk to you about,' I say. 'I'd like to offer *you* a promotion… and a pay rise.'

'Really?' Damien nods slowly, letting my words sink in.

'But it would also mean a lot more responsibility.'

He leans back in his seat and runs a hand through his hair. 'Wow. I didn't expect that.'

'I was thinking that as my PA, you almost know my job as well as I do. You're resourceful, hard-working. You come up with good solutions and you're organised.'

'Josh always says I'm *too* organised.'

'You can never be too organised.' I flash him a quick smile. 'So how does the title Business Director sound to you, on a six-month trial basis? You would report directly to me and have seniority over all the other staff. Your salary would reflect that.'

'What? *Seriously?*' Damien shakes his head in disbelief. 'That sounds… I mean… that sounds amazing. But what would the other managers have to say about it? Surely they'd be annoyed to have a lowly PA start telling them what to do? Wouldn't they expect to be promoted over me?'

'They don't know the inner workings of the business like you do. They only deal with certain parts of it. And anyway, it's my company, my decision. It would mean that we wouldn't need a new facilities manager immediately, as that position could now be covered by both of us.'

'Gemma, I don't know what to say.'

'Say yes.'

'Well, I mean… *yes*. Thank you. I can't believe it.'

'So the idea appeals to you?'

'More than that. I'm stunned. I feel like this is a dream. Business Director? Are you sure?'

'You're the best person for the job. You know what most of my job entails, and I can train you up on the parts you don't know.'

'This is… this is incredible.'

'There's one condition, though.'

'What's that?'

'You'll have to hire me a new you and train them up, okay? I need a PA who's as good as you are.'

'Not sure if that's possible,' he jokes.

'Okay, well someone who's almost as good as you.'

'Deal,' he says.

I feel a lightening in my chest. This could work out brilliantly. I don't know why I hadn't thought of this before.

Now that I've started to set my working life in order, it's time to sort out my domestic life.

When I get home, the house is calm. A tantalising smell of lasagne pervades the downstairs. Robert is out with a client. I know I should probably wait for him to get back before I do this, but he'll only try to talk me out of it. He's adamant that we keep Sadie. I know what he means when he says that everything runs more smoothly with her around. But in certain circumstances, there's a lot to be said for a bit of well-ordered chaos.

Could there be something going on between Robert and Sadie? If not a full-blown affair, then some mild flirting. Some unrequited lust? I don't know, but Diane's words at the golf club shook me up a bit. She hinted that her husband cheated on her and she let him get away with it. She thinks Robert might be doing the same thing and she wants me to turn a blind eye too. Ironically, her comments have made me more determined to act. I won't be like Diane, keeping everything going for appearance's sake. And I won't allow Robert the opportunity to talk me out of this decision again. Things still aren't right between us since the dinner dance. I need to do this before he gets home. He isn't due back until after eight.

I was going to arrange to meet up with Rebecca – see if she actually knows anything. But what if she really was just talking nonsense at the dinner dance? If I go to her with questions about Sadie, it will be all over school by the end of the week. Rebecca will take huge delight in spreading that kind of gossip. She'll pretend to be sympathetic, all the while loving every minute of it. And I can't afford for the girls to hear a whisper of this. *No.* The best thing to do is to take action and face this head-on.

I go upstairs. Sadie and the girls are in Eva's room doing homework. I walk in and the girls jump up and come over to give me a hug.

'Hello, babies, how are you?'

'We're not babies!' Eva says, extricating herself from my arms.

'I know.' I stroke her cheek. 'You're already a mini-adult,' I say.

'Am I a mini-adult?' Katie asks.

'You're the mini-est adult of all.'

Katie beams.

'Eva's doing really well with her test papers,' Sadie says, her voice neutral. 'Her English and Verbal Reasoning are wonderful. We just need to concentrate on her Maths now.'

'That's great to hear.' I give Sadie a measured smile that doesn't reach my eyes.

'We're finished now,' she says, standing up. 'We can carry on tomorrow.'

'Thanks, Sadie. I'll take over with the baths and bedtime stories.'

'Are you sure?'

I nod, irritated by the suggestion that I wouldn't want to do this. We have the same exchange almost every evening. And she always asks me if I'm sure.

Sadie kisses the girls goodnight and leaves the room. I hear her climbing the attic stairs and exhale once she's gone, my limbs losing their tension. When we first hired her, I had visions of us sharing cosy cups of tea and chatting about the children together. Of her becoming a friend, like part of the family. Instead, she's become someone I want to avoid. Somehow, she makes me feel uncomfortable in my own home.

While I run the children's bath, I think back to that unfashionable, greasy-haired, innocent girl who came for an interview with us a few weeks ago. It's like she's metamorphosed before our eyes. Was it all just an act to get herself hired? I really think it might have been. I don't care if she wasn't that girl, but it's the pretence that bothers me. Why couldn't she have come here as herself? Did she think she was too pretty to be hired as a live-in nanny? Maybe. And, if I'm honest with myself, would I have hired her looking as she does now? Maybe *I'm* the problem? Perhaps it says something about mine and Robert's relationship that I don't trust him around a pretty girl. But would any woman want temptation put there? And aren't I just assuming that Sadie is equally untrustworthy? I push these unpleasant thoughts away. It makes no difference. However right or wrong I am to assume, I still don't trust her.

I want Sadie to leave our house right now, but she hasn't actually done anything overtly wrong. I can't just sack her without pay; there are laws against that type of thing. But now that I have Damien to take over some of the heavy lifting at work, it will free me up to spend more time with the girls. My heart flutters with excitement at the thought of reclaiming my house, my children, my husband.

Once the girls are bathed and in their pyjamas, I tuck Katie into her bed. Eva comes and crawls under the duvet at the opposite end and I sit and read a chapter from a book in their latest favourite series, *The Twins at St Clare's*. Katie is almost asleep by the time I've turned the final page.

'Can I have a few minutes on my phone to chat to Lauren?' Eva asks.

I kiss Katie goodnight and get to my feet, taking Eva's hand and pulling her up. 'You know the rules; no devices after seven o'clock. I'm probably not as exciting as Lauren, but you can chat to *me* if you like? Or you can have some time in your room to read.'

'Okay,' Eva says with a sigh. 'Can we chat? And then I'll read?'

'Yes. I would love that.' Hopefully I can coax a smile out of my eldest daughter. I miss her smiles.

I lead her out of Katie's room, switching off the light.

'Can you leave the hall light on?' Katie calls out sleepily.

'Okay. Night, night.'

I follow Eva into her room, where we spend the next half hour chatting about school and her friends and how many likes she got on her last Instagram post and what she's going to dress up as for Halloween. Apparently, Sadie has offered to help the girls make their costumes. I make a mental note to sort out Halloween costumes with the girls at the weekend.

Pretty soon, Eva is yawning and I'm tucking her into her bed, resisting the urge to climb in with her and fall asleep myself. But then I remember I have something urgent I need to do.

CHAPTER 43

Before I have a chance to lose my nerve, I begin to make my way up the attic stairs. I haven't been up here since Sadie moved in. And although it's still part of our house, it feels as though I'm entering someone else's property.

'Hello!' I call. 'Sadie? Are you up here? Can I have a word?'

She appears in the doorway of her makeshift lounge. 'Hi, Gemma. Everything okay?'

'Have you got time for a chat?' I ask.

'Uh, yes, sure. Do you want to come in?' She stands back from the door and invites me in.

The room looks the same. I don't know what else I was expecting. It seems like years since Robert and I were up here preparing it for Sadie's arrival. She sits on the day bed and I perch on the edge of one of the dining chairs. Now that I'm here, faced with her, I wonder if I'm making the right decision. She seems small and harmless. Vulnerable even. Her blue eyes questioning.

'Is everything okay?' she asks.

'Yes, fine. Um…' I need to be decisive. Act quickly, like ripping off a plaster. 'Sadie, the thing is… we employed you because Robert and I both work long hours and we needed someone at home with the girls. But my circumstances have recently changed.' I take a breath.

A flash of something passes across Sadie's face – anger or disappointment – but it's gone before I have the chance to decipher it.

'I'm actually going to be at home a lot more, so, the thing is… I'm sorry, but we won't need you any more.'

Sadie's eyes widen further and start to glisten. I hope she's not going to cry. 'You mean… you want me to leave?'

'With immediate effect. We'll pay for another month in lieu of notice, plus an additional month's salary for the inconvenience of leaving so soon. But there's no need for you to stay now that I'm going to be at home more. I'm sorry.'

'But… what about Eva's studies? We're making such great progress. I could stay until the entrance exam, if you like. I mean, if you're paying me for the extra month, you may as well get your money's worth.' She gives a small laugh, but it sounds more like a sob.

I feel awful, but I don't want her to stay for another month. I remember the perfume and her hair in my bed. I picture her and Robert cosily sharing a bottle of wine. Their trip to the theatre. It hits me that she could have engineered that whole thing – messed up the theatre dates on purpose. But, looking at her now, she seems so innocent. And I feel like the Wicked Witch of the East. 'That's okay,' I say, forcing myself not to cave in. 'I can take over their tutoring myself. I'll have the time to do it now.'

Sadie exhales and leans back against the sofa. She presses her fingertips to her forehead. To my dismay, a tear slips down her cheek. She wipes it away and gulps. 'Sorry,' she says. 'It's just a bit of a shock, that's all. I've grown so fond of the girls and I'm really going to miss them.'

Oh no. Have I got this all wrong? Should I not have done this? But I can't go back now. I need to stay strong. 'They'll really miss you, too, Sadie. You've been brilliant with them.'

She takes a tissue out of her pocket and blows her nose. 'I hope it's not because you're unhappy with me in any way. I pride myself on my professionalism. I'd hate to think that I did something to—'

'No, no, not at all,' I lie. I can't come out with all my suspicions. There's no point. Not if she's leaving. And if I'm wrong it will just lead to a great big mess. It's not like she would admit to any of it anyway. 'Like I said, I'm going to be having more free time, so we don't need a nanny any more.'

'And Robert feels the same?' she asks.

My hackles start to rise at her presumption. 'Yes, of course.'

'Okay. It's just, he was only saying the other day how much he values me and the time I spend with the girls.'

'Yes,' I say, swallowing down a flare of temper, 'we both value you. That's not the issue. The issue is that I'm going to be home more often.'

'Okay…' Her face closes down. 'So when do you want me to leave?'

'Do you have somewhere you can go?' I ask, feeling heartless once again.

'Not really. But I can rent somewhere, or check into a B & B while I look for another position.'

I resist the urge to say that she can stay until she finds a new job. Kicking her out goes against all my usual instincts. But I can't have her here, messing up my relationship with my family. I can't give in to those wide, china-blue eyes. It's a good job Robert isn't here with me now, because I know he would tell her to take as long as she needs. I'm sure Sadie knows this too. It's why she asked me about him, just now.

'Stay for tonight, obviously,' I say. 'I'm sure you'll have no problem finding a new position.'

'I hope so.' She sniffs and her face hardens further. 'I turned down two other jobs to take this one, you know.'

'Well, there you go,' I say, purposely misconstruing her meaning. 'Hopefully one of those jobs will still be available.'

'I doubt it,' she mutters.

I pretend not to hear.

'So, can I at least say goodbye to the girls before I go?'

'I think it would probably be better if you don't. They're both asleep now, and if you said goodbye just before school tomorrow morning it would be a bit disruptive.' I couldn't cope with a tearful goodbye. I have the feeling Sadie would make a show of it and the girls would end up begging her to stay.

'But won't they wonder why I've gone?'

'Don't worry, I'll explain it to them. Thanks for being so understanding,' I add, trying to cut our conversation short. I get to my feet. 'We really are very grateful for everything you've done.'

'Please don't sack me,' she begs.

My heart sinks. I feel like such a heartless bitch. But what's the alternative? Keep her here while I watch my family fall deeper and deeper for her charms, edging me out. Making me feel like a stranger in my own home. I have to stay strong and follow this through. 'I'm not sacking you, Sadie. We're letting you go. It's nothing to do with your work. Your care for the girls has been brilliant.'

'So keep me on! I can help you out. You can give me more chores to do. I don't mind.'

'Sorry. I can't.'

'You mean you won't.' She clenches her fists and sits back down, her whole body sagging. 'Fine. I'll leave first thing in the morning before the girls are up.'

'That's probably best.' I can't think of anything else to say, so I give a small nod and leave the room. Walk back down the stairs to the rest of my house. A house I can start to reclaim tomorrow. This whole encounter has left me feeling wrung out and guilty. Like I'm some evil stepmother who's mistreating a stepchild. But I'm not convinced Sadie's distress is even genuine. The girl is a chameleon. I don't trust her and I need her to leave as soon as possible. I wish she would go right now. But I guess tomorrow morning will have to do.

As I reach the landing, I hear the front door open and then close with a bang. Robert is home. I take a breath and prepare to tell him what I've done. I only hope he doesn't try to talk me out of it.

CHAPTER 44

As Gemma's footsteps recede, I begin pacing the attic room. I had to force myself not to yell at her when she was giving me that ridiculous story about no longer needing me. Of course she needs me. I've made myself indispensable. And I bet Robert doesn't even know what she's done. He'll stick up for me. He won't let her get rid of me, will he? Ugh, I know he's not likely to side against her. She'll twist him around her little finger.

I pick up a cushion from the sofa, press my face into the soft cotton and let out a muffled scream of frustration. I can't believe I haven't managed to do what I set out to achieve. I've failed yet again. I shouldn't have wasted so much time being so cautious, but I thought I had weeks, months to accomplish my goal. Now it's all been for nothing. Again. It should have been so easy. I was halfway there. Robert trusts me, I know he does. And I've seen the way he looks at me. At my body. But it had to be done slowly. My first impression of him wasn't quite right. He's more loyal, more sincere than I hoped. Which is why I was moving slowly. If I'd launched myself at him, he would have recoiled, bolted.

But bloody Gemma has ruined everything. I think I overplayed my hand with the perfume. I wanted to sow a seed of doubt between them, increase the tension. But I didn't think it would end up with me being booted out. I'm so angry with myself. But I'm angrier with her. I thought she was wedded to her career. She's changed. I've forced her to change. Nothing like an interloper to make you re-examine your priorities.

I thought my tears might sway her, but she's tougher than I thought. Hard as nails, actually. It made her uncomfortable to see me cry like that. To know she was the cause. But she held firm anyway. Part of me admires that about her. Maybe that's why she's a successful business-woman – you have to think with your head rather than your heart.

I take a few deep breaths and try to think rationally. Okay, I might have to leave here, but it's not over yet. I can spin this to work in my favour. There are still one or two last opportunities open to me...

CHAPTER 45

'What are you talking about?' Robert says, pouring himself a glass of water.

'I've decided to work fewer hours. So we won't need Sadie any more.'

I've just told Robert that I've promoted Damien at work, which means I'll be able to devote more time to the children at home. He doesn't look impressed.

'Is this because you smelt her perfume in our room?' Robert asks. 'Is this some misplaced jealousy thing?'

'No. It isn't.'

He lowers his voice. 'Where is she, anyway?'

'Up in her room.'

'So you didn't kick her out onto the street, then.' He scowls.

'Robert!' I shake my head, annoyed.

'What? I'm just checking.' He leans back against the worktop while I stand in the doorway. 'You've had it in for her for weeks, Gem. It's not like you to be so... mean.'

'I'm not mean!'

He raises an eyebrow. 'She's just a young girl who we gave a job to. And who, by the way, is doing that job brilliantly. I don't think she deserves to be sacked.'

'Not even if we don't need her to do that job any more?'

'What about Eva's studies?'

'I can help her with them.'

'Can you? What's changed, Gemma? Before we had Sadie, you were adamant that you couldn't cut down your hours. You were stressed and overworked. Now, all of a sudden, you say you're going to work less and manage everything yourself – the business, the house, the girls?'

'I told you, I've promoted Damien.'

'I know you. There's no way you'll relinquish any control at work. Especially not to your PA.'

'I've had a change of heart. People can change, you know.'

'Not that much. Why didn't you talk to me before telling Sadie we don't need her? You'd have gone mad if I went behind your back and did something like that.'

'I know,' I reply sheepishly. 'I should have spoken to you first. But I wasn't thinking straight. I just assumed that now I've fixed my work situation, you'd be pleased we can get our house back. Our privacy. You have to admit, it's been odd having another person living in our house.'

Robert shrugs. 'She's not that intrusive. Half the time I don't even notice she's here. And you have to admit, it's been great having the house spotless and our dinner cooked for us every night.'

'I'd rather have our house back. And I feel like the girls have been relying on Sadie too much. They're talking to *her* about their issues rather than to us. That's not right. I want to be the one to give our children guidance.'

'Well, that's because she's the one picking them up from school.'

'Exactly! It should be us. And anyway, I don't know about you, but I don't feel comfortable leaving our girls alone with her. I think she's having a negative influence on Eva. She's not the same girl she was before Sadie came along.'

'Hormones?' Robert says. 'Puberty? She's almost a teenager.'

'It's more than that. Eva ran away over a mobile phone! Does that sound like our daughter? She would never have done that a few months ago.'

'Okay,' Rob says grumpily. 'So when's she going? You know you have to give a month's notice, right? And Mum will be disappointed. She loves Sadie.'

Everyone loves bloody Sadie.

'Mum's paying her salary,' he adds. 'So we'll have to tell her soon.'

'I said we'd give her two months' salary.'

'Oh.' Robert's face brightens. 'Well that's good. So she's staying for a couple more months?'

'Well…' I shift from one foot to the other.

'What?' Robert's eyes narrow.

'I'm paying her two months' salary, but she's actually leaving tomorrow.'

'Tomorrow? Why on earth—'

'Because it's awkward. I thought it would be best to have a clean break, for the kids' sake.'

'You know they're going to be gutted.'

'Yes!' I cry, suddenly sick of trying to explain myself. 'I know the kids will be gutted, and I know you're gutted, and I know your mum thinks she's amazing! But don't you think that's part of why I want her gone? I feel like a spare part in my own house. My own family prefer her to me. It makes me feel like shit, and I'm sick of it!' I draw in a huge breath and exhale slowly, my body trembling.

'Okay.' Robert comes over to where I'm standing and pulls me into a hug. 'Sorry, Gemma. I didn't… I didn't know you felt like that.'

'Well,' I sniff, 'now you do. Now you know exactly how I feel.' I lean into his chest, listening to the regular beats of his heart, his breathing slow and steady while I can barely breathe at all.

CHAPTER 46

'Have you had enough to eat?' I ask for the hundredth time as Eva sits on the stairs to put on her shoes.

'Yes, Mum. I'm not hungry,' she replies, her thin face pale and drawn.

It's the day of the entrance exam, and we're about to leave the house to walk to the girls' grammar school where the exams are being held. Eva hasn't seemed nervous at all, until this morning when she barely touched her breakfast. Just nibbled on a few corners of toast.

'Just relax and do your best, okay?' I say. 'You'll be brilliant.'

'What if I don't pass?'

'Don't think like that,' Robert says. 'Like Mum says, you'll be brilliant!'

'She hasn't eaten anything,' I whisper to Robert. 'What if she faints?'

Robert goes into the kitchen and comes back with a small bowl. He hands it to Eva.

'What's that?' I ask.

'Ooh, blueberries!' Eva crams a handful into her mouth. 'Thanks, Dad.'

'Can I have some?' Katie asks.

'When we get back,' Robert says, kissing the top of her head. 'Those ones are for Eva to give her super brainpower.'

I check my watch. 'We'd better go. We've got to be there in fifteen minutes.'

We all pile out of the house into the chilly November morning, wrapped up in scarves and hats and mittens. We figured there was no point driving as the roads will be gridlocked with stressed parents, and the parking will be horrific. The walk will only take ten minutes, so we all begin striding down the pavement.

'Why does it have to be on a Saturday?' Eva asks. 'They could have at least done it on a weekday so I got to miss school.'

'That's the point,' Robert says. 'They have it on a Saturday so you *don't* miss school.'

As we draw closer to the grammar, we see other families walking in the same direction, their daughters clutching pencil cases and water bottles. The traffic is indeed gridlocked and – noting the faces of panicked parents stuck in their cars – I'm relieved we chose to walk.

The past month has been tricky. The girls were distraught at Sadie's departure. At one point, Eva refused to even sit the test unless Sadie came back. I tried tutoring Eva myself, but she just ended up snapping and telling me that I was too bossy. Eventually I hired the original tutor I found online – Louise Martin. I did a thorough background check and it turns out she's a good friend's younger sister. She has turned out to be lovely and patient and – most importantly – Eva likes her. It was a tough decision for me to allow another person into our house and into the children's lives, but I made sure that either Robert or I were at home while Louise was in the house. The balance was better with a tutor than with a live-in nanny. I should have gone this route in the first place – it would have saved me a lot of sleepless nights.

As well as the girls being grumpy about Sadie leaving, Robert has been sulky too. Every time I'm late from work, or there isn't anything interesting for dinner, he gives me a look as though to say, *If Sadie were here things would be running a lot more smoothly.* Although, perhaps I'm imagining that. Perhaps it's my guilt at not being able to organise the house and children as well as Sadie did. Even though the rational part of me knows I have nothing to feel guilty about.

The one good thing to come out of this is that my own work–life balance is improving. Promoting Damien has proved to be the best business decision I ever made. He is competent, reliable and professional and I know that when he does something, he will do it brilliantly. My other managers were a little put out at first, but Damien hasn't taken any crap from them. He has focused on the job and ignored any underground grumblings. His professionalism has meant that he's been accepted a lot more quickly.

We turn into North Road to see that it's lined with cars and thronged with families, as though it's a festival rather than an exam day. The wind whips down the long street as we walk past the deserted boys' grammar and towards the bustling girls' building. I realise suddenly that I'm not even in favour of segregating boys and girls. It's not exactly preparation for real life, and most of the girls I know who went to single-sex schools ended up either incredibly awkward around the opposite sex, or boy-mad. Rebecca informed me that they now have lunch and break times together, it's just the lessons that are separate. So I suppose that's something. And I do want her to get the best education. Most importantly, it's where my daughter wants to go.

'Are you feeling okay, Eva?'

She nods, but I can tell she's nervous. Not surprising really. This is her first taste of exams. Of 'big' school.

'You'll be great.'

'Eva!' A woman's voice calling out behind us. 'Hi! Eva!'

I know that voice.

Eva's face lights up. 'Sadie!' She turns and runs.

'Eva! Come back. We've got to go in in a minute.'

Katie lets go of my hand and follows after her sister.

'Katie!' Robert calls. But, unlike me, he's smiling indulgently.

I run along the pavement after the girls, weaving between families. I see Sadie jogging towards us, waving, excited. Eva reaches her and flings herself into her arms. Katie gets there next. And for a brief moment, I swear I see a look of triumph in Sadie's eyes.

'Hi, Gemma,' she says. 'I hoped I'd catch Eva to say good luck. Hope you don't mind!'

Yes I bloody do mind. 'Hi, Sadie. I didn't realise you were still in the area.'

'Oh, I love it down here, so I decided to stay.'

A thud of unease beats in my chest at the knowledge she stayed in Bournemouth. It's a free country, but I wish she'd gone back to wherever she came from. It's unsettling to find out she's living locally. 'Are you with a new family?'

'No. I'm just doing some childcare and tutoring at the moment. A few of my students are taking the test today so I'm here for moral support and last-minute tips.'

'Oh, which students? Anyone from Eva's school?'

'No. I doubt you know them.'

'Hi, Sadie,' Robert says warmly. 'Lovely to see you.'

'You too. I was just saying to Gemma that I've come down to lend my support to a couple of students I'm tutoring. I hoped I'd catch up with Eva to wish her luck.'

'You've got a new job?' he asks.

She looks at the ground for a moment. 'Not a proper job, no. Just odds and ends. It's harder to find a job when you're not currently in employment.' The accusation hangs in the air.

Robert shakes his head. 'You can say you're currently employed by us, can't she, Gems? It's the least we can do. We feel bad about letting you go, but Gemma was missing the kids too much.'

'I understand,' Sadie replies. 'They're such lovely girls. I miss them to bits. I hope you're not cross with me for saying hello. It's just, I put so much work into the preparation, I just wanted to wish her luck, you know?'

'We miss you too, Sadie,' Eva says, her eyes brimming dangerously with tears. This isn't good for her just before she's about to go and sit the tests.

'I miss you too, sweetie. We had fun, didn't we?'

'Can't you come back? She can come back, can't she, Mum?'

I ignore my daughter's plea. 'Lovely to see you, Sadie, but we'd better take Eva in now.'

'No problem, I'll walk down with you.'

I clamp my lips together, hoping Sadie's intrusion hasn't distracted Eva too much. Both my girls are now holding Sadie's hands, chattering away to her, leaving me and Robert to walk behind.

'Sadie looks well,' Robert says. 'But it's a shame she hasn't managed to get another job yet. Do we know anyone who needs a nanny? Maybe we could help her find a new family.'

'What the hell is she doing here?' I hiss.

'She said she's come to support some other children, didn't she?'

'So where are they then? These mythical other children?'

'They've probably gone in already. Why are you getting so stressed? Eva seems happy to see her.'

I can't explain that the presence of this woman has set my heart racing and my head buzzing. That seeing my girls with her gives me a physical pain in my gut. That Robert's defence of her feels like a betrayal. If I say any of this aloud I will come across as paranoid, jealous and bitter. So I stay quiet and hope and pray that this is the last we will see of Sadie Lewis.

CHAPTER 47

Women like Gemma think they have it all. They parade around with their families like they hold the keys to the kingdom. So smug with their sickly sweet children and attentive husbands… but I know how quickly that can end.

And I can't believe she hasn't worked out the truth.

CHAPTER 48

FOUR MONTHS LATER

We pull up onto Diane's vast driveway, which is already crammed with vehicles. Although it's almost April, there was a hard frost this morning and the air still crackles with winter. The sky is a bright, arctic blue that looks solid enough to smash with a hammer. We get out of my Honda, pulling our coats tightly around our flimsy party clothes. I hope Diane has the central heating turned up high.

Life has settled down into a new pattern. Things are better than they've ever been. My relationship with Robert is flourishing. After his initial disappointment at Sadie's departure, he seems happier than ever. Paying me more attention, buying me flowers and gifts. We train together two mornings a week and I almost feel like we're returning to those passionate months when we first met.

'It was lovely of your mum to do this,' I say.

'You know how much Mum enjoys hosting a party.'

'I love parties too,' Katie says. She's wearing a frothy pink creation that Diane bought her especially for today. Eva chose a more demure dress – navy with white polka dots.

'We're so proud of you, Eva,' I say, giving our eldest daughter another hug which she accepts with good grace. We found out last week that Eva passed the grammar-school test with an exceptionally high grade, and so Diane has arranged a party in her honour. It's probably going to be mainly my mother-in-law's friends, but that's fine. Eva will be made a fuss of, and she deserves it after all her hard work.

Over the past few months, Eva has finally returned to being the sweet girl she used to be. I've had no more worrying calls from the school. At her latest parents' evening, Mrs Slade said how kind and helpful Eva is being towards her fellow classmates. There was no mention made of last year's awful behaviour.

'Is Maya here yet?' Eva asks.

I glance around Diane's drive. 'I can't see their car, but maybe they walked.'

Eva no longer hangs around with Lauren and Emily, and instead has become best friends with Maya again, after they discovered a shared love of singing. Consequently, Suri has forgiven Eva (and me) for the bullying Maya was subjected to last year. Even better, both girls passed the test, which means they'll be moving forward to senior school together.

Maya was the only friend Eva wanted to invite today and I'm looking forward to catching up with Suri this afternoon, away from the busyness of the school gates.

Robert doesn't bother ringing Diane's doorbell. The front door is on the latch so we just walk in. The entrance hall is already crowded with people. Multicoloured balloons are tied to the polished banisters and a sign has been strung out across the width of the hallway with 'CONGRATULATIONS EVA' written in colourful letters.

As the four of us walk in, all the guests cheer and shout 'congratulations' to our daughter. She presses herself close to my side, but her cheeks are pink and she smiles shyly. Maya rushes over and the girls hug.

'Congratulations to you, too, Maya,' I say.

'Thank you,' she says.

Suri, Steve and their eldest daughter Jade are here too. We all hug and congratulate one another on the achievements of our daughters, not caring about bragging today. After all, this is supposed to be a celebration for them.

'Have you seen who's here?' Suri whispers to me.

My mind scrolls through possibilities. 'Not Rebecca? That would be a bit awkward.'

'No, don't be daft.' Suri gives me a look. 'There's no way she'd come. Not after Lauren failed the entrance test.'

Unfortunately, although Lauren hit the pass mark, she still didn't make the cut as there were other children who managed to get higher grades. Rebecca is furious and is appealing to the admissions board, citing the unfairness of letting children who live outside the local area attend the school. I'm sure she's also secretly mad at Eva for getting in despite only being tutored for a couple of months as opposed to the eighteen months of hard work Lauren put in. Not to mention the hundreds of pounds spent on her tutor's fees.

'Who are you talking about then?' I ask.

Just then, Katie's high voice cuts through the hubbub. 'Look, Mum! It's Sadie!'

My hackles rise. Suri puts a calming hand on my arm. Over the past few months, I've confided all my insecurities about our former to nanny to Suri, so she knows what my feelings are about the woman. Inviting her here today must be Diane's doing.

'Is she here?' Eva gasps, her eyes bright. 'Maya, you have to come and say hi to Sadie. She's the best.'

'Deep breaths,' Suri says.

My heart is racing. I turn to my husband, who was chatting to Steve but is now glancing across the hallway to where Sadie is emerging from the kitchen. She is wearing a figure-hugging black pencil skirt and tight powder-pink blouse with a pussycat bow, her hair again caught up in an elegant chignon, which has the irritating effect of looking demure and vampish at the same time.

'Did you know she was going to be here today?' I hiss at Robert.

'Who, Sadie? No, of course not.'

'There she is!' Diane sweeps out of the kitchen behind Sadie. 'There's my clever granddaughter.' The two of them walk over to us.

I realise my whole body is rigid and I have to force myself to relax my facial muscles into some semblance of a smile.

'Well done, Eva!' Diane says, handing her an envelope. 'Here's a little something to go in your bank account. A prize for doing so well.'

I have to stop myself from saying that passing the test itself is reward enough. I don't want my children to receive a gift every single time they do something. It drives me mad that she keeps giving them money and buying them stuff. Pretty soon Diane will be giving them gifts for getting a gift. I just hope it isn't too much money. If it is, Eva can put it towards her university fees or something.

'Thank you, Grandma!'

'It's my pleasure, darling. And look who I invited!'

The girls are a little shyer in Sadie's presence today. They haven't seen her for four months and the easiness they once had has faded.

'How are my favourite girls?' Sadie asks, her eyes alight.

'Fine, thank you,' the girls reply.

'I had to invite the person responsible for getting Eva through her exams,' Diane says. She turns to a cluster of her golf-club friends. 'This is the nanny who tutored Eva. Brains as well as beauty.'

Sadie blushes and looks down at her feet.

'Don't be bashful. You made a deep impression on my granddaughters' lives. Today is a congratulation for you, Sadie, as well as Eva.'

'Well,' Sadie says quietly. 'I don't know about that. I was only her tutor for a few weeks.'

'And look how much you achieved in that time,' Diane says. 'Robert and Gemma are very grateful to you. We all are.' Diane raises her glass. 'To Sadie!' she cries.

The cluster of people around us also raise their glasses. 'To Sadie!'

Luckily, I don't have a drink yet, so I can't make the toast. But I'm now desperate for a glass of something cold and alcoholic. Suri has read my mind and lifts a glass of champagne from the tray of a passing waiter, depositing it in my hand. Luckily, Diane's parties are always well catered, with the booze flowing freely. A legacy from her husband's days, who was partial to a drink or five.

I down half the glass and plaster a smile on my face.

'Hi, Diane. Hi, Sadie.'

'Lovely to see you, Gemma,' Sadie says. 'You're looking well.'

'You too.' I'm not going to ask her what she's doing these days. I don't actually want to know. I drain the rest of my drink and reach for another.

Thankfully, Amelia comes over and my attention is taken away from our former nanny for the moment. While I chat with Amelia and Suri, I spy, on the edge of my vision, that Robert and Sadie are now deep in conversation. And it doesn't look like a light-hearted, social chat either. It looks more intense than that. What could they possibly be talking about?

The champagne has gone straight to my head. I should probably eat something. I glance around for a waiter with food, but another tray of drinks come past so I swap out my empty glass for another new one.

'You're knocking them back a bit,' Suri says with a grin.

'I need anaesthetic against Diane and Sadie,' I say a little too loudly.

'Shh.' Suri puts a finger to her lips and giggles. 'You'll get into trouble.'

'I'm fine,' I reply, realising that my words are a little slurred.

'Just going to nip to the loo,' Suri says. 'Stay there, and when I get back, I'm going to get some food inside you. It's dangerous being drunk around you know who.' She tips her head in the direction of Sadie. 'Where's the loo anyway?'

I point out the downstairs cloakroom and then turn back to Amelia, who has a strange expression fixed to her face.

'You okay?' I ask.

'Promise not to say anything to anyone,' she murmurs.

'Of course. About what?'

'I wasn't going to tell you today, because this is Eva's day and I don't want to steal her thunder...'

'You're not stealing anything. Just tell me,' I say, excited by the possibility of what I think she might be about to say.

'I'm pregnant,' she whispers.

I let out a muffled squeal, excitement distracting me from thoughts of Sadie and my husband.

'Only eight weeks, so it's early days, but I can't quite believe it.'

'Oh wow, Amelia. I'm so happy for you. I didn't know you were doing another round of IVF.'

'That's the crazy thing. We're not doing it at the moment. It happened naturally. Don't tell anyone yet. We're going to wait until the three-month mark before we tell people.'

'How about Robert? Can I tell him?'

'James is going to tell him today.'

'Ah, that's such fantastic news.' I give her a hug. 'I'm over the moon for you both. You really deserve this. The girls will be so excited to have a cousin. Don't worry, I won't mention it to them yet. Katie hasn't quite mastered the art of keeping secrets.'

'Ha, yes, she's a bit of a chatterbox, my little niece.'

'How are you feeling anyway?'

'Fine actually. A little nauseous and tired, but nothing too bad. Look, I'll be back in a minute, Diane wants me to bring down a box of wine glasses from upstairs.'

'What? No, I'll go,' I don't want Amelia to be lugging heavy boxes if she's pregnant.

'Oh, it's fine, I can manage.'

'No way,' I reply. 'You need to look after yourself. Where's this box? I can get it.' Although I am feeling a wee bit unsteady in my heels.

'In the study, under the desk. Apparently the dishwasher's on the fritz so the caterers need more glasses.'

'Okay. I'm on it. We'll meet for a cuppa next week to have a proper talk, yes?'

'Definitely. But no tea or coffee for me. I just don't fancy caffeine at all at the moment.'

'Lunch then.'

'Yes. Perfect.'

'Okay. Back in a mo.'

I weave my way a little unsteadily through the hall and up the curved staircase to the first floor, sliding my hand up the banister for support. When I reach the spacious landing, I head over to Terence's old study, but the sound of familiar voices coming from one of the bedrooms makes me pause. I stop where I am and listen. It sounds like Robert and… Sadie. My eye twitches.

'We should go back down,' Robert says.

What the hell are they doing up here together? I suddenly feel hot, my skin prickling with sweat. I pad over to the door, which is slightly ajar.

'Can you just listen to me for a moment?' she says.

My heart is banging against my ribcage. Don't let this be what I think it is.

I push open the door just in time to see Robert sink down heavily onto the double bed with Sadie beneath him. Her arms circling his body.

CHAPTER 49

I make an animal sound in my throat. 'Robert!' I stagger backwards a couple of paces as he pushes himself up off the bed.

'Gemma!' he cries.

'Oh my God!' I gasp. 'I don't believe this.'

Sadie is still lying there, her skirt hitched up around her thighs, her pussycat bow undone, her cleavage spilling out of a pale pink lacy bra. She seems unperturbed by my arrival. She simply sits up and starts rearranging her clothing.

'Gemma,' Robert says, his hands out towards me in a calming motion.

'What the fuck, Robert!' I cry. 'How long has this been going on?' My mind reels backwards. 'That night I smelt her perfume on our bed... I've been so stupid, so naive.' The room is spinning and I don't care that my voice is becoming louder, that people downstairs might hear.

'Nothing happened, Gemma,' Sadie says, getting to her feet, her clothes all done up once again.

Her voice makes me want to scream. 'Just shut your mouth, Sadie. I never trusted you. And now I know why.'

'Gemma,' Robert says, trying to sound matter of fact, 'I promise you, you've got this all wrong. It's not what it looks like. Not at all.'

'Oh, right. So you lying on top of our ex-nanny on a bed while half her clothes are undone is not what it looks like?' I snarl. And then I gasp and double over as the reality starts to sink in. I'm one of *those* women. One of the ones whose husbands have an affair with a younger woman. But this is *Robert*. My soulmate.

He comes over and puts an arm around my shoulder. I flinch and jerk away.

'Don't touch me! Not with those same hands that were touching *her*. Don't you dare…' But I can't say any more. I'm still trying to let this sink in. Trying not to break down and sob. I can't give Sadie the satisfaction of seeing me broken. Of letting her know she's won. Because I realise now, in my drunken haze, that this whole thing has been her plan from the start. To take my husband from me. To steal what was never hers and leave me discarded by the wayside.

'Gemma, what you saw,' Robert tries to explain, 'I know it sounds crazy, but when you pushed open the door, Sadie tripped backwards and fell onto the bed with me on top of her. I swear that's all it was.'

'You're right,' I reply. 'It does sound crazy. It sounds like the most *pathetic* excuse I've ever heard. You actually expect me to believe that? You were both up here, in a bedroom, on your own… and then you accidentally fell onto the bed. Do you think I'm stupid?'

'He's telling the truth,' Sadie adds. She's standing behind Robert. Her voice sounds distraught, but the look she's giving me is halfway between pity and triumph.

'You're a conniving little whore,' I hiss. And then I turn to Robert. 'And you're a weak bastard for falling for it. Well done, Robert. You've just screwed up your marriage and destroyed your family. Well fucking done.' I clench my fists, yearning to punch Sadie in her perfect little face. To shake Robert until his bones rattle. But my children are here. I can't unleash my emotions. Not yet.

With massive self-restraint, I spin on my heel and walk away across the landing towards the staircase, my fury blazing like an August sun. But Diane is coming up the stairs towards me, her nostrils flaring. I can't deal with my mother-in-law right now.

'Gemma, what's going on up here?'

'You can tell your son to bring the box of glasses down,' I say through clenched teeth. 'I'm going home.' I make to walk past her, but she moves to the left, blocking my escape.

'What are you talking about?' She frowns. 'Are you drunk, Gemma? We can all hear you shouting obscene language. It's not appropriate. Especially not when I've got a houseful of guests. Your young daughters are downstairs, for goodness sake. Is this how you behave at home?'

I turn to Robert and give a sarcastic laugh. 'It's not appropriate. Did you hear that? My language is inappropriate.' I turn back to my mother-in-law. 'Tell me, Diane, is it appropriate for my husband to be having sex with the nanny in the spare bedroom during our daughter's party? Where does that sit on your scale of appropriateness?'

Diane's mouth falls open as she looks from me to Robert, and then to Sadie. Sadie shrugs and shakes her head as though she has no clue what I'm talking about. Diane puts her bony fingers to the diamond pendant at her throat and starts fiddling with it.

'Gemma's got it wrong, Mum. She's had a bit too much to drink and she's got the wrong end of the stick.'

Diane's shoulders relax. 'I thought that must be the case. Robert, why don't you take Gemma home? Leave the girls here to enjoy the party. I'll simply tell everybody that Gemma's not feeling well and you've had to leave.'

'Well done, Diane.' I start to clap. 'That's a nice, neat explanation for "Gemma's discovered her husband shagging the nanny".' I yell the last part.

'For God's sake, Gemma,' Robert says. 'Keep your voice down. Do you want to upset the girls? Let's go home, have a strong coffee and talk about this sensibly.'

'I'm going home. But you feel free to stay here and carry on with what you were doing. I think I interrupted you just as you were getting to the good part, didn't I?'

My husband's face turns crimson. He grabs my upper arm and starts marching me down the stairs.

'Get off me!' I yell. But he ignores me and keeps going. Ignores the faces that are turned towards us in fascinated horror to witness the breakdown of our marriage. Or perhaps they think it's just me having some kind of nervous breakdown.

'Please, be quiet, Gemma,' Robert says under his breath. 'Wait until we get home. You can yell at me then.'

'You'd like that!' I cry. 'You'd like me to stay nice and quiet so your dirty secret doesn't come out in front of all Diane's prim-and-proper golf-club cronies.'

'The girls,' he hisses.

'Mummy!' Katie calls out across the hall, silencing everyone.

Robert and I freeze on the staircase. My eyes are drawn to my daughter, her eyes glistening with tears. Next to her stands Eva, her face pale and drawn, hurt and confusion etched across her features. The red mist dissipates for a moment while my maternal instincts take over. I wish with all my heart that my daughters hadn't seen me like this. Seen their mother's fury laid bare. But I won't take the blame. Not for something Robert did.

'It's okay, sweeties,' I call out, my voice shrill and quavering. 'Stay and enjoy the party. Mummy's got a bit of a headache, that's all.'

Amelia gives me a worried, sympathetic glance and mouths, *Are you okay?*

I give a quick shake of my head. She nods and ushers my girls out of the hall and into the lounge, closing the door behind them.

'Get off me, Robert.' I shake my arm free. 'I'm quite capable of walking down the stairs on my own.' I keep my eyes fixed on the front door, unwilling to catch anyone else's eye. Robert walks down the stairs with me. I wonder if Diane and Sadie are following us or if they're still up on the landing. I refuse to turn around and check. I couldn't bear to see the smug expression on Sadie's face.

And I'll bet she's feeding my mother-in-law some nonsense about poor Gemma having too much to drink and imagining things.

Well, unfortunately, I didn't imagine it. It was all too real. And now I have to work out what the hell I'm going to do about it.

CHAPTER 50

I fumble with the key in the lock.

'Here,' Robert says, 'let me do that.' He reaches out to take the key from my shaking fingers, but I swipe his hand away, my whole body bristling. The girls are still at the party. It's better that they don't have to witness the fallout from this.

On the short car journey back from Diane's, I didn't utter a word to Robert. He tried to tell me again that it wasn't what it looked like. But I've ignored my instincts about Sadie before and I'm not going to do it any more. Diane was right when she said that to keep my family intact, I would have to ignore certain things. But I'm not like her. I can't pretend things are not happening. I can't live a lie. What's the point of that? Of enduring this churning, sick feeling in my belly every day? *No.* If Robert wanted to keep this family intact, he would never have done what he did.

I eventually get the door unlocked and head straight upstairs without looking to see if Robert is following. I hear the front door close with a bang. The house feels different, like the soul has been ripped out of it, leaving a cold, empty shell. A meaningless collection of bricks and timber and slate. Square rooms that represent nothing. That contain only the dead, stale air of a life that no longer exists. I stifle a sob, open the airing cupboard and pull out the telescopic metal rod that we use to open the loft hatch.

'Gemma, what are you doing?' Robert asks, as he reaches the top of the stairs. His voice is like a buzzing fly that I want to swat and silence with a rolled-up newspaper.

I reach up and unhook the square hatch. Then I use the pole to pull down the aluminium ladder. Kicking off my heels and hitching up my skirt, I climb the ladder and switch on the light to the tiny loft space in the eaves. Next, I haul myself up and crawl across the boards towards a covered mound. I pull off the dust sheet to reveal a pile of suitcases. As I tug out two of the older cases, the ones on top slide off into a messy heap. Diane bought these particular two for us. They're expensive leather, but they're heavy and don't have wheels, so although they look smart, they're completely impractical.

I drag the largest one over to the open hatch. Robert has started to climb the ladder and I'm tempted to chuck the suitcase at his head and knock him off balance. But I don't think being accused of attempted murder will help me.

'Can you take this down?'

He does as I ask, lifting the case and putting it on the landing.

'I've got another one. Hang on.' I go back to retrieve the medium case and shove that into his hands a little too violently. But he manages to keep his balance.

'Gemma, don't do this,' he says as I switch off the light and climb down the ladder. 'Don't leave. There's no need. What you saw… it wasn't like that.'

'Leave?' I say, stepping back onto the landing and grasping the handles of both suitcases. '*I'm* not leaving.'

I go into our bedroom, set both cases on the bed and flip them open. Then I pull open the wardrobe door and start transplanting Robert's clothes from the wardrobe to the suitcases. Shoving them in, complete with their hangers.

'What are you doing? Put those back! I thought we were going to talk about this?' He closes the wardrobe door, but I yank it back open. 'Gemma, for Christ's sake, talk to me!'

I straighten up and stare at Robert for a moment. At this man who I thought I would spend the rest of my life with. 'Okay. You want me to talk? I'll talk. I thought I could trust you. I thought you loved me. But I was obviously mistaken. You've torn my heart out and stamped on it, and I will never, *ever* forgive you. Is that enough talking?'

'But I've done nothing wrong!' he cries, taking an armful of his clothes out of the case and trying to shove them back into the wardrobe. I snatch them back, ripping one of his shirts in the process.

'Your definition of wrong and mine are obviously two completely different things,' I say, my voice shaking with anger. With disbelief. With sadness. The image of him and Sadie, their bodies pressed up close, playing over and over on a loop in my head. I wrench open a drawer and start pulling out handfuls of his underwear and socks, stuffing them into the cases.

'Listen to me!' he cries. 'I love you, Gemma! I love our family! Do you really want to throw all that away?'

'*Me* throw it away?' I haven't managed to pack all his things yet, but it's taking too long so I figure he's got enough for now. I close up the cases and start lugging them out of the room. 'I should have kicked you out the night of your mother's golf-club do. When I found Sadie's hair in our bed.' I give a bitter laugh. 'There were so many other signs, but I was stupid. I ignored them. Not any more, *Rob*. I'm not going to disbelieve what I've seen with my own eyes.'

'I know what you saw, Gemma. And I know how it looked. But like I keep trying to tell you, I didn't—'

'Just shut up! Stop lying. Can't you hear yourself?' I drag the cases down the stairs, bumping them down each step, Robert's clothing half hanging out of them.

'You can ask Sadie,' he says again. 'She'll tell you the same thing.'

'What? You mean, ask the woman who was lying under you? Whose breasts were hanging out of her top? Yes, I'm sure she can be relied on to give an accurate account of what happened.' I pull open the front door and dump the cases outside on the step. One of them tips over onto its side. Robert doesn't move.

'Get out,' I say.

He looks at me, pleading with his eyes, but I keep my expression hard. 'Think about how happy we've been,' he says. 'Our marriage has been so good, and it feels like it's been the best it's ever been recently, don't you think? Why would I throw that away to sleep with someone else? Think about it.'

'I have no idea. Maybe you thought you could have it all. The wife and kids, plus a hot young nanny on the side.' Something occurs to me. 'Maybe that's why you've been especially nice to me these past few months. All the flowers and the sex and the affection. Was that just your guilt? Or was it because she makes you happy so you could afford to throw me a few crumbs? Just… please, get out. Get out! GET OUT!'

'You're wrong, Gemma.' Robert shakes his head and steps outside. 'I'll go, for now, but we're going to talk about this again once you're calmer. And you can speak to Sadie. She'll tell you that it's all been a misunderstanding.'

I throw my husband a venomous look and slam the door in his face.

I stand in the hallway trembling, listening to my heart thumping. To my ragged breathing. To the boot of his car opening. To the thuds as he throws in both suitcases and then closes the boot. To the car door slamming, the engine starting, and the hiss of the tyres as he pulls out of the drive. I don't want him to go. I want him to stay and convince me that I didn't see them together. That it was, like he claims, a misunderstanding. But if I let myself believe him, then I'm a fool who deserves to have a cheating husband.

My legs buckle and I sink to my knees, pressing my palms against the gritty hall floorboards, just breathing in and out for a moment. Then I let my whole body collapse onto its side.

I don't know how long I lay there on the hall floor, but eventually I must have hauled myself up. Now, some hours later, I'm sitting in the dark lounge, staring out of the window, the streetlamps casting an eerie glow across the bushes and trees beyond the drive.

Diane texted after the party to say that the girls could stay with her overnight. What she actually said was that I was in no fit state to look after the children so she would keep them with her until tomorrow. I was going to protest and type back a snotty reply. But, actually, she's right. I'm too over the limit to drive and I would be no good to the girls in this mood. I'll pick them up first thing in the morning, when I will also have to try and figure out how to tell them that Daddy won't be living with us any more. This is the end for us. I can't tolerate any kind of reconciliation with Robert now. Not after seeing him cheating on me.

With a dull ache of dread, I wonder if he and Sadie will move in together. If that happens then Eva and Katie will see her on a regular basis. They may even end up living there part-time. I can't let that happen. I can't have that woman in our lives. The thought of it gives me a pain in my chest. I snatch up my phone and call her number. I have no idea what I'm going to say, but I need to know if she's with Robert now. If her plan is to be with him permanently.

It rings twice. She answers.

'*Hello, Gemma.*' Her voice is clipped. Neutral.

'Do you love him?' I ask.

There's a brief pause where I hear her breathing. And then, '*Yes.*'

I go cold. My breath catches. I inhale to try to keep the tears from falling. I can't let her hear me crying. I can't believe Robert lied to me. That it wasn't an accident that he and Sadie ended up on the bed together. Deep down I knew it. Of course I knew it. But I had desperately hoped that Sadie would corroborate his story. That she would be adamant that I had simply witnessed an unfortunately embarrassing situation. Now she's telling me that they actually have feelings for each other. She's admitting it. How can this be happening?

'*I'm sorry,*' she says. '*We never meant for it to happen. We just… we tried to fight it, but the tension between us had been building for weeks. And we… we eventually gave in. And I know it was wrong. But now…*'

I swallow. 'If he loves you, why was he just here begging me not to throw him out? He denied that there was anything even going on with you.'

'*He's a good man,*' Sadie says softly. '*He doesn't want to hurt you and the girls.*'

'Well it's a bit late for that!' A sob escapes and I'm furious with myself. She can't hear me like this. Sadie may sound apologetic on the phone, but I don't believe she is. Not for one moment. No. She's loving every minute of this. I end the call and throw my phone across the room, watching it smash into the windowsill. I get to my feet and give a howl of anguish. How can this have happened? How can everything wonderful have turned so dark and painful in the space of just a few hours? How can this heartache have turned into my life?

CHAPTER 51

Sun streams through the bedroom window where I forgot to draw the curtains last night. I wake with an unnamed feeling of anxiety, turn to Robert… and then I remember.

Robert is not here.

He betrayed me. I kicked him out. He will never sleep in this bed again. Robert and Sadie… no… it will be *Rob* and Sadie. The children might even call her *Mummy*. I close my eyes again, wishing I could return to the oblivion of sleep. But my brain is moving too fast for sleep, cataloguing everything that has happened. Dredging up the sickening vision of Robert and Sadie on the bed. Their bodies close. I snap open my eyes to dispel the image, and sit up, focusing on what I'm going to do now.

The girls are still at Diane's. I need to bring them home. I wonder if they have any idea of what happened yesterday. Probably not. But they're not stupid. They heard me shouting at the party. Eva is probably old enough to put two and two together. They'll ask questions and I will need to answer them. I'll have to work out what I'm going to say. Of course, Diane will want everything to continue as before. She won't want a whiff of any scandal. She'll want us to pretend it's all happy families as usual. *If only it could be.*

I get up, wash, and dress in jeans and a sweatshirt. I'm appalled at the yawning space in Robert's half of the wardrobe. At his lone burgundy hoodie lying forgotten at the bottom, like a congealed wound. I close the wardrobe door and go downstairs. The stillness of the house a silent reminder that all is not well.

Breakfast is the furthest thing from my mind, but I want to be sharp for my encounter with Diane, so I make myself a strong coffee and force down a small finger of shortbread, its texture like dry sand in my mouth, but at least the sugar helps to wake me up. I glance around the kitchen for my phone. Perhaps it's in the lounge. As I walk into the front room, I remember my despair after speaking to Sadie. I remember hurling my phone across the room. I spy it on the floor by the window, wondering if it's damaged beyond repair.

Bending to pick it up, I see that the screen guard is cracked, but apart from that, the phone appears to be intact. I have five voice messages.

Message one: "*Hi, Gemma. Suri here. Just calling to see if you're okay. Not sure what happened upstairs at Diane's, but I saw that Sadie was there, and… well, it's none of my business, but if you need to talk, I'm here for you. Lots of love.*" This message was left on Saturday at five fourteen p.m.'

Message two: *beeeeeeeeep*

Message three: *beeeeeeeeep*

Message four: "*Gemma? It's Amelia. Hope you're okay. The girls are fine, they enjoyed the party. They were a bit worried about you, but I just told them you had a headache and would be better tomorrow. Hope that's okay. Call me if you need anything. And I mean anything.*" This message was left on Saturday at six fifty-five p.m.'

Message five: '*Gemma, it's Robert…*'

My breath hitches at the sound of his voice.

'*… I wasn't going to call. I was going to give you some space. But… please, just phone me. We need to sort this out. I'm worried about you.*'

There's a pause, as though he's going to say something else. But then the call ends. '*This call was left today at seven fifty-two a.m.*'

He's worried about *me*? Worried about himself, more like. Worried that I've kicked him out of the house and he won't get to see the girls whenever he likes. I shove my phone in my bag, shrug on my coat and leave the house.

Driving over to Diane's, the sun is low in the sky and every few seconds I have to slow down as the glare blinds me. Yesterday, when I pulled onto Diane's driveway, I was surrounded by my family. I was happy. Today, I am alone and I feel as though there is a rock in my stomach and poison in my veins.

Diane's front door opens before I'm even out of the car. She's standing on the front step, dressed in navy slacks and a white sweater. I wonder if Robert is here, too. I realise I don't want to see him. Not yet. I don't quite feel strong enough. But his car isn't in the drive so hopefully I won't have to. But then the awful thought hits me that if he's not here, he's probably with Sadie. Perhaps, right at this minute, they're in bed together, ecstatic to finally be free to shag each other senseless. I swallow down the nausea rising in my gullet.

'Gemma, come in. It's freezing out here.'

I do as Diane asks, looking forward to seeing the children, but also bracing myself for their inevitable questions.

'Shall we have a cup of tea?' Diane asks, walking through to the kitchen without waiting for an answer.

I glance around, giving a small shudder at the sight of the stairs. Remembering walking up them to discover my husband and Sadie. And then walking back down, my voice loud and hysterical, attracting the attention of all our friends and family. Letting them witness the ugly breakdown of our marriage. I shake away the raw memory, listening for the sound of the girls running to greet me. But apart from Diane's neat footsteps, the house is silent. All traces of yesterday's party removed.

In the kitchen, Diane is filling up the kettle.

'No tea for me, thanks. Where are the girls?'

'Sit down, Gemma. You've got time for a quick drink, surely?'

'No, not really. We've got to get back, finish homework and get ready for school tomorrow.'

'Robert's taken the girls out for breakfast.'

I stiffen, my mind immediately leaping to conclusions. Are they out with Sadie? Are they already making up a new family without me? 'Where have they gone? Are they at Crumbs? I can go and pick them up from there.' I turn to leave.

'No!' she says, a little too quickly.

'What do you mean, *no?*'

'I just mean, they're not at Crumbs. Robert said he was taking them to a beach café, but he didn't say which one.'

'No problem, I'll call him.' I pull my phone out of my bag.

'Just let them have their breakfast, Gemma. They'll be back in half an hour. Surely you can wait that long.' Diane gets out two china cups and saucers from a glass-fronted cabinet. I reluctantly sit at the table, realising she wants to use this opportunity to talk to me. To make me see things from Robert's point of view. She'll be wasting her breath. But perhaps I can find out what she knows about Sadie.

'What did Robert say to you?' I ask. 'Did he tell you what happened?'

'Of course. And I must say, Gemma, you're completely over-reacting. Nothing happened between them.'

'So you haven't spoken to Sadie?' I say, folding my arms across my chest.

'No. I believe my son when he says nothing happened. I'm not about to start cross-examining the nanny!'

'Well I spoke to her on the phone last night.'

Diane's face takes on a pinched expression.

'Sadie said that she and Robert are in love.'

'That's nonsense!'

'She also said that they've felt this way for weeks.'

'Rubbish! Robert would have told me.'

'Would he?'

'We have a very close relationship. He tells me everything, Gemma. I know you were having delusions about Sadie and

Robert when she was working for you. It was making Robert very unhappy.'

I take a deep breath, trying to keep my temper under control. 'Well, it looks like I was right, doesn't it?'

She sets the tea on the table in front of me. 'You're making a big mistake, Gemma. Whatever has happened or not happened, it's done now and you need to move forward. You need to stop this selfish, dramatic behaviour and think about the children.'

I get to my feet. 'And I need you to mind your own business and stop treating Robert as though he's an eight-year-old prince who can do no wrong!'

'If you split up this marriage, you'll regret it, Gemma.'

I grip the edge of the table. '*He's* the one splitting the family up. *He's* the one who's had the affair. This is his doing, not mine.'

'It doesn't matter whose fault it is,' Diane says calmly. 'What matters is what happens next. And that's up to you, Gemma.'

'I bet you wouldn't be saying that if it was me who'd been sleeping around. *He's* made this mess. He's ruined everything!' I need to leave here. I feel shaky and sad and furious and heartsick and I can't bear Diane's cool composure. 'Tell Robert to drop the girls at the house before lunch.' I march out of the kitchen and back through the hall.

'Gemma, come back.' She sounds regretful now, but I know it's just an act to make me stay longer so she can try to change my mind. However, I'm not as malleable as Robert. Diane can't bend me to her will – she's never been able to control me – and it infuriates her. I hear the swish of her trousers and the clop of her heels as she hurries out of the kitchen to catch me up. 'They're having breakfast at Marco's restaurant,' she says.

I stop and turn around. 'At Marco's? So why didn't you tell me that in the first place?'

'I thought it would be better if you both had some space.'

'Why didn't you go with them?'

'I offered to stay home in case you came round.'

'Thank you,' I say grudgingly.

She nods, her composure slipping. 'Give him another chance, Gemma.'

'Goodbye, Diane.'

'Don't do anything you'll regret.'

I don't bother answering this time. I just get into my car and head down to the seafront, barely able to concentrate on the road.

The traffic is frustratingly busy, the sunshine drawing everyone to the coast despite the chill in the air. Finally, I make it down to the beachfront car park, managing to slip into a newly vacated parking spot. I leave the car and walk the few minutes to the restaurant, feeling set apart from everyone. Removed from all these people enjoying the weekend sunshine. Going about their lives without any cares – or maybe that's just how it looks to an outsider whose world is imploding.

I worry that I'm going to walk into the restaurant and see Sadie sitting with my family. That I won't be able to control my emotions. That the girls will see Mummy losing it for the second day in a row. I try to breathe normally. I'll simply go in, take my daughters by their hands and lead them out of the restaurant without a fuss. If the girls complain about not having finished their breakfast, I'll bribe them with a Mr Whippy ice cream.

Marco's is packed. It looks like every spot inside and out is full. I wend my way through each table, searching out my family. But after two sweeps of the place, I conclude they aren't here. *Damn.* I must have missed them.

I catch sight of Marco behind the bar. He looks busy, but I make my way over.

'Gemma!' He kisses me on both cheeks. 'You are here with your family, yes? You want a table? Of course. But we are a little busy. Can you wait ten, maybe fifteen minutes?'

'Hi, Marco. No, it's fine. Robert's already been in for breakfast with the girls but I must have missed them. Do you know what time they left?'

'Robert and the girls? No, they haven't been here today.'

'Are you sure?'

'Positive. Hundred per cent.' He calls over one of his waiting staff and speaks to her in rapid Italian before turning back to me once more. 'No. Lucia says they haven't been here today.'

'Okay, no problem. Maybe they saw how busy you are.'

'Always we make space for you. You tell him to come back, okay.'

'Thanks, Marco. I'll see you soon.' I hurry out of the restaurant, past the families and the couples, their laughter sounding hollow to my ears, their happy chatter an insult to my broken heart.

Back outside, I call Robert, but it goes to voicemail so I leave a message. 'Are you still out with the girls? Your mum said you were coming to Marco's, but you're not here. Let me know where you are and I'll come and get them.'

I bash out a text with the same message.

There's no point hanging around down at the beach. I may as well return to the car and head back home.

It takes me ages to get out of the car park, and I'm starting to get an uneasy feeling in my gut. I've put my phone on the passenger seat in case Robert calls to tell me they're at a different café and I have to turn around. But I'm starting to wonder if I've been sent on a wild goose chase.

My need to get back home suddenly becomes urgent. Once I'm on the dual carriageway of the A338, I press my foot down hard on the accelerator, darting between lanes and earning a few flashing lights and beeping horns from other drivers. I've probably got a speeding ticket from that last camera, but I don't care. All I know is, I have to get home. Something isn't right. Why did Diane wait until I was leaving her house to tell me they were at Marco's?

I eventually manage to get home in one piece, without getting into an accident or being arrested for reckless driving; which is a miracle. But Robert's car isn't here. Maybe they're still having breakfast. Or maybe they walked over here from Diane's.

My pulse is racing, my breathing shallow. I almost fall onto the driveway in my haste to get out of the car.

Don't let me be right. Please, don't let me be right.

I let myself in and immediately sense there is no one home. But I can see that they've been here since I left this morning. The girls' school coats and bags are missing from the hallway.

No, no, no.

I scramble up the stairs and go into Katie's room. It's been stripped of all her favourite toys. I throw open her wardrobe – empty.

How could Robert do this! What is he playing at?

I go into Eva's room and it's the same thing. Her room is decimated. Her clothes are gone. What the hell?

He can't do this, can he?

CHAPTER 52

Robert has taken our children without my consent. I sit on the floor in Eva's room and with shaking fingers I put a call through to him. As expected, it goes to voicemail.

'Robert? Where are you? What the hell are you doing taking the girls' things? Is this your mother's idea? Why would you do this? I've done nothing wrong! You're the one who's had an affair. If you don't bring the girls home now, I'm calling the police.'

I call again, and again, but every time it goes to voicemail. He must have it switched off so he doesn't have to speak to me. Well, if my husband won't talk to me, maybe Sadie will. I call her number and wait, expecting her to pick up, or for the call to go to voicemail. Unfortunately it does neither. A pre-recorded voice tells me: '*The number you have called has not been recognised.*' *What?*

I call again and get the same thing. Sadie has obviously ditched her number. Has she gone off with Robert and the girls somewhere?

I race downstairs into the dining room, where we keep all our paperwork. I haven't done any filing for months, and piles of unsorted letters and papers sit on the dusty dining table waiting for the twelfth of never when I'll finally get around to putting it all in its proper place. Right now, I'm regretting my lack of organisation as I begin frantically searching through the first pile. But I find what I'm looking for almost immediately – Sadie's résumé.

There's no address listed on it, and the phone number is the same as the discontinued one. My laptop is on the table so I open it up and go into my emails. I find her email address and tap out a message:

> *Sadie, can you contact me ASAP. Your phone number isn't working and I need to talk to you urgently. Please don't ignore this!!!!*

I press send.

But I can't just sit around waiting for a reply. I call Diane's mobile. It goes to voicemail. They're all dodging my calls. I try not to think about what this means. That they've made a plan to keep the children from me. To make sure everything works in Robert's favour.

I try to get my breathing under control and check my emails again. I have one new message. Please let it be from Sadie.

I read the subject line:

Message Undeliverable

Fuck! She must have closed down her email account too.

I do a quick check on social media for any sign of Sadie Lewis, but I can't find mention of her anywhere. It's as though she's disappeared off the face of the earth. Or like she never existed in the first place…

I leave the house and get back in my car. I'm shaking so much that I'm not safe to drive but I have no choice. I tear back round to Diane's ready to scream at her if she doesn't tell me where Robert has taken my children. Her car is missing from her driveway, but I get out and ring her doorbell anyway. No reply. I hammer on the door with my fists and scream her name, even though I know it's useless. She's not here.

I stand on the doorstep pulling at my hair and dragging my nails down my cheeks. I've entered a nightmare. What am I going to do? *Think. Think.*

Okay, so the girls have school tomorrow. Once Robert has dropped them off, I'll go to the school office and say we've had a family emergency and I have to take them out. It's the last week of term before the Easter holidays so I can change the door locks and keep the girls home until I've worked out what to do. Three weeks should be enough time to figure something out.

But I want them home with me *now*. Why did I leave them at Diane's last night? I should have anticipated she'd suggest something like this. It's not Robert's style to be so devious. So calculating. So *cruel*.

I leave Diane's place for the second time today, and head back home. At a loss for what to do. Maybe I really should call the police?

As I let myself back into the house, my phone pings with a voice message. I stand in the hall, call my voicemail and with a thumping heart, I listen. It's a message from Robert. *Finally.*

'*Hi Gemma, I'm sorry for giving you the run-around this morning. I thought it would be best if I looked after the girls for the next few weeks.*'

What? Next few weeks? Best for who exactly? It sounds as though he's on speaker phone in the car. I can hear the girls in the background and my heart aches to have them with me. I try to concentrate on what he's saying.

'*You're always so busy with work that it makes sense if I take them for the holidays. Nothing happened between me and Sadie, but you're not willing to believe me and after you threw me out of the house... I couldn't risk you keeping me from the girls. I've always been their primary carer, so I should be the one they live with while we're sorting things out.*'

Primary carer? My pulse is racing now, the blood whooshing in my ears.

'*I'll keep in touch via phone. Don't worry about the girls. They're absolutely fine. Happy as anything.*'

Happy without me, you mean. Well we'll see how long that lasts. I'll give it a day before they start missing me.

'*I mean it, Gemma. Don't worry. I love you. But you've totally overreacted. We'll talk when I get back.*'

Get back? Get back from where exactly? I have a horrible feeling about this.

'*Mum has come with me to help out. We'll be back before school starts up. Okay, I'd better go.*'

The voice message ends and I immediately call him back. But, as always, it goes straight to voicemail. As I leave him a furious message I head back into the dining room to see if my suspicions are right.

'I've just listened to your message. Why are you doing this? Was this your mum's idea? Is Sadie with you? Her mobile isn't working. Nor is her email. *Why* won't you speak to me properly instead of leaving messages? I need to talk to you Robert! You can't just ignore me!'

Back in the dining room, I pull open the filing cabinet and check the hanging file where we keep our passports.

No!

Only my passport is here. Robert's and the girls' are missing.

CHAPTER 53

It's Monday evening and I'm lying on my bed still wearing the same clothes as yesterday. The past thirty-six hours have been a living hell. I haven't slept. I haven't washed. I've barely eaten. I can hardly hold myself upright. I have no idea where Robert and Diane have gone, or if Sadie is with them. Would Diane even condone that? She may not particularly like me, but I can't believe she would accept Robert shacking up with the nanny.

But the more I've tried to find answers, the more dead ends I've come up against.

The doorbell rings, a harsh, hollow sound that only serves to ramp up my anxiety. I don't have the energy to get up, but it could be important. Maybe it's Sadie... I jerk upright and head downstairs, pulling open the door.

It takes me a moment to register that it's not Sadie. It's Amelia, looking her usual glamorous self, a bottle of rosé in her hand. She holds out her arms and I step into them, finally letting out the tears that I've been holding on to.

'It's okay,' she says, coming inside and leading me into the lounge. 'It's okay, Gemma.'

'Oh, Amelia. It's not okay. It's all awful. Everything's gone wrong. And Robert's taken the girls. I haven't seen them since Saturday!'

'Have you eaten anything?'

I shake my head. 'Not hungry.'

'You need to eat, or you'll be no good to anyone.'

'You brought wine. I could definitely do with a glass of wine.'

'Not a good idea on an empty stomach. Come on, let's go into the kitchen and see what you've got in the fridge.'

I follow her in like a helpless child – a feeling that is totally alien to me. I'm usually the one sorting out problems and taking charge, but it's as though the life has been drained from my body.

She opens the fridge and peers in. 'Fresh pasta. Perfect. That'll take five minutes. Right, you sit at the table.'

I do as Amelia says, watching as she glides around the kitchen putting a pan on to boil and looking in cupboards for other ingredients.

'Here, eat these.' She passes me two cheese crackers.

I nibble at them slowly. Not tasting, just chewing and swallowing, chewing and swallowing. Trying to force each mouthful past the lump in my throat, tears still trailing down my cheeks. 'Does James know where Robert is?' I ask, my voice small and croaky.

'I'm sorry, he doesn't. Robert left James a message to say he'd taken the girls on holiday and that Diane's gone with them.' Amelia takes a wine glass from the cupboard and places it on the table in front of me.

'So you have no idea where they've gone?' I ask again.

'None. I'm sorry.' She pours me a large glassful and I take a deep draught of the cold, sharp liquid. 'I left you a message on Saturday; did you get it?'

I nod. 'Sorry I didn't call you back. I just... I couldn't face talking to anyone and—'

'No, of course, it's fine. I just hope you know I'm here for you whatever you need.'

'I need my kids back! I need for Robert not to have slept with Sadie.'

'So... did he... really? Are you sure they actually...?'

'I saw them on the bed together, at Diane's party.'

'Shit. I'm sorry, Gemma.' Amelia pours herself a glass of water and drinks it down in one. Then she pours herself another. 'I seem to be thirsty all the time,' she says. 'And then peeing all the time.'

'I shouldn't be stressing you out with all this,' I say, guilt flooding me. 'Not with you being pregnant. You should be sitting down and taking it easy while *I* cook.'

'Don't be silly. I love to cook. You sit there, have a drink and let me look after you.'

'Thank you.' Her kindness is making me teary again. 'How are you anyway? Sorry I'm putting such a downer on your happy news.'

'I'm absolutely fine. Don't worry about me. I'm here for *you* today, okay? So, has Robert really not told you where he's taken the girls? That seems a bit extreme.'

'He's angry. When we left the party, I packed a couple of suitcases with his stuff and kicked him out of the house. Maybe it was harsh, but what would you have done if you'd found James with another woman?'

'I'm not criticising, Gemma. I probably would have done exactly the same. Worse. I'd have got the scissors out and shredded the lot.'

'I'm pretty sure this was Diane's idea. I think she's made Robert paranoid that I'll deny him access to the girls. Which is absolute rubbish. I would never do that.'

'But you've spoken to him about it, surely?'

'I've left tons of messages and texts, but the only reply I've received is a message to say they're fine.'

Amelia is still bustling around the kitchen, chopping and grating. I don't have the heart to tell her I'm not hungry. It was all I could do to force those two crackers down. 'Want me to call Diane?' she asks. 'See if I can find out where they are?'

'Would you?'

'Of course.'

'I already messaged her to ask which of her friends recommended Sadie as a nanny – you know it was one of her friends from the golf club. I figured if I could speak to them, maybe they could help me track her down. But Diane sent me a text saying she wasn't prepared to put me in touch with her friends for me to harass them! Can you believe that?'

Amelia gives a dry laugh. 'Actually, I can believe it. Diane won't want to be shown up. You'll have to learn how to get her on your side, Gemma. You always tend to rub her up the wrong way.'

'I know. I can't help it.' I sigh and pull at the skin around my eyes.

'Look,' Amelia says, draining the pasta, 'I know this sucks. I know you're missing the girls. But Robert isn't heartless. He'll bring them back. You know he will.'

'I thought about calling the police, you know.' I watch Amelia's face as I drop this piece of news. Wondering if she'll think this is a step too far – reporting my own husband. But she simply nods. 'But I'm nervous about involving the authorities. What if they get social services involved, or they decide Robert should have full custody? Diane knows everyone in this town so I'm sure she can twist things to make me look bad. Like I'm this working mother who doesn't care about her children.'

'Oh, Gemma. It all sounds so serious. But I'm sure Robert will bring them home soon and you'll be able to work things out. He'll want what's best for the children, and they'll want to spend time with both of you.'

'It's only been two days and I'm already missing them so much it's making me sick. I need to know they're okay. What Robert's doing now is almost worse than his betrayal with Sadie. What if he moves in with her and she gets access to my girls?'

Hysteria claws its way through my veins. Can this really be happening? I feel like I'm trapped in a nightmare. How can Robert not see what this is doing to me?

'Have you spoken to her?'

'To Sadie? Yes. She said she loves him.'

'Shit.'

'But when I tried to call her again today, it says her number isn't available. Same with her email address.'

'What do you mean?'

'I mean, she's not contactable any more.'

'That's odd.'

'I know. But it gets worse. Today, I messaged Sadie's families – you know, the ones she used to nanny for before us. I used the email references she gave on her résumé, but both addresses have come back as undeliverable. Which means that they were probably fake references.'

Amelia's eyes widen and she sits down heavily. 'That's…'

'I know. Scary, right. I mean, who the hell even is she? Did she get fired from her last job? Is she a danger to the girls?'

'Surely Robert knows where she is? I mean, if he and she are… you know.'

'He says he doesn't know where she is, but I don't know whether he's telling the truth or not. Maybe he's with her, or maybe he's covering up where she is to protect her from me. My only option now is to try to find her.'

'I agree. You need to have it out with her. Are you sure you and Robert can't put all this behind you and work it out? I mean, Robert's always been a bit of a player.'

I look at her, not sure if I've heard her correctly. 'A player? No he hasn't!' I'm surprised at Amelia for saying that. 'Sorry, didn't mean to snap, but Robert is most definitely not a player.'

'Oh. Well, it's good to hear that he's changed since *we* were together.' She inhales and raises her eyebrows.

'Changed?' It always makes me feel weird to remember that Robert and Amelia used to be an item.

'You know… that he's grown up since then. I loved him, but he used to be the biggest flirt on the planet. James is less… confident, shall we say, around women.'

'I've never thought of Robert as flirty,' I reply, a little surprised by Amelia's analysis of him. 'That's why this has all come as such a shock.'

'So, did you...' She breaks off.

'What?' I prompt. 'Did I what?'

'Did you trust him with his clients? All those fit, powerful businesswomen with their killer bodies...'

'... and men,' I add. 'It isn't just women he trains.'

'I know, but his job means he's getting up close and personal with a lot of women. That would test even the closest relationships.'

'It's never been an issue,' I reply. 'The truth is, until Sadie, I've never had any reason to doubt him.' But I'm now wondering if that's true. I cast my mind back over our marriage years and think about how charming Robert is with everyone. How women are always drawn to him. Is that because he encourages it? Surely not.

'You need to find Sadie,' Amelia says, jolting me from my dark thoughts. 'Find out the truth about what's gone on. She might even be lying.'

'Do you think?'

'Until you speak to her, you won't know.'

Amelia is right. I need to track down Sadie and confront her face to face. I need to know whether or not she's lying. Then maybe I'll be able to accept things and move on. One way or another.

CHAPTER 54

The day after my talk with Amelia, I go into the office with renewed purpose. First, I tell Damien that he will be running things for at least the next two weeks. Then I call two of my most trusted staff into my office.

A few minutes later, I'm sitting at my desk opposite Dave Ristretto, Head of Security, and Gary Marshall, Head of IT. Appearance-wise they are the polar opposites. Dave is six foot two and broad shouldered with a buzz cut. Gary is five ten, chubby and balding. Both men are fantastic at their jobs.

Normally I would make polite small talk, ask after their families and how everything is going at work. But right now I can't work up the enthusiasm and I'm far too impatient. Instead, I cut straight to the main event.

'I need to ask you both a favour.'

Dave raises an eyebrow. 'Is this a work-related favour?'

'No. You can pursue it during work time, but I'll pay you separately, on top of your salaries. It's an urgent matter.'

'Is it legal?' Gary asks with a chuckle.

'Ye-es.'

'You don't sound too sure, boss,' Gary says, still smiling.

'I'm sure.' I take a breath. 'I need you to find someone for me.'

Neither of them reply.

'It's a woman. To be precise, it's the woman who used to look after my kids. She's a nanny, but she seems to have disappeared without a trace. Her phone number's dead, her email is saying undeliverable, and there's no forwarding address. Do you think you can help? Or should I hire a PI?'

There's a brief silence.

'What's her name?' Gary asks.

'Sadie Lewis.'

'That her real name?' Gary adds.

'I don't know. It wouldn't surprise me if it was fake.'

'I'll need a photo,' Dave says.

'Okay. I've got a few on my phone.' Thankfully, Eva took a few selfies with Sadie, so I can lift them from her private Instagram feed. 'I'll forward them to you. Does that mean you're both on board?'

'Sure, why not,' Dave replies, inclining his head.

'Are the girls okay?' Gary asks with a frown. 'She didn't hurt them, did she, this nanny?'

'They're fine,' I say, swallowing down the words. 'They're with Robert at the moment. I just… I need to find her.' I try to keep my voice as neutral as possible. The urge to go off on a rant is strong, but I'm trying to keep this on a professional level. Like I would with any other job. The other *greater* temptation is to ask them to track down Robert and the girls, but I don't want my staff to know *all* my private business. And at least I know my children are safe. And I really believe he'll be true to his word and bring them back. I'll find Sadie first, then deal with my husband next. Of course, there's always the possibility that Sadie is with Robert and the children. But that doesn't even bear thinking about.

'I hope it goes without saying that I want this kept quiet. I don't need the rest of my staff knowing—'

Dave raises a hand. 'I'm offended you'd even ask.'

I manage a grim smile. 'Thanks. Can you make this your top priority?'

'Above regular work?'

'Yes, but don't let clients suffer. If you need to hire some temps, that's fine.'

'Is she still in the country?' Gary asks.

'I honestly don't know. I guess she might have gone abroad.'

'You better hope she's still in the UK,' Gary says. 'It'll be harder to trace her if she's gone overseas.'

'Let's assume she's in the UK,' I reply, wanting this desperately to be true. If she's here, then the chances are she isn't with Robert.

'What sort of timescale we talking?' Dave asks.

'Today wouldn't be too soon,' I reply.

'Ha. That might be tricky, but we'll give it a good go,' Gary replies. 'Send us the photos and everything else you've got – her old phone number, emails, messages. Nothing's too trivial, okay?'

I nod, feeling a tiny bit lighter. If anyone can find her, these guys can.

After a nail-biting and distressing week of little sleep, I finally get the news that I've been waiting for. Dave and Gary have found Sadie. Working together with a freelance team, they eventually managed to track her down via a security camera in west London, using facial recognition technology. Once they found her image on a few cameras, they narrowed her location. Then travelled up to London to confirm where she's living.

Now, back in my office once again, they're briefing me on their discovery.

'She's got no regular internet presence,' Gary says. 'Nothing at all. She also has no registered phone or email. So it got me thinking—'

'Before we go on,' Dave interrupts, 'are you sure you want to know all the details? We weren't exactly... by the book with this.'

'I'm sure,' I reply, scratching at my ear. 'You didn't try to make contact with her, did you?' I'm suddenly worried that they might have scared her off.

Dave gives me a look. 'Give us some credit, boss. We're confident she's got no idea we're watching her.'

'I definitely want all the details.' I lean forward in my chair, nervous but excited that I might finally be getting somewhere. This has been the longest week of my life. Robert leaves me text messages each day to say that he and the girls are fine, but he won't answer my calls. Neither will Diane. And Amelia has had no luck finding out where they are. My heart aches at being separated from my daughters for so long. If he doesn't bring them back to me by the end of the holidays, I'm going to ask Dave and Gary for their help once more. This time to track down my family. But I'd rather not get them involved in that. I still don't want my private family issues entangled with my business.

'Have you heard of the dark web?' Gary asks.

His question prompts a feeling of unease. 'I've heard of it, but I'm not entirely sure what it is…'

'Okay,' Gary says. 'So it's a collection of websites that are highly encrypted, meaning its users are anonymous and their activities are hidden.'

My scalp prickles. 'That sounds creepy.'

'It can be,' Gary says. 'It looks like the regular internet, but instead of ordinary, innocuous businesses and social media sites, you can get pretty much anything you want. And I mean *anything*. Think of all the dark and depraved and illegal stuff in the world and imagine there's a menu for all that crap. Well, that would be the dark web. Anyone can go on there, but you need to download particular software to access it.'

A chill enters my bloodstream. 'This isn't to do with Eva and Katie, is it? Sadie isn't going to—'

'No, no. Nothing like that,' Gary jumps in. 'Sorry, I should have put your mind at rest before talking about all this stuff. This is nothing to do with the girls. We couldn't find anything specifically about *them*. But…'

'But what?'

'…it is to do with *you*… and with Robert.'

'What is? Sorry, I don't quite understand what you're telling me. And what has Sadie got to do with the dark web?'

'She's got a website on there,' Gary says. 'Don't ask us how we found out.'

It hadn't occurred to me that I would be asking my employees to engage in potentially illegal activities. I like to think of myself as a good, law-abiding citizen. But I've been pushed into this situation. When it comes to protecting my family, I've discovered I'm willing to cross lines.

'What's the website for?' I ask.

'Come and have a look,' Gary says.

I get up and walk around the desk as Gary flips open his laptop. Leaning forwards, I stare at the screen while he opens a browser and clicks onto a site called 'Relationship Assassin'.

'This is her site?' I ask.

'Mmhm.'

'What is it?'

'It's exactly what it says it is. She's paid to assassinate relationships – break them up from the inside.'

'So she's not a nanny?'

'Doesn't look like it. But maybe she used a nanny persona to get close to your family.'

'Fuck.'

'Indeed,' Gary replies.

I cover my mouth with my hand. My heart is banging in my chest and my vision blurs as the seriousness of what they're telling me sinks in.

'On here, she goes by the name Kelly Parker,' Gary continues. 'But that's probably just another alias. I highly doubt she'd use her real identity for any of this stuff.'

My brain judders, trying to make sense of what Gary and Dave are telling me. That Sadie, or Kelly, or whatever her name is, is not a nanny. She was never qualified to take care of our children. She was in our house. Paid by someone to do a job. Paid by someone to ruin my marriage. The idea makes me feel physically sick.

But who would want to break me and Robert up?

Whoever it is, they've succeeded. Whoever it is, I'm going to find them. I'll find out the truth and then I'll make them sorry they ever messed with me and my family.

CHAPTER 55

I sit in the café trying not to catch anyone's eye. My back is to the door so she doesn't see my face and then bolt. I'm wearing jeans, a white sweatshirt and a dark brown wig braided in a single plait down my back. In my message, I told her to look out for the braid and the white sweatshirt. It makes me stand out from everyone else. Ensures she'll come and sit at my table. I told her my name was Linda, and I wanted to divorce my husband. That I needed her to set a honey trap for him so that I can cite infidelity as my reason for divorce. She wanted five hundred quid up front just for this meeting.

Dave is sitting at a table diagonal to me. He starts tapping his fingers on the side of his coffee cup to alert me to the fact that Sadie has just walked in. I swallow and put a hand on my knee to stop it bouncing up and down. I shouldn't be anxious. I should be furious. I take a breath and will myself to stay calm.

I sense someone coming up behind me and I take a sip of my tea as she walks up to the table and smiles questioningly.

'Linda?' Sadie asks. Her hair hangs down like a curtain of dark silk. Her make-up is flawless and she's wearing a beautifully tailored trouser suit that shows off her cleavage. I put my cup back down on the table and stare up at her, watching with satisfaction as her expression clouds with puzzlement. She's trying to work out where she knows me from. But the wig has confused her.

'Hello, Sadie,' I say. 'Or should that be *Kelly?*'

It only takes a split second for recognition to set in. There's a fleeting expression of shock but she quickly composes her features and remains standing. 'Go home, Gemma. You're out of your depth.'

'You'd like to think that, wouldn't you?' I say, my words slow and measured. 'That I'm some naive mother who doesn't have a clue. Well maybe that was once true. But now you've broken up my family, I'm not going to let you get away with it.' I stare at this sleek, composed woman and wonder who she really is. Does she work alone? Does she have any kind of conscience?'

Sadie shrugs. 'But I have gotten away with it, Gemma. Your family is… broken.' She sits opposite me. 'What? You think you can report me to the authorities, is that it? By the time you can convince anyone to take you seriously – which I highly doubt you will – my website will have disappeared. You won't be able to trace me. And then I'll pop up somewhere else with a new name and a new site. Simple.'

'I don't care about you or your site,' I snap. 'I don't care what you do next. I just want to know who hired you. Tell me that and I'll leave you alone.'

She smiles and shakes her head. Gets to her feet again. 'You've had a wasted journey.'

I tell myself to stay calm, to not raise my voice. 'If you leave, I'll follow you. And I'll keep following you until you tell me who hired you.'

'That's very dramatic, Gemma.' She smirks, but I can tell she's rattled by the tightness of her jaw and the stiffening of her shoulders.

'Not dramatic. Just the truth. Look around the room. I have plain-clothes security here.'

Sadie's smile falters. She does as I suggest and glances around. Dave gives her a wave, and a couple of my female security officers nod in our direction.

'You think you're the one in control here,' I say, my confidence growing. 'But you're not. You actually don't know who you're dealing with, Sadie, or whatever your name is. I have over two hundred security staff on my books, most of them ex-military. I could make you disappear if I wanted. No one would miss you… you don't exist, remember?' I'm surprised at how steady and authoritative my voice sounds, considering how on edge I feel. I would never do anything approaching what I'm threatening, but I figure this is the only language Sadie will understand. I hold my breath, waiting to see if she'll heed my bluff or walk away.

'Do you know what?' Sadie says, sitting opposite me once more. 'I've already been paid my fee, so what the hell. Whatever happens now is none of my concern. You want to know who hired me…'

'That's why I'm here.' My palms are sweaty and my body starts to tingle with anticipation. Who would do such a terrible thing?

Sadie fixes me with a stare. 'My client was Diane Ballantine.'

I feel my jaw drop and I immediately clamp it shut. 'Diane?' Can Sadie be telling the truth?

'Your mother-in-law paid me a ridiculous fee to split up you and Robert.'

I know I'm not Diane's favourite person, but for her to do something like this… it's wicked. It's outrageous. For the moment, I have no words as her revelation sinks in.

'I'll tell you something, that woman really hates you.' Sadie leans back in her chair and slowly shakes her head. 'But Robert… well, he can do no wrong. Diane didn't think you were good enough for her youngest son. She wanted you out of the picture.'

'But… it makes no sense!' I cry. 'She kept telling me to stand by Robert. To do the right thing for the sake of the children. For the family.'

'It's what's known as a double bluff, Gemma. Diane knows you can't stand her. She knew that trying to push you one way would make you lean in the other direction. She used that to her advantage – with my guidance, of course.'

'But why wait this long to do it? Robert and I have been together for years.'

'I don't know.' Sadie shrugs. 'My job isn't to find out why. I just do what the client asks.'

I narrow my eyes. 'How do I know you're even telling the truth? You could be saying all this simply to get me off your back.'

'I've got no reason to lie.'

I can't take my eyes off Sadie. Off this confident woman who is so different from her previous persona. This Sadie is a professional. A businesswoman. She's talking about the wreckage of my life as though it was a game of chess, a series of moves and counter moves. But she's mistaken if she thinks the game is over.

'You know,' she says, 'before she hired me, Diane tried a honey trap on you first.'

'She did *what*?'

'She invented a handsome businessman who would take you out to dinner and put a move on you. She had someone positioned at the restaurant to take photos of the two of you getting cosy. Only you didn't bite.'

I run a hand over my hair, surprised to find it's the wig. I feel like ripping the damn thing off. 'I just… I can't believe…' I clench my fists. Bloody Mick Cosgrove! It had to be him, didn't it? I can't think of anyone else who's made a pass at me recently. That man really shook me up. Diane must have a low opinion of me if she thinks I would be seduced by anyone, let alone by Mick Cosgrove's vile groping. It dawns on me that he probably wasn't even the real Cosgrove. The whole thing must have been a set-up. All those hours I spent working on a fake pitch… I'll strangle the woman when I next see her. How dare she treat me like that!

Something else hits me. 'The graffiti!'

Sadie frowns. 'The what?'

'Someone spray-painted my car—'

'Oh, the "bad mother" thing? Yeah, Diane arranged that too. She was just trying to rattle you. To put you under pressure. See if you and Robert would start getting snippy with one another. Nothing to do with me. That was before she secured my services. If she'd asked my opinion, I'd have told her that was a waste of time. Attacking you like that would only rouse Robert's protective side and bring you closer together. Anyway, when her attempts weren't working, she decided to go all out and break up your relationship from the inside. That's when she got in contact with me.'

I have so many thoughts racing through my head, but there's one other thing I really need to know. 'So let's say I believe you, and Diane really did put you up to this. Did you and Robert actually have an affair?'

She purses her lips and gazes up at the ceiling for a moment. 'Look, Gemma, I wouldn't usually undo everything my client has paid for. But she won't be able to trace me and I never liked her anyway. Condescending woman.'

I can't disagree with Sadie on that point.

'Your mother-in-law has paid me enough to get out of the business for a while. I'm retiring, moving abroad. Leaving this life behind me – for now at least. So, I'm going to break my golden rule and tell you what happened. I tried pretty much every trick in the book to seduce your husband. He. Did. Not. Bite. Not once. I did it in a subtle way, to get him to make the first move. In every other job I've had, it's worked. The guy always falls for me. And if he doesn't, then he'll at least want to have a quick, no-strings fuck. But Robert…' She shakes her head. 'That man loves you. Don't split your family up over something you think you saw. Because it wasn't real. None of it was real.'

My heart is beating so loudly that I'm sure everyone in the café can hear it. I really want to believe her. But I can't get my hopes up. Not yet.

'You can't expect me to swallow that – not after what I saw at Diane's house.'

'What did you see?' Sadie smiles. 'You saw Robert on top of me on a bed in Diane's spare room. If we were having an affair, do you seriously think he would do something as stupid as that, in his mother's house while his wife and kids and family and friends are there?'

'I… I don't know. Maybe you encouraged him? Maybe he liked the excitement. The risk of being discovered.'

'Does that sound like Robert to you?'

'Not really. But I assumed he was having some kind of midlife crisis.'

'Gemma, what you saw was very simple. I asked Robert to help me bring some coats upstairs. Diane said she would arrange for you to come up while we were there. As soon as I saw you push the door open, I pretended to stumble and fall backwards. I grabbed hold of Robert in the process, pulling him back onto the bed with me. As he was getting up, I pulled at the bow on my blouse to make it look as though I was half dressed.'

I listen with a certain amount of scepticism. It must show on my face because she continues trying to convince me.

'Why would I lie? What could I possibly have to gain? You can believe me or not believe me. But I'm telling you, hand on heart, your husband is not a cheater. And if you let him go because of something you thought you saw, well… more fool you.'

I scratch at my arm and try to rationalise it all. If what Sadie is saying is true, then I've accused my husband unfairly, and I've kicked him out of our home for no reason. But it also means that my family can be put back together again. I won't need to lose Robert or the girls. There won't be any separation or divorce. If this was really all Diane's doing, if we've been in the grasp of her manipulation, then Robert and I can surely move past all this and get back to how we used to be. That is, if I can forgive him for taking the children. Which I'm not sure I can. I hardly dare hope that Sadie is telling the truth.

'And try not to work so hard,' Sadie adds. 'I'd kill for your life. Your husband, your family. You're so lucky and you don't even realise it. It's partly why I'm giving up what I do. I want my own version of what you have.'

I still can't speak. This woman is not what I thought she was. Not at all. I need to talk to Robert. Tell him what I've discovered about his mother. He'll be gutted when he hears of her betrayal. But will he even believe me?

'So,' Sadie says, getting to her feet. 'I've told you what you wanted to know, so I'm leaving, okay?'

'No,' I cry. 'Not yet.'

Sadie raises her eyebrows. Over on the other table, Dave gets to his feet at my outburst, and mouths to ask if I'm okay. I nod.

'Please. Sit down,' I ask her.

'Why? What else do you want? I've told you everything.'

I take a deep breath and look Sadie in the eye. 'I think I might have another job for you.'

CHAPTER 56

Everything is immaculate. After ignoring all the housework since Robert took the girls, I've now dusted and hoovered and cleaned and scrubbed every surface and corner of our neglected home. My family is due back any minute and I want them to return to a sparkling house with a well-stocked fridge and fresh flowers. I keep looking out of the window, and when that gets too frustrating, I leave the house, walk down the drive and stride out onto the pavement, squinting through the sunlight in the direction I think they'll be arriving from.

After I left Sadie at the café, I sent Robert a long, heartfelt email telling him that I'd been wrong to accuse him. I told him I'd spoken to Sadie and she had told me the truth about what had happened at the party. I begged him to please come home. I didn't tell him *exactly* what I'd discovered. I left out the part about Sadie manipulating us both, and the other more horrifying fact that it was his mother who had hired her. I don't want him speaking to Diane before we can both figure out what to do about her.

Robert called me as soon as he read my email. We cried down the phone and he said he was miserable without me, and so were the girls. Apparently his mother had rented them a gîte in France, but he didn't think he should leave the country so they ended up in a cottage in Cornwall. He said it had rained every day and it was awful. I almost told him about Sadie. But I managed to stop myself. It's better if I explain the whole thing face to face, showing him the emails and evidence to prove it's all true. And I couldn't risk him giving Diane a chance to talk her way out of it.

That was yesterday. Today Robert and the girls are driving home. He sent me a text to say he's back in Bournemouth, but he has to drop his mother home first. I'll bet she's not happy about that. In fact, I'll bet she's furious that he's coming back to me at all.

I'm in the kitchen distractedly surfing the net when I hear the car doors slam – one, two and three. Little footsteps slapping the concrete. The doorbell ringing repeatedly.

'Mummy!'

'Mum! We're home! Open the door!'

Happiness bubbles up through my whole body. I run through the hall and pull the front door wide. Two small bodies throw themselves at me. But they seem taller, stronger, more grown-up.

'Oh my goodness, I've missed you two monsters!'

'We missed you too, Mum,' Eva cries.

I kiss them and hug them, basking in the exquisite pain of holding my girls once more. Breathing in their scent and feeling like I never want to let them go. This is the longest we've ever been parted. And my thoughts can't help but turn to the reason why… *Diane.* This is all her doing. She planned this. She arranged for Robert to spirit my babies away. How dare she!

'Why didn't you come with us, Mummy?' Katie asks crossly. 'You should've come.'

'Dad said you were working,' Eva accuses.

I stare over their heads to the driveway, where my husband stands, the keys in his hand, a sheepish expression on his face. As though he's waiting for my permission to be allowed back in. I banish all my negative thoughts towards him. We were both the victims. We were both played. And Diane is not going to have the satisfaction of seeing our marriage disintegrate. I love Robert. I love my family. And no one is going to take them away from me again.

*

The girls are asleep in bed. After supper and baths, Robert and I let them stay up late to watch a movie, but they were both so exhausted from travelling that they were asleep within half an hour of the film starting.

While the girls were awake, I didn't say anything to Robert about Sadie or Diane, or any of the stuff that's sitting on my brain like a giant bug. It's not a conversation we can have in whispers over our children's heads. I realise I'm terrified about telling him his mother's part in all of this. How do I say all that without hurting him? I can't. He's going to be devastated. But I can't put it off either. He needs to know.

We sit in the lounge with a glass of wine. Now that the girls are no longer with us to act as a buffer, the atmosphere between us is awkward and strained.

'It's good to be home,' Robert says. 'Back with you. I missed you so much, Gemma. I'm sorry I took the girls, but I was desperate. I thought… when you threw me out of the house, I was worried you wouldn't let me see them. Mum said I had to keep them with me in case you denied me access. I was scared—'

'Robert—'

'What made you change your mind? You said you spoke to Sadie – did she explain that it was all a stupid misunderstanding?'

'Robert,' I repeat his name more forcefully. 'There's something you need to know. And it's not an easy thing to tell you. It will all sound far-fetched and unbelievable, so will you just listen to me while I explain the whole thing? And know that I have the evidence to back up what I'm saying.'

Robert frowns. 'You're scaring me now, Gemma. This isn't about us, is it? You don't want us to split up? Because I swear nothing happened—'

'I don't want us to split up either. Just listen, okay?'

He gives me a nod and I go on to tell him about meeting up with Sadie, about her not really being a nanny, about her being hired to break up our marriage.

'You're joking, right?' he says, interrupting me.

'I wish I was.'

'But that sounds… like something out of a movie. We're just regular people, Gemma. Sadie was just a nanny, that's all. Are you sure she's not messing with you? Or maybe she's having some kind of breakdown. You know, perhaps she might need psychological help.'

I fetch my laptop so I can present him with the evidence, explain about her website and what she does for a living, showing him screenshots of her site. We google the dark web and it becomes apparent that Sadie's business is only the tip of a toxic iceberg. In the murky depths of the cyber-underworld lies a solid mass of darkness and terror. All the while, Robert's face is becoming paler and paler as it's starting to sink in that what Sadie has done is very real. Finally he is white with anger, his body rigid, his eyes blazing as he is finally convinced.

'What an absolute bitch!' He stands and paces around the sitting room, his eyes glazed, his breathing heavy.

'I know, Robert. The whole thing was a set-up.'

'If this really is true, it makes no sense. I mean, who would want to split us up? And *why*?' He snaps his head around to face me. 'Do you know who's behind it?'

I nod my head slowly, unwilling to say.

'Tell me, Gemma.'

'Sit down first.'

'I don't want to sit down. Just tell me.'

'Okay, but it's going to shock you. You won't like it.'

'Please, Gemma.'

'The person who hired Sadie… it was your mother.'

I'm surprised to see Robert's shoulders relax. He gives me a look. 'Come on, Gemma. You don't believe that.'

'I didn't want to believe it either, but it's true.'

'I know that you and Mum aren't exactly best friends, but come on, this is bloody ridiculous. No way. No way is that true.'

I show him the evidence that Sadie gave me – printouts of the emails between Sadie and his mother. He reads them with scepticism at first, and then with a growing expression of horror on his face. I then present him with copies of Sadie's bank statements, which show payments being deposited by Diane.

My husband shakes his head, and my heart goes out to him at the devastating news he is being forced to process. Although I've never liked Diane, I wouldn't wish this revelation on my worst enemy. To find out that your own mother could be so calculating and callous.

I go on to tell him about her also being responsible for the graffiti on my car. And then I admit what happened with the fake Mick Cosgrove – something I had wanted to keep secret from him, but it's all wrapped up with this incident, so he needs to know just how low his mother has stooped. This last revelation seems to make him more furious than all the rest of it put together. Or maybe it's just the straw that breaks the camel's back.

'How could she do this? I'll kill her.'

CHAPTER 57

ONE WEEK LATER

We stand on Diane's front step, waiting for her to come to the door. She thinks we're here for a social visit. She couldn't be more wrong. I was a little nervous that Sadie wouldn't show up today. But, true to her word, she's here with me and Robert, prepared to face Diane and get the woman to admit what she's done.

The door opens, and Diane's smile becomes a frown. I have to keep from smirking at her discomfort. I have to remember that this is Robert's mother, and none of this can be easy for him.

'Sadie…' Diane says before faltering, her fingers flying up to touch her lips.

'Hello,' Robert says. 'Are you going to leave us outside on the doorstep, or can we come in?'

'Of course, yes, come in. I wasn't expecting… I didn't realise…'

We follow her into the lounge, none of us offering an explanation as to why Sadie is with us. I have to admit, I'm enjoying Diane's discomfort.

'Robert,' Diane says, 'will you come into the kitchen and help me bring out the tea things?'

I know what her game is. She wants to question her son out of earshot. 'That's okay, Diane,' I say brightly. 'I'll help,'

'But Robert...'

I bustle out of the room and lead the way to the kitchen. Diane has no choice but to follow me, unless she wants to make an embarrassing fuss, which of course she won't. Once we're there, I deflect any chance of conversation by taking hold of the tray, which is already set out with cups, saucers, plates, cake and biscuits. 'This one, yes?'

'Oh, wait a moment,' she says, 'I'll need to re-boil the kettle and put the teapot on the tray too.'

'No problem, I'll take this. You can bring the teapot separately.' I pick up the tray and sweep out of the room without giving her the opportunity to speak further.

It's been a feat of massive self-restraint for me and Robert this past week, trying to pretend that everything is fine between us and Diane. Every time she calls, I feel like screaming at her. Calling her out for the evil witch she is. But Robert wanted us to wait until Sadie could come with us to confront her. That way, we would have her testimony too, and his mother wouldn't be able to deny it.

I don't know why we're even going through with this afternoon-tea charade. None of us will be eating any of her homemade-bloody-angel cake, that's for sure. But Robert thought this was the easiest way to do it. The girls are with Amelia and James. We haven't yet told them about any of this. Robert is dreading telling his brother. But we'll save that conversation for another day. Right now, we need to confront Diane.

I dump the tray on the coffee table, catching Robert's eye and giving him what I hope is a supportive smile. Moments later, Diane appears with the teapot. I must say, my mother-in-law now appears remarkably calm. She must be wondering why we're here. She must suspect something. I wonder what she'll say when we present her with the stark reality of our evidence. I wonder how she's going to try to worm her way out of it.

Robert does the talking while I restrain myself from chipping in. Sadie keeps her silence too. We agreed that he would do it. He said it was only right that he's the one to confront her.

'You seriously expect me to admit to this hogwash?' Diane snaps, directing her gaze to me and not to Robert, who has just spent the past five minutes telling her that we know what she did.

'You don't need to admit it, Mother,' Robert says, his voice low and even. 'We have all the evidence. I haven't come here to ask you if it's true, I've come here to ask you what the hell were you thinking, meddling in my life like this. Subjecting Gemma to all that harassment and fear. But worst of all, hiring a woman who could have been dangerous – no offence Sadie – to come and live in our house and take care of our children. I mean, who does that? Who puts their own family at risk like that?'

'I don't know, Robert. I don't know who does that. But it certainly isn't me. Are you really going to believe the word of a virtual stranger, a *charlatan*, over the word of your own mother?' She stares from him, to me, to Sadie. 'You!' She points at Sadie with a pink-polished fingernail. 'I don't know what your game is, young woman, but you've obviously made my family believe your fairy tales. So answer me, why are you doing this?'

'I'm sorry, Diane,' Sadie says, flushing a little. 'I know I shouldn't have told them. It was unprofessional. But, look, I fulfilled my part of the deal. I broke them up for you. That particular job… it's finished. Then another job came along and I took it, simple as that.'

'Talking of which…' I pull a cheque out of my bag. 'Your fee, Sadie.'

She takes it from me. 'Thank you, Gemma.'

I turn back to face Diane. 'You hired Sadie to split us up, which she did. And then I hired her to get us back together again, which she did. She also showed us all the emails and bank statements relating to your transactions, so don't even try to deny what you've done.'

Diane's mouth is opening and closing, but no words are coming out.

'What's the matter, Mother? Don't you like it when people go behind your back? It's not very nice, is it?'

Diane is shaking her head. Her face is pale and I notice her hands are quivering. But I can't feel sorry for my mother-in-law. She's brought this upon herself. She's been found out and she knows that Robert will never forgive her.

Diane comes over to stand before him. 'Robert, you're my son, and I love you—'

'That doesn't give you the right to try to run my life! I'm not a child any more, I'm a grown man, for Christ's sake!'

'But you can't possibly believe—'

'Don't even bother TRYING!' Robert's face is crimson. I've never seen him so angry. His hands are balled fists and a muscle in his cheek pulses and twitches.

I take his hand and uncurl his fist, slipping my own into his. Putting my other hand on his arm. 'There's no point getting upset,' I murmur. 'We've said what we came to say. We should just leave.'

'You're enjoying this!' Diane cries, pushing at my shoulder. 'You've poisoned him against me. You wicked, wicked little bitch!'

I gasp at her outburst. I don't think I've ever heard Diane swear. It's like a slap in the face. I take a breath and tell myself to rise above it. She doesn't have the power to hurt me any more.

'Right,' Robert says, pulling me to my feet. 'That's it, we're leaving. You don't talk to my wife like that. In fact, you don't talk to Gemma ever again, full stop.'

'Robert, don't do this. You're making a terrible mistake...'

'Goodbye, Mother. We're going now and we won't be coming back. Don't come anywhere near me or my family again. You've just lost your son and your grandchildren. Good job, *Diane*. I hope it's made you happy.'

Robert and I are both trembling as we leave Diane's house with Sadie. I feel as though we've been through a war. As Sadie drives away, I'm left with mixed feelings about the woman. Her job, her website, must be the cause of so much misery. I bet no one else on the receiving end of her 'work' has managed to discover that they've been played. How many relationships has she destroyed? How many happy couples and families has she torn apart because of some bitter, unhappy individual who has paid her a fee? I realise it won't do me any good to dwell on it. All I can do now is thank God that I've been granted a second chance. And I'm not about to waste it.

EPILOGUE

ONE MONTH LATER

She's never been to East Anglia before. Strange, but the stormy sky seems bigger here, like the darkening clouds could swallow you up and you'd never be seen again. Dusk is falling as she pushes open the door to the wine bar, the soft, warm lighting beckoning her in. This is her second trip to visit Sadie. Of course, that's not the woman's real name, but she's grown used to it now. She can't think of her as anyone else. It's funny to think they won't be in contact again after this final meeting. Oddly, she feels like they're kindred spirits, set apart from the rest of the world, moving through life in their own separate orbits. Their first meeting took place up north last year after she stumbled upon Sadie's website. It's amazing the sorts of things you can find on the dark web.

She checks her watch. She's early, but Sadie is already here, sitting in a dim corner at the back, a glass of something clear in front of her. It could be water, it could be vodka. Weaving her way between the tables and past the busy bar area, she places a hand protectively over her bag, nervous about carrying so much cash out in public. But she had to bring the final payment along today. And it was worth every penny. She's impressed with how everything has worked out exactly as Sadie promised. Well, *almost*. She would have preferred it if Gemma and Robert had actually split up. That would have been the icing on the cake. But Sadie warned against pushing it further. She advised keeping an eye on the original brief. Not to get distracted. Sadie cautioned that it would be tricky, if not impossible, to get between Gemma and Robert, and that it could ruin everything they had worked so hard towards. She was right, of course, but it still galls that their marriage is as solid as ever.

She reaches Sadie's table, sits opposite her and takes a deep breath, stretching out the cricks in her neck from the long journey. She's not used to driving this far. Usually, she just potters around Bournemouth, but at least she had a good audiobook to listen to, so that helped pass the time and keep her calm. She won't bother with a drink. She was going to try to find a B & B after this meeting, but she decides she'll probably just get in her car and drive straight back home.

'Hello,' Sadie says without getting up. 'We're all done then?'

'Yes, all done,' she replies, taking a seat opposite and crossing her long legs. 'Robert's had no contact with his mother since he found out what she supposedly did. They've refused all Diane's attempts at any kind of reconciliation.'

'I'm pleased for you.' Sadie takes a sip of her drink. 'It was a long road, but we got there in the end.'

'We did,' Amelia replies. 'Thanks to you.'

Sadie dips her head in acknowledgement.

Amelia was first alerted to the dark web while searching for some contacts for her husband's business. She had the idea that he could diversify from antiques to something less legitimate. James is not a successful businessman. He plays at being a big shot, but it frustrates Amelia how utterly business illiterate he is. She's always having to guide him away from bad deals. Away from people who would take advantage of his good nature. If he didn't have her at his shoulder, they'd be more broke than they already are.

Anyway, she came across Sadie's website, 'Break-Up Babe', after it was mentioned in an online chat forum. Someone with the username 'PissedOff555' was searching for Sadie after she'd destroyed his family somehow or another – Amelia can't quite remember the details. Sadie later changed her website name to 'Relationship Assassin', as this disgruntled client was getting too close to her. Now she's shut that site down too. She must have to keep doing this in order to protect herself. Amelia realises it will probably be impossible to contact her again after today.

Poor Diane, being falsely accused when all along Sadie was working for *Amelia*. But then, that was the point – for Gemma and Robert to believe that Diane was behind everything. It was all part of the game plan for them to be so outraged by Diane's despicable behaviour that they would sever all contact with her. Amelia almost feels sorry for Diane. The woman has no idea what she's been accused of or what she's supposed to have done wrong. The shock of it all has sent the silly old bat a bit loopy. She's lost that steely look in her eye. This estrangement from her son and her grandchildren has aged her.

Meanwhile, Amelia has become Diane's shoulder to cry on. Her rock. The one she turns to for comfort. Diane is convinced that it's Gemma who's turned her son against her, so Amelia has acted outraged on Diane's behalf. And she keeps pouring a little more fuel onto the flames, just to help keep the heat up. Amelia is the daughter-in-law who can do no wrong. And she's achieved what she's been working so hard towards – Diane has finally written Robert and his family out of her will. Now, when the old witch dies, her entire glorious fortune will go to James and, by extension, to his wife.

Amelia was sceptical of Sadie's plan at first. It seemed a long-winded way to get between Robert and his mother. Surely there was an easier route to reach the same outcome? It seemed there was so much that could go wrong. But Sadie explained that in order to make the rift permanent, Diane would have to be seen to be utterly calculating and evil, carrying out not just one act against them, but multiple events, each one worse than the last.

Sadie is the supposed expert in relationship break-ups, so Amelia trusted her judgement. She wanted Robert and Diane's mother–son relationship annihilated. And at the same time, she wanted to cause him and his family the maximum hurt and distress that she could get away with. In the same way that Robert hurt *Amelia* when he dumped her and shattered her heart. He was her first love. In fact, the only person she ever loved. But she doesn't want him back, not after he left her and then hooked up with Gemma. No. Amelia simply wanted him to feel the pain that she felt. She wanted them all to feel it. She hates that sickening family, with their successful businesses, their beautiful character house and their perfect little children.

So Amelia told Sadie to inflict serious damage on the family. Make them all suffer. And once she got started with the idea, she couldn't seem to stop. Even before Sadie arrived, Amelia was already underway with her campaign.

Aunty Amelia may have whispered to her youngest niece that it would be fun go out into the street to look out for her daddy coming home from work. She may have told little Katie that it would be a wonderful surprise. That Daddy would love to see his little girl outside the house, smiling and waving. And if she couldn't spot him right away, she could always have a little wander down the road, where she would definitely find him. She added that it had to be a secret or it would ruin the surprise. And that she mustn't tell anyone about it. Katie could pretend it was her own grown-up idea. Of course, Amelia didn't know if Katie would actually do it, or if there would be any sort of drama. But it was just one of many little seeds she sowed.

She also arranged for Gemma's car to get a makeover, and swapped out her house key to mess with her mind. Poor Gemma.

And then there was the faked commercial developer, Mick Cosgrove. That was fun.

The computer virus was a stroke of genius – Amelia didn't want Gemma to employ a tutor. No. She wanted her to hire a nanny. She wanted her to hire *Sadie*. So, having the virus wipe her computer files every time she typed the word 'tutor' was a way to make it harder for Gemma to find one. Plus, there was the added bonus of the fast-acting virus being a terrible shock.

Eva's dramatic suspension from school gave Amelia the idea for Sadie to turn Eva into one of the school bullies. Turns out children are like sponges, whatever ideas you put into their heads, they soak them up; unless you want them to eat their vegetables, of course.

Splitting Gemma and Robert up would have been the final wonderful achievement. And Sadie gave it a damn good go. But alas, it wasn't to be. At least it soothes Amelia to know that she caused Gemma an awful lot of sleepless nights. And Sadie updated Amelia every step of the way, so she always knew what was going on.

Volunteering for the charity golf-club dinner was the easiest way to get Diane to transfer money into Sadie's dummy bank account, RA Holdings. She simply told Diane that RA Holdings was the trading name for a supplier they used at the event. She explained that Diane needed to pay them herself and that the golf club would reimburse her later. It didn't have to be a large amount, just enough to show Robert and Gemma that the two of them were linked. The emails were forged by Sadie easily enough.

At the party, Amelia lied when she told Gemma she was pregnant. She needed her to believe she was so that Gemma would offer to bring the box of glasses downstairs, and accidentally stumble upon her husband and the nanny having sex in the spare room. Unfortunately, Robert didn't oblige with the having-sex part, but at least Sadie was quick thinking and made it look as awful as she could.

It should have been *Amelia* that Robert married. Instead, she ended up with second-best James. The ill-favoured son. Not as bright or funny or intelligent or handsome as his younger brother. A shadow. And Amelia deserves compensation for having to marry a shadow. Compensation that will soon be forthcoming.

'Have you got another job to work on now?' Amelia asks, curious to discover a little about the other woman's life.

'Possibly,' Sadie replies. 'Can I put you down as a reference?'

Amelia stares at her, a little shocked, imagining the sorts of people who would want to get in touch… and then she sees that Sadie is smiling. She exhales and returns the smile. 'I almost thought you were serious for a moment.'

'Sorry, bad joke. No, like I told Gemma, I'm retiring from the business. Or having a long break at least. I might go abroad, do some travelling.'

'Sounds nice,' Amelia replies.

Sadie shifts in her chair. 'So…'

'Oh, yes.' Amelia pulls a large envelope from her bag and passes it across the table. 'The final instalment. It's all there. Anyway, if it isn't, you know where I live.' She quirks an eyebrow.

'Yes,' Sadie replies without humour. 'I do.'

There doesn't seem to be anything left to say, other than their goodbyes. Amelia gets up and leaves the crowded bar, walks away from this episode of her life feeling lighter.

She thinks she'll have a break from all this intense activity for a few months. If she hadn't had to re-mortgage the house to pay Sadie's fee, maybe she and James could have booked themselves a little holiday. But they haven't got a penny left and the credit cards are all maxed out.

Amelia isn't worried though. There'll be plenty of time and money for holidays soon enough. Once everything has settled down again, she'll pay another visit to the dark web.

Because Christmas would be the perfect time for Diane to meet with a little accident…

A LETTER FROM SHALINI

Thank you for reading my seventh psychological thriller, *The Perfect Family*. I can't believe I've written seven already – I had to double-check that was the right number! I do hope you enjoyed Gemma's story as much as I enjoyed writing it.

If you'd like to keep up-to-date with my latest releases, just sign up at the link below and I'll let you know when I have a new novel coming out.

www.bookouture.com/shalini-boland

I love getting feedback on my books, so if you have a few moments, I'd be really grateful if you'd be kind enough to post a review online or tell your friends about it. A good review absolutely makes my day!

When I'm not writing or spending time with my family, I adore chatting to readers, so please feel free to get in touch via my Facebook page, through Twitter, Goodreads or my website.

f shalinibolandauthor

🐦 @shaliniboland

g 4727364.shalini_boland

🌐 shaliniboland.co.uk

Thanks so much,
Shalini Boland x

ACKNOWLEDGEMENTS

Thank you to my sensational publisher, Natasha Harding. It's always such a pleasure and a joy to work with you. Long may it continue!

Thanks also to the wonderful team at Bookouture, especially Ellen Gleeson, Peta Nightingale, Kim Nash, Noelle Holton, Natalie Butlin, Alex Crow and Jules Macadam. You are the dream team.

Thanks to my brilliant copy editor, Fraser Crichton, for your honest comments and suggestions. To the fabulous Lauren Finger (I'll miss you!) and Alexandra Holmes (lovely to start working with you) for their eagle-eye proofreading and perfect suggestions. Also thank you to Emma Graves for my favourite cover yet.

I feel very lucky to have such loyal and thorough beta readers. Thank you Terry Harden, Julie Carey and Amara Gillo. I always value your feedback and opinions.

Thanks to all my lovely readers who take the time to read, review or recommend my books. It means so much.

Finally, I want to thank Pete Boland who is the most supportive husband ever.

Made in the USA
Columbia, SC
17 June 2019